This work is dedicated lovingly to my mother,

Nancy.

She really is the badass she is in the books.

# ~ 2 ~

## Immanuel

The paramedic had quickly and professionally checked Him over. She had carefully checked his pulse, listened to his heart, and asked him questions about his medical history. She had even given him something cold to press against the spot on his head where that cop had hit him before she had moved off. The name on her badge had read Suarez, and she was a probably the prettiest paramedic he had ever seen. Her delicate features and dark skin would have been very appealing to a normal man, but the voice had gifted him with the other kind of sight. He could see past the pretty veil she cast and to the demon underneath, controlling and possessing her. The black aura gave it all away. The blackness surrounding her was so deep it seemed to draw in the light from the room, making him need to strain his eyes to see. She was surely meant to be one of his angels, like all the others.

His angels were special and missed each one of them, but his most recent had left him feeling ashamed. He had been careless and gotten caught before he could finish purifying her, and as such, had let not only her, but god down as well. Her name was Lily, and she had been beautiful before he had begun to cleanse the beast inside away. Her looks had been what corrupted her, he was sure of that, so full of the sin of pride and vanity. He had been working on removing the source of her problem when the F.B.I. had burst in and taken her away from him. The last he had seen of her was as she was loaded into the ambulance, and he had not even been allowed to say goodbye to her.

It wasn't until later that night that he learned that she had died. He had grieved for her soul, he had been so close to saving her, so close to finally cutting away her sin, so close to making her into one of his true angels, and it had all been for nothing. Instead, he had found himself in handcuffs in a cold cinderblock room.

Men in suits had come and gone, asking him questions, making threats and sometimes acting like his friends for hours, trying every trick they possessed. “Are you the Greenfield Gasher?” one would demand, “Did you kill those girls in Denver?” another would ask. They showed him hundreds of pictures of beautifully purified women and girls from all over the country, most of which he had helped into heaven, but a few he did not know. Did the voice speak to another? He had always figured he couldn’t be alone in his work. So many possessed and corrupted people out there, and he was but one man. It warmed him to know that as usual, God had provided him with help. Though all the detectives, policemen, agents and investigators tried, he would not speak to them. One unpleasant brute from Oregon had even forced his mouth open to verify that he had a tongue. The lord would provide for his continued work, and this was just a delay. There was no need to speak to those that wouldn’t understand, couldn’t understand, the plans of the lord god almighty.

It had gone on like that for over a full day before he was taken to a medical facility where he knew that more questions would be asked by doctors and still be ignored. They Gave him a shot and he was left alone, and that gave him time to close his eyes and pray. He was handcuffed to the bed, so the proper genuflection could not be achieved, but he knew God would understand.

It was during this prayer that the screaming in the hallway had started, and then the gunshots. He prayed harder, knowing that Satan was at hand, what else could it be… he heard a loud bang as the door to his room was thrown open, and then the voices of the officers sent to guard him, panicking as they spoke of monsters and things coming down the hall. He kept his eyes shut tight, and prayed to the father and son, repledging himself to their work. Still, more crashing followed and then more gunshots. They were so incredibly loud that they almost startled him out of his prayer, but he persevered. Something heavy fell across him, struggling at first, but then laying still. He felt the presence of other things in the room, and then the weight across him started to shift back and forth, as if being pulled at by several hands. His body was quickly drenched in a something sticky as the smell of blood filled his nose. He continued to pray, listening to the chewing sounds until he finally lost the fight with the medications they had given, and darkness took him

When he had woken up, the sun was shining through his window. The room was hot and smelled horribly of death. He looked around, but saw no one. The power seemed to be off in the building, and though he listened as hard as he could, there was no sound he could detect from anywhere nearby.

He sat up, displeased to see that he was still handcuffed to the rail. His arm was black with dried blood, as was almost every other inch of his body. His legs were crusty and had something sticking to them, using his free hand, he peeled up part of a blue uniform shirt, and under it, part of a policeman's belt. He remembered the weight that had fallen upon him during the prayer, the lord's wraith had been messy and terrible, he must be covered in one of the officers sent to guard him. But He saw gods true gift to him when he lifted the belt, several keys dangled from a ring attached to the side.

He had wandered the hospital in shock. Everywhere the dead littered the floors and rooms. These dead didn't have their evil carefully cut away, they seemed to have been devoured! He had stopped at one such gruesome scene, a waiting room strewn with the dead. As he stood contemplating the tableau of gore, A body in its midst began to move. The voice awoke and whispered a word in his ear.

"Stillness".

He watched the cadaver as it twitched, randomly moving first one part of itself, and then another. It soon began to coordinate its twitching into efforts to stand. He could tell it had once been a pretty young woman of about 30. He could see the thick layer of darkness surrounding her. This destruction couldn't be the work of God, these things must be sending's of the other. Satan had reanimated the dead and sent them forth to consume the living. She gained her feet and begin to shuffle towards him. Fear built in his chest like an icy lump, but he held his ground. The torn woman drew near, but then stopped, staring at him and through him at the same time, before losing interest and wandering away. He followed the woman, maybe he could save her.

"Ma'am," He called softly, "I am Immanuel, and I have been sent to bring you out of the darkness."

She turned back slowly towards the sound of his voice. Her eyes met his and focused a thousand miles away at the same time in a way that brought a chill racing down his spine. He expected her to attack, his angels always fought at first, but the thing took an unsure step towards him, and then halted, sniffing.

It must be the blood, he thought to himself, I am covered in blood and chunks of that officer, so she sees me as one of her own. He stepped up to her, and cautiously reached down and took her hand. She did not react.

"What's your name?" He didn't really expect an answer, but at the sound of his voice, she snarled and lunged for him. He quickly stepped away, raising his arms to shield himself, but before she could come at him again, she lost interest.

'Very interesting' he thought to himself, 'I look and smell like one of those demons, but when I talk, she can tell. I think I will hold my tongue.' He again reached forward and took her hand.

When he began leading her down the hall, she followed meekly, offering no real resistance. He slowly led her down the corridor reading the signs by each door, until he found what he needed. He soon had her strapped down to a small conference room table. 'I wish I had my tools...probably all in little plastic baggies by now in some room at the police station.' He lamented to himself. He began to search and soon had found a wide variety of blades and instruments

"The good Lord provides!" he exclaimed as he laid out his bounty. His voice energized the woman, who moaned loudly and began to strain at the restraints.

'Be quiet ... I must come up with a name for you. You look like a Jennifer, is that it?" He asked. The creature before him moaned again. "Maybe a Sarah?" the woman did not make a noise, she just struggled to rise again.

"Sarah, it is then," he pronounced as if making a great proclamation. He reached to the table and drew out a large scalpel he had found, "Let's see what we can do about removing this evil and saving your immortal soul."

Standing at the window later, he noticed how far the sun had moved across the sky. "Several hours trying to help you Sister Sarah, and I don't think I am any closer to helping you." He turned back towards her. She again turned her head to the sound of his voice and tried to moan, her jaws opened and closed, but no sound escaped. He wasn't surprised, she had not been able to make any noise since he had removed her lungs, indeed all her organs now laid neatly beside her. He peered into her open chest, searching for anything he might have missed, but finding nothing.

"WHERE IS IT HIDING!? I KNOW ITS IN THERE SARAH!" he brought his fists down on the table with a resounding bang. But all her eyeless sockets did was stare at him from her skinless face. His rage grew within him. He forced himself to take several deep breaths and count to ten." It must be inside your head my dear," he said threw clichéd teeth, "no other part of you has not been laid open by my hand."

He looked at the pile of tools he had gathered and closed his hands around a curve clawed hammer he had taken from a toolkit in a utility closet. "I am sorry for failing you Sister Sarah, and I forgive you for failing me. May the Lord protect, purify and keep you, Amen." As he said this last word, he brought the hammer down as hard as he could at the center of her forehead.

The impact brought a satisfying crack to his ears as the skull gave way and released its contents in a spray across the table. He let the hammer slip through his hands to the floor and began to shift through the remnants of her brain. He found nothing and could feel the rage building again. "What have I done wrong dear lord, how did I fail you?" he asked the empty room. He waited for an answer, but none came. He reached for the hammer again, and swung it at the body on the table, striking her jaw and shattering it in a spray of blood and gore. There was no satisfaction in the destruction. He had yet to feel any satisfaction with Sarah, maybe that was God's punishment for failing to find the evil. True, Sarah had lived longer than any of his other angels, but there had been no begging, no pleading, no confession of her sins. Gods work had always left him fulfilled before, but now he felt forsaken and empty. He looked down at her again.

"ITS YOU, YOU HAVE FAILED GOD, NOT I!" he swung the tool down again. "YOU WERE UNWORTHY OF MY ATTENTION, YOU WERE SENT TO DISTRACT ME, SO YOUR CREATOR COULD ESCAPE!" he brought the hammer down again and again until finally, it smashed through the table where her skull had been and lodged in the wood.

He yanked it free and hurled it at the large window, watching the glass shatter and fall away. Beyond it he heard the moans of thousands of the infected in the street below. He walked over and looked down at the things wandering aimlessly up and down the roadway. As his rage ebbed, he tried to figure what to do. "Somewhere out there is the one that created all of you," he whispered to the things, "And that's the one I must find."

He picked up a gym bag someone had left in the corner and dumped out the sweaty clothing inside. It would fit all his new tools nicely, and then he would work his way downstairs, searching for food and water and anything else useful as he went.

On the ground floor, he found a young girl, cowering in a closet. She was wearing the pink and white stripes of a candy striper. She didn't speak as he reached for her hand, but her eyes grew wide in terror as she took in his appearance. Only then did he realize that he must look just like one of those demons, covered in blood and pieces of dried flesh.

"It's ok my dear, "He said in his most charming and harmless voice, "I am not one of those things, I just want to help you."

"Oh, thank god!" She exclaimed, and threw her arms around him, even as bloody as he was.

"Thank god indeed, let's get out of here... I am Immanuel, and I have been sent to bring you out of the darkness." He replied and pulled her behind him down the hall.

'Tomorrow morning will be soon enough to start on my journey'. He thought to himself, 'now to find a table.'

***

*Maria Suarez glanced at the clock built into the dashboard, it showed less than ten minutes until eleven. The ambulance was parked in the side lot of a shuttered grocery store that appeared to have closed long ago.*

*Her partner, Jenny, slept in the seat next to her. Maria wished she could sleep also after the night they had just had, but one of them had to stay awake in case another call came over the radio, and it was her turn.*

*The whole department had been swamped all night, the panic of the pandemic being pushed by the media had led to everyone who felt sick calling 911. Despite their assurances, most had insisted on being transported to the emergency room.*

*She had thought back on the night, the first call had been to the scene of a grisly murder, not to save the victim, it had been too late for that, but to check out the perpetrator. Maria's skin had crawled every time she had to touch the man. Then she had to transport the man to the hospital in restraints accompanied by no less than three agents from some government agency or another. It was the first of three times she had had to tie someone to the gurney.*

*The last had been a woman in her seventies. They had been dispatched to her house after a neighbor had bit her. The wound itself had not been that bad, but the woman must have had some underlying psychiatric problems because she was going nuts by the time they arrived.*

*Several Police officers were holding the woman down when they arrived, and still, they could get a pulse because she was thrashing so much. Jenny had injected the women with a double dose of Versed, and she fought through it.*

*The cops did their best, but the old crone had still managed to get a hand free and raked three deep scratches down Jenny's arm as they had tied her down. The Emergency room doctor had wrapped the arm, and said it wasn't that bad, but advised her to see her physician in the morning. He promised to let them know if the woman tested positive for anything infectious.*

*Maria looked over at her partner's arm, the bulky gauze covered the wound, but Maria was sure she could see a tinge of redness on the arm. She realized her partner's steady breathing had stopped.*

*She looked up at Jenny's face, and saw her eyes were open, staring back into her own. "How is your arm?" Maria asked, concerned. But Jenny just sat motionless, staring back.*

*"Jenny!" Maria said, alarmed. "Are you okay?"*

*Across the cab, Jenny Lunged towards her. On the other side of the parking lot, a stray dog looked up at the sudden screams, and quickly scampered off.*

***

**Brandy**

Brandy stood beside their car watching her mother pace back and forth. They had been on the road for two days, listening to the situation deteriorate on the radio, but had made it to less than 30 miles from grandma and granddads before they had come across one of the military roadblocks they had heard about. Armed soldiers had made it quite clear that they would open fire on anyone attempting to push past, and had directed ever one back a few miles down the road to a red cross camp sat up inside a rest area off the interstate. The area was already overcrowded when their sports utility vehicle had pulled in and been directed to park in a jumble of other vehicles.

They had been assigned to a tent with seven other people, and even though the tent was large, it was still crowded. And there they had stayed.

Two days passed before her mother couldn't take the confinement and confronted the elderly army major that seemed to be in charge. The gray-haired man had listened wearily to her demands to be allowed to continue, no doubt having been cornered like this before.

“Listen, ma’am, you are safer here...” He started to explain before he was cut off.

“Don’t ma’am me, I have to get into Milwaukee and check on my family. I can’t sit here and do nothing anymore!” Her mother said in an exasperated voice.

“I understand how you feel, my family all lived there as well” The officer’s shoulders drooped when he said this and seemed to age another ten years, “but you have to know it’s just not possible.”

“And why the hell not?” said a nearby man who, like the group of people gathering around, had been listening in.

The colonel thrust a finger into the sky north of them, obviously tired of the conversation, “Do you see that glow on the horizon? There is no Milwaukee anymore.” He gave them a minute to allow the news to settle in. “Both Milwaukee and Chicago were so overrun that we have no reason to believe that any survivors are still in those areas. Milwaukee started burning 24 hours ago, but we have no idea why, they suspected an industrial accident. The area around Chicago is undergoing what the Pentagon is calling thermal decontamination. We are making plans to move all of you to an emergency shelter set up in a middle school a few miles away, you should be settled there this time tomorrow.” He turned and walked away, leaving them all stunned.

“What does he mean ‘thermal decontamination’?” Derek asked their mother, but it was someone in the gathered crowd that answered.

“Firebombs, Young man,” Said the older man, “We heard it on that little radio we brought with us, the air force has been firebombing some of the larger cities to stop those… things… from getting out.”

“How can they do that? There have to be living people in there, how are they supposed to escape?” asked a middle-aged woman.

“The bigger cities are death traps, the infection spreads so quickly that it would take a miracle for anyone to stay alive, much less get out.” He explained. “We were in a quiet little suburb of Chicago and we barely got out, hell the neighbors pulled out right behind us and they didn’t make it two blocks before they were swarmed. Watched the whole thing in the rearview and couldn’t do a damn thing. It was the worst thing I have ever seen.”

Brandy looked around the crowd, some of those gathered were weeping openly, all looked shocked.

"Dad would have stayed at home, that's far enough out of town, right?" Brandy asked.

"I hope so dear, I hope so." Her mother said assuredly, as if trying to convince herself as much as her children. "I am sure he is fine."

Brandy again looked at the glowing sky north of them and felt a tear building in her eye. This whole thing was overwhelming her, she was supposed to be playing pool in Grandads basement and shopping at the outlet store her mother had bragged about, not living as a refugee in some damned tent city.

She pulled the cell phone from her pocket and glared at its glowing display, 'no signal' filled its screen, as if taunting her. "All I want is one damn bar, one phone call!" she held the phone up, searching for a signal, but finding none.

The cell towers had stopped working the day before and no one seemed to know why, whether they had been shut down or destroyed no one could even guess at. Only the soldiers seemed to have any form of communications that carried farther than a shout.

Brandy put the phone back in her pocket and began to walk towards the tent they called the orphanage. It was where the children that had been brought in alone, or whose parents were in quarantine for bites and scratches were kept. She had been working there as much as they would let her, anything to keep herself busy.

# ~ 14 ~

## Derek

Derek woke up before daylight and lay there thinking. He hadn't liked the way his mother seemed to have already written off their father, yeah, she had said she thought he was okay, but she didn't seem to believe it. Derek had faith that if anyone could survive this, it was Dad.

The sunrise found him up and it wasn't long before he ran across Chad sitting on the edge of the pond behind the rest area. Derek sat down beside him and picked up a handful of rocks. They sat together quietly for several minutes hurling rocks at the floating garbage before Chad finally broke the silence.

"Sucks" was all he said.

"Sucks" Derek agreed.

"I saw everyone having a pow wow last night, learn anything new?" Chad asked.

"Not really, same shit different day." Was all Derek could bring himself to say, he knew Chad's mother was in New York City, his grandparents were in Milwaukee. He didn't want to be the one to tell his new friend that they were probably all gone. Derek got the feeling his friend had already come to that conclusion anyway.

Chad had been traveling on the big greyhound bus that was now parked a few hundred yards away to see his grandparents when it had been stopped by the military roadblock. On the outside, he seemed to be handling the situation well, but as Derek grew to know him better, he could see the cracks in that facade beginning to show.

"So, what's G.I. Joe's big plan then?" Chad asked.

"They are going to move us to some big shelter with a bunch of other people, but I think that's all they have figured out at this point." Derek shrugged. "I guess we just wait."

The silence drug out again, neither boy knowing what to say. They heard footsteps behind them and turned to see a man approaching them dressed in a polo shirt and khaki shorts.

"Hey boys, I hate to ask this, but do either of you have any cigarettes?" asked the man. Derek noticed that he seemed nervous and a little shaky.

"Sorry, I don't smoke," Derek responded quickly, embarrassed. But chad reached into his pocket and withdrew a crumpled pack.

"I think there's like three or four in there, help yourself," Chad said as he tossed the pack to him.

"Bless you!" the man exclaimed, "You sure you don't mind? I'd hate to take the last of your stash." The man asked concern on his face.

Chad chuckled, "Nah go ahead, I don't smoke, I just swipe my mom's all the time trying to get her to stop. I got this pack from her purse at the bus station."

"Well thanks again, my names Jack, and I owe you one." The man said and fumbled one from the pack.

They watched the man walk away, puffing on his freshly lit cigarette and sighing audibly.

"Isn't your mom going to be mad when she finds out you took those?" Derek asked.

"I doubt she is mad at much of anything anymore," Chad said and went back to staring across the pond.

Derek swore at himself for mentioning Chad's mother. “Maybe she’s okay,” Derek said, trying to force a little hope into his voice.

Chad turned and looked at him, Derek thought he saw a spark of rage in the other boy’s eyes for a split second, but then his eyes softened. “Maybe,” he mumbled, “let’s get out of here, go sneak into the mess tent and try to nick some food.”

Chad rose with the other boy and the wandered towards the smell of breakfast cooking. Off in the distance, they heard a barrage of gunshots and paused to listen. “Maybe it’s one of the infected?” Derek wondered aloud.

“Infected?” Chad asked sarcastically, “you still believe that infected crap? Whatever it was, sounds like they got it.” Chad started walking towards the large tent again.

“Yeah,” Derek agreed, halfheartedly, “Or maybe IT got them.”

***

*The giant of a man stood to the side of the door waiting for the officer to give the word. He could feel the tenseness that radiated off the men standing behind him. On the other side of the door, the lieutenant nodded her head sharply.*

*The sergeant stepped up and slammed his shoulder into the door and felt the hinges pop free of the wood as the screws were ripped out. “Go! Go! Go!” he urged the squad and led them into the room.*

*He scanned the living room of the house, the walls bore bloody handprints and the air held a sticky metallic smell. He knew the smell well from his last tour overseas, but he did not see the source. To His right stood the opening to a kitchen area, and to his left another opening that he could see the beginning of a hallway.*

*Instinctively he knew that this was a waste of time. The chances of finding a survivor in a building with one of them were low, but they had to look. They were already here after all.*

*Someone stepped up from behind him. He could make out a lock of auburn hair hanging loose, having escaped the confines of the helmet. He waited for her order. She signaled him to take his squad and move into the kitchen, and then for Sergeant Anderson to take his towards the hallway and its many doors.*

*He stepped quickly towards the gaping opening, confident that his men would move with him. They spread out, and moved into the room. No one was there. He could hear the other team knocking down doors on the other side of the house.*

*"Clear!" He called loudly, letting everyone else know they could move on. As they started to turn, the staccato rattle of gunfire echoed through the house. He saw two of the figures with him go down into heaps on the floor, and from the other team, a gurgling scream rang out.*

*He looked around the room, Corporal ward was down in a spreading pool of blood, and Lieutenant Kelley was writhing on the floor, clutching her chest. He called for a medic and knelt beside her, trying to pull her hands from the wound so he could see it.*

*"It hit the plate, it didn't penetrate." She gasped out, trying to catch her breath. "It just hurts like hell! Go check on Anderson."*

*He ducked as he rushed through the doorway out of the habit of a tall man and made his way towards the hallway. He found it a bloody scene, several soldiers lay prone in the first room on the right unmoving, and a line of jagged holes stitched the walls on both sides of the hallway.*

*He felt a hand on his shoulder and knew the others had caught up with him. He ducked low and rushed into the room the shots had come from before tearing through walls and men. Inside he found Lt. Anderson sprawled across the blood-soaked bed, a moving mass of human flesh writhed above him, tearing flesh from his body. Still clutched in his hand was the rifle, thin wisps of smoke issuing from its barrel.*

*Calmly He drew his pistol and shot the two infected in the back of the head. They had been so consumed with their meal, they hadn't bothered to turn around. He stepped forward and fired another round through the head of the soldier, guaranteeing that he would never rise again. They cleared the rest of the house and found no more people, other alive or infected.*

*He met his leader back in the living room when it was over. "Lt. Anderson, he was surprised and emptied his clip. The shots went thru the walls, killed two of his, injured three more. That's what hit you and the corporal." He reported.*

*She shook her head disgustedly. "Five dead, four injured. For nothing." She said sadly, "Load everyone up and let's get the hell out of here."*

***

**Immanuel**

The sun was just beginning its flow over the rooftops in the east when he emerged from the hospital the next morning. He stood for a moment on the sidewalk, watching the demons wander aimlessly and was glad he had applied a fresh coat of the camouflaging gore.

He had thought about what he was going to do after he had helped his newest angel last night. He had been relieved when he had found her evil and cut it away, and only slightly disappointed in her for not surviving. He could tell by her screams that it had been a difficult procedure for her, but he knew she had died with heaven in her future. Already he could hear her voice whispering in the back of his mind. After his inability to help the demon, he had worried that THE voice had forsaken him, but he felt confident that he was meant to carry on now.

The voice had even granted him a vision, he had seen himself spreading its work south and outside the city. This was a major step, for the voice had always wanted him to stay hidden amongst the large crowds that cities had offered, but to avoid smaller towns because he was more likely to be noticed, and the lord's work couldn't be interrupted.

'South it is then' he thought to himself, and stepped from the curb. He knew it would be many miles before he could rest, and he had to stay alert. With so many demons, he couldn't become careless; he couldn't give in to the urge to argue with the newest angel's voice. She didn't understand what had happened to her yet; she was still weak and untrained, still angry. They always started out that way right after they moved in, it would just take a little time, sometimes as much as a few weeks, before she would accept the gift he would give her. He would explain it to her, and she would eventually understand

and join her voice to those of the other angels in song and praise of his good deeds. This was just the price he paid to do what he must. He had to tame this angel before THE voice would give him another.

He walked through the milling crowd, heading south. The sun was now up, and its heat beat down on him. He noticed a smell, not completely unpleasant at first, but as the day warmed, more and more putrescent. At first, he assumed it was the beings that surrounded him, but as their numbers thinned in the outskirts of the main city, he realized that it was in fact, him. He was further dismayed when he realized that he was beginning to sweat, and that liquid would carry the blood and gore he had coated himself with into his eyes and mouth. He had to make it to the suburbs where he could find somewhere to wash and hide and make a new plan. The area around him was less densely populated by the abominations, but there was still a large number.

He quickened his step, he knew now that he had been too casual about escaping the city, and that time was a factor in his safety. Should he risk trying to steal one of these cars parked haphazardly about? Many were damaged, but he felt that some looked like they were still road worthy.  Some were even sitting beside the road with the door open, ghouls straining against the belts that held them in place.

His eyes settled on a ford ranger that looked like it had been parked rather than abandoned. It was a smaller vehicle, and he hoped that he would be able to maneuver it around the many roadblocks and obstructions he had seen so far as he had walked south. It was locked, which did not surprise him, no one left a vehicle unlocked in downtown Milwaukee, but that was easy to fix, there was after all no police to worry about anymore. He had not seen another person all day that look capable of calling the authorities, and the things that walked around him seemed to not care about the laws of man.

He reached into the bed of the truck and lifted out a large wrench that had been left there amidst some other tools. He smashed the window closest to him, the passenger side window. He looked around to see if he had been spotted, but as usual, the possessed paid him no attention. They didn't even look up at the noise, just carried on about their mindless rambling as he worked with the wiring until he found what he needed and was rewarded by the engine trying to turn over. A few more tries and the engine purred to life.

Over the sound of the engine he heard a moan, one at first, but then a chorus of them as the others took interest in the rumble of the truck. He listened and heard them coming, lots of them. He tried to right himself from the cramped floorboard, but he was wedged. Strong hands closed on his foot and he looked up into the shredded face of a muscular man dressed in the remains of a postal uniform. He kicked as hard as he could; the creature was shoved back and fell to a sitting position, still clutching the shoe it had ripped from his foot.

He managed to lift himself to the seat as another came into view, without thinking, he pulled the shifter on the column down and jammed his foot down onto the gas pedal. The pickup shot backward and into the vehicle parked behind it. He thanked God that it had only been a few feet, and moved the shifter into drive. He again pushed the gas down hard, cutting the wheel to the right and out into the street. He felt the thumps as he hit several of the creatures, and the following bumps as the wheels ground over the tops of them. As he sped away, he saw those same creatures struggling to rise from the pavement. He said a prayer for their immortal souls, even as he struck another, and then another with the vehicle. He had soon left the mob behind.

He made it less than a dozen blocks before he found the first roadblock, police cars sat nose to nose across the traffic lanes, their doors open and abandoned. He narrowly made it by them on the sidewalk, but was forced to slow. He was amazed that even this brief delay allowed a crowd to form and he was forced to power the vehicle through and even over them.

"The city is definitely not the place to start my work again," he said allowed "I have to get out of town and find somewhere safe." He listened for THE voice to confirm, but all he heard was the candy strippers screams still ringing in his mind.

# ~ 23 ~

## Brandy

The headlights of the vehicles arriving and departing the school made the rafters cast odd undulating shadows that writhed on the sickly tan ceiling. The caged clock on the wall indicated just after three in the morning, but brandy had not yet been able to fall asleep. She sat up on her cot and looked at the sleeping form of her younger brother and at her mother beyond him. She could tell by the slow rise and fall of the thin green blanket that her mother had finally drifted off to sleep.

'Good', Brandy thought, it was the first time her mother had slept since the colonel had broken the news to them about the cities destruction six days ago. Brandy envied those sleeping around her, their rhythmic breathing and occasional coughs were soothing to her, but not enough to lull her to sleep. She slid quietly into her shoes and made her way across the gym floor towards the double doors leading outside.

She stepped out into the courtyard surrounded by the buildings that made up the school. Every building was full of sleeping people. For almost the last week, no less than a thousand people had called the middle school home. Besides the travelers diverted from the interstate and the locals that had been using this as an emergency shelter since the nearby towns had been overrun, there were roughly two hundred soldiers here to protect them. Brandy glanced at the small groups of people sitting around the picnic tables playing cards or talking, but decided she didn't really feel like company. She started for the covered walkway that would lead her to her destination beyond the courtyard. A soldier stopped her as she neared the courtyards boundary.

"I'm sorry miss, civilians have to stay in the buildings or courtyard." He said in what she took for an attempt to sound official. The soldier was tall, but skinny and wore thick black rimmed glasses. Brandy eyed him for a second, wondering what he would if she tried to just push past him, but decided it wasn't worth it. At the very least it would mean a commotion that would draw a crowd, and with the soldiers as tense as they seemed to be, she didn't want to risk it.

"I am on duty in the library this morning," she explained and pulled the small clip on badge they had given her from her pocket and held it up for him. He studied it for a second, making a show of comparing her photo to her face.

"Proceed." His word said brusquely as he stepped aside, allowing her to pass. She kept her badge, complete with its photo, the colonel's scrawled signature and bright red letters indicating her as status 'CV', a civilian volunteer in her hand.

The large numbers of refugees already here, as well as those still being brought in, were taxing to the military personnel available, especially with the large numbers needed to guard the perimeter. The lack of manpower at the shelter had quickly led to a call for volunteers to free up soldiers for whatever it was that the army did during the apocalypse. She had volunteered as soon as she had learned that the volunteers would be allowed to go beyond the normal confines of the courtyard if their duty called for it.

Now instead of being stuck in the gym most of the time, she got to spend 8 hours a day in the library. There were even rumors that civilians would be allowed to go out on some of the rescue and scavenging missions once the area was deemed safer. From what she could gather though, that wasn't going to be anytime soon. Every time the army went out, it seemed they would lose another soldier, and at least once she had heard that an entire unit had been overrun. It was getting rough out there.

The entrance ahead was dark, but she could still make out the two figures watching her approach. She held up her badge as she drew near, and squinted as the powerful flashlight burst flared to life directly into her eyes her.

“Halt! Stop and be recognized.” The speaker’s voice reminded her of huge slabs of granite shifting far beneath the earth’s crust and not for the first time she thought again about the huge amounts of money this guy could have made doing voiceovers in scary movies.

“Geez, Sarge, it’s way too early in the morning for that,” she complained, “I haven’t even had coffee yet!”

“Many apologies Ma’am,” responded a voice from behind the flashlight, “Better safe than sorry.” The light shifted to her feet and the man came dimly into view as her eyes readjusted to the low light.

“Thank you, Sergeant.” She said, favoring him with a smile as she watched him pull a clipboard from a hook in the wall beside him, “carry off any fair maidens yet today?”

The huge man met her eyes with a stern look, and for a second she was intimidated, but then a smile cracked across his face. “You have got to stop calling me Shrek, little lady. You have no idea how easy it is for a nickname like that to stick in the military.”

The man was almost seven-foot-tall, and his shoulders were wide enough that he looked like he didn’t fit through doorways. “How have you been in the military this long and not already gotten one? Besides, it makes the kids feel better to know that an ogre is standing guard outside the door.”

“Speaking of which,” he says brushing off her comment “I’m not showing you on duty for another four hours, shouldn’t you be asleep?”

“Sleep isn’t happening tonight, thought I might as well come here and let someone else go to bed and make the attempt. Besides, I was hoping to make a pot of coffee, want some?”

“No thank you, ma’am, getting relieved soon and looking forward to sleeping myself, but go on in. Ms. Cramer is on duty and will be thrilled to see you. You wouldn’t believe the racket in there last night, somebody got the idea to give them the last of the ice cream and played some kind of space movie. I swear I heard them making ray gun sounds and arguing about who got hit until an hour ago. It’s been pretty quiet since them.” He explained, reaching to open the door.

“Oh, Joy!” She patted him on the arm as she passed, “Sleep well, Sarge.”

As the door close, she heard the other man snicker and say something, but all she could make was the word ‘Shrek’. The big man’s voice carried farther, “Well I guess that makes you the damn donkey then doesn’t it?”

The Library was quiet, thankfully, when she entered. She scanned the room and saw that the floor around the shelves was full of cots for the children. On about half of these, she could see the shapes of sleeping children, and she knew the empty ones each had a child sleeping under it. The library was now the home for the orphans that were found, twenty-six at last count. The youngest was four, and it seemed that that was about the minimum age that a child could escape a turned parent or be separated and survive at least long enough to find help. The thought made her sad, but then again, millions were dying every day, you just had to not think about it.

She turned her attention to the large desk in the middle of the room and the figure slumped over it. That would be Julie Cramer, fast asleep despite the rules against it. Brandy walked over to the desk and lifted the belt that had been set beside the sleeping figure and put it around her waist. "Not only asleep, but you left the gun laying around in a room full of kids," she kicked the chair, making it slide a little on the carpet and jerking the sleeper awake, pleased that it slid quietly.

Julie gasped, but brandy had already put a hand across her mouth to stifle it. "Shhh!" brandy urged, not removing her hand until she could tell the older women was more awake.

"You fell asleep, AGAIN, you left the gun out, AGAIN," Brandy whispered harshly, "do you have any idea what could have happened?"

Julie's eyes showed anger, but she managed to whisper instead of yell, "I fell asleep because these damn brats wore me out, even after I gave them treats last night if they promised to sleep early, which they didn't I might add." She pushed her hair back out of her face and stood, "and as to the gun, it was perfectly safe, I unloaded it and locked the bullets in the office!"

Brandy stood aghast at what the woman had said, "This isn't your law firm, you can't negotiate with scared little children, and an unloaded gun is just about the stupidest thing you can have now. Just get out, I'm here to relieve you."

"We will see how the general feels about this, no one talks to me like that," the woman started gathering the few things she had brought with her, "when this is all over, I'll make sure you pay for the way you have treated me." She stormed towards the door.

"He is a colonel, not a general, idiot, but be sure to tell him I said hello." Brandy retorted, but the woman paid no attention as she stormed out the door and into the night.

Looking around the room, she saw a few kids moving around, but she didn't think the commotion had truly woken any of them. She headed into the office and found the clips to the gun in the top desk drawer, locked but thankfully with the key still hanging out. She reloaded the gun and placed the spare clips back into the pouches on the belt before settling down at the desk in the main room.

"Seventeen years old, two thousand miles from home, and standing armed guard duty over two dozen newly orphaned kids, amazing the twists and turns one's life takes." The oddness of the thought amuses her for a moment, but then she thinks "God that's depressing…"

The time passed slowly in the quiet darkness of the room. It seemed to be several hours before the high windows started to lighten from the rising sun, but shortly thereafter she started to hear people moving around outside. She looked at the clock and realized the breakfasts would soon arrive, pushed most likely by either her brother or one of the others assigned to the kitchens. She also noted that the second person was late to help her get the children ready. One person could watch over the children at night, but you needed several when those kids were up and moving. Oh well, nothing to do now but go for it.

"Wakey Wakey time, children," she called in her most pleasant voice, trying to sound cheery despite her fatigue, "got to get ready, breakfast will be here soon."

Around the room, several voices said weakly "Good morning Ms. Brandy." But most of the children would require more effort to be woken up, so she started those already awake towards the bathrooms and began to wake the others.

When the last one was finally on her feet and shuffling towards the line formed outside the bathroom doors, the entrance swung open and her help rushed in.

"I am so sorry," the women said in her southern drawl, "I tried to get her on time but it just seemed that everything had worked against me. What can I help you do?"

Brandy looked the girl over, noticing that her outfit was perfectly coordinated, her hair was freshly styled, and her makeup had been applied this morning. If she had skipped any of these steps, she could have been early, but Brandy saw no reason to start trouble by bringing it up. "Good morning Linda, Help the kids get their bathroom stuff taken care of and make sure they don't stay in there forever playing. When they are done have them come make their beds, I will start setting up the tables for food. Did you happen to see if it was being made yet?"

"I did, looks like powdered eggs and sausage again, oh, and those cracker things." Linda made a face that brandy returned, military crackers were so bad that even the kids wouldn't eat them and mostly just used them as toys and Frisbees.

"Lovely," said brandy, as she began to set up the folding tables in the open area. The library wasn't big enough for tables and cots at the same time, so they had to be swapped out. The older kids usually helped with this, so it was a quick transition. They had just finished when the door banged open and a pudgy man pushed a large insulated metal cart into the room. The smell of food filled the room causing brandy's stomach to growl.

"Good a- morning bambinos!" boomed the man's voice, in a poor imitation of an Italian accent, "Boy do we-a have some good-a food for you today!"

He then whispered to Brandy as he passed "Same old crap, but fake it until you make it, that's what granddad always said."

Brandy chuckled, "Good morning Rob, how are things going for you today?"

"About the same, sleep, cook, guard duty, sleep, cook, guard duty. End of the world or not, it seems a cooks life never changes." He beamed another smile at her, "Us old army cooks never liked change anyway... which explains the food for the last two hundred years, HA, beat ya to that one."

Brandy laughed with him, "They have you on guard duty now?"

The man's face grew serious as he opened the doors on the steam cabinet and started to remove trays of food. "Everyone is pulling double duty now; we are getting so short staffed. Hell, I haven't done anything but cook since Desert Storm and I have been told I am going on a patrol this afternoon!" He glanced around him to make sure no one else was nearby, "now this is just between you and me. There is even scuttlebutt that the colonel is going to start a civilian guard; arm some volunteers to help take up the slack. Turns out that unit that we were expecting from...", he suddenly broke off as Linda walked up and took the tray from his hands.

"What are you two over here gossiping about when we got hungry mouths to feed," Linda clucked her tongue in mock disapproval, "is it about anyone I know? I could sure use some good gossip."

"I was begging Chef Rob here to tell me we weren't having that gray stuff for dinner again, not sure I can eat that more than once a week." She said, covering.

Rob removed the last of the food from the warmer and sat it on the table. "I will have you know, young lady, that creamed beef on toast is not only a delicacy but a tradition!" his mock anger as overdone as his earlier Italian accent. "To you, I say adieu!"

He turned and pushed his cart towards the door "We will talk later." He mouthed to brandy before whistling and heading back to the kitchen.

Brandy and Linda passed out the food, and then sat together eating and making small talk, but inside she was worried, the chef had been about to tell her something bad, she could feel that in her bones, but what? She didn't have to worry about it long before the first of the children was done eating and the day's true chaos, fed and rested toddlers, began.

# ~ 32 ~

**Derek**

Chad shook him awake. "Hey, Derek, come on, we are going to be late for the kitchens."

Derek sat up and fumbled in the dark for his shoes. Chad handed them to him and then sat down on the bed next to him while he finished getting ready.

"I can't believe you talked me into volunteering for this," Chad complained like he had each of the mornings since they had volunteered together.

Derek yawned again and said in a gruff voice. "Get over it, it's something to do other than sit around and stare at the walls. We were both going crazy." He stood, and they quietly went outside.

They made their way out into a courtyard being transformed by the lightening sky; the sun would be up soon. Across the grassy area, they could see the open doors to the kitchen, its bright glow contrasting invitingly against the shadows around the yard.

"Too bad they never let me deliver the food to the daycare, I was getting ready to make my move on your sister," Chad said, and Derek punched him in the arm.

"I said stop saying stuff like that, it's creepy," Derek complained to his friend.

"Yeah, I am creepy, you are creepy, and it's creepy, but she is hot!" exclaimed Chad softly, keeping his voice down so as not be heard by those already wandering the area.

Derek tried to give him his best glare, but soon a smile broke through. Derek knew Chad had a thing for his sister, but he was scared of her at the same time. The two boys harassed each other over it constantly.

"I think the next time I see her I will go for it, maybe take her out to a movie and then take her to do a little undead hunting." Chad continued.

"I say go for it, watching movies and feeding you to the ghouls would probably be a lot of fun for her." Derek retorted, and the boys laughed.

The boys were no sooner in the door when the head chef found them. "Thank goodness! I am so glad to see you two. Chad, I am out of pans, can you help with that? Derek, help Jack with the eggs." Chad groaned at the prospect of washing dishes yet again.

Derek found Jack near the large cooktop stirring water into the army's egg powder. The two had just started ladling the goop onto the griddle when Jack leaned over and whispered, "I think I found a way to get out."

Derek knew exactly what he was talking about. Since they had arrived, Jack had been on a constant search for cigarettes. He had got all the way up the chain of command, but neither the Army, the Red Cross, nor the local authorities seemed to care. Lately, he had even tried to bribe the members of the search and rescue parties that went out each day, but had yet to procure more than a single pack.

"Are you still going on about that?" Derek asked, amazed by the man's stubborn persistence.

"You don't understand, I need more tobacco, I've been rationing that pack I traded my golf clubs for the other day. But I am almost out." The golf pro explained.

"How are you going to do it? Is it safe?" Derek whispered back, afraid that the military personnel would overhear and spoil the man's scheme.

"I was up on the roof sneaking a smoke, and two of the soldiers were up there having a joint, pissed me off, can't get a legal cigarette from anyone, but they managed to find pot, but anyway, they got loose-lipped and started talking about some big mission coming up and about how most of the soldiers were going to be gone all night tonight. He said that they wouldn't be walking the fence line tonight. I figure if I can get outside the perimeter, I can find a way and head into town. There's got to be a gas station or something I can hit."

Derek pondered for a second, "That sounds awfully dangerous. Even if you get outside, there is no guarantee you can find a car, and even if you did, we don't know how dangerous it is out there."

"We will see, need me to bring you back anything? I am going to take off as soon as we are done here." The older man asked.

Derek couldn't think of anything, so he just shook his head. Chef Rob chose that moment to appear, approved the eggs as finished, and told them to pan them up and start delivering.

Derek and Jack were almost finished with their rounds when they heard a big convoy of vehicles arrive at the front of the school. Jack looked at Derek, and Derek knew the man wanted to go investigate, so he nodded that it was okay with him, and pushed the empty food cart towards the kitchen. With any luck, Chad would be almost done and they could try to get off a little early.

**Immanuel**

"The military is much more efficient than the police about roadblocks." he said aloud to the empty cab as he looked out the ranger's window towards the huge green vehicles sprawled across the middle of the bridge. Less than two feet had been left between the bumpers and the concrete side rails of the span. He stepped from the truck to further survey the area. Two hundred yards behind him, the things that had been following him had already made it to the bridge, he knew there was no going back that way, the little truck could never power through that many of them. He guessed he had maybe five minutes before they would make it to his current location, but also that he could walk faster than the shambling pursuers.

All about him laid bodies and he took time to thank god that these at least weren't moving. He saw no weapons of any kind, even though several of these were soldiers, and almost all the bodies had their pockets turned out. Someone had been here before him, probably fleeing the city the same as he was. More people would mean more safety, and would increase his likelihood of regaining civilization. A larger group could mean he could get back to his true calling.

"I have to find them." he told the voice, "I have to find people to survive and continue my work." He waited for THE voice to answer, but still he could only hear the newest angel, her screams were giving way to steady sobbing, 'good' he thought to himself, 'she's coming along nicely'.

He moved from vehicle to vehicle, he couldn't get any to start, and found almost nothing to help him on his travels. He found an empty duffle bag and transferred his tools to it, a single bottle of water from the cab of one of the trucks went in also. Behind him, he heard the moans of the things getting closer.

He lifted his bag of tools and began walking away swiftly.

# ~ 36 ~

**Brandy**

Her back popped as she stretched as the cramps were finally beginning to unwind. The library had finally fallen quiet as the children gave in to the afternoon naps.

"Coffee?" she said to Linda, who was beside her applying fresh make-up, "I'm going to make a run, do you want some?"

"No thanks girl, don't you know that stuff will give you wrinkles?" Linda asked back, appalled at the suggestion.

"I will risk it." Brandy stood and removed the gun belt and sat it on the table in front of the other woman. "It's loaded and ready."

Linda sat down her compact and picked up the gun belt, studying it like she expected it to start moving and bite her. "I know it's necessary, but I have never liked these things, you sure you don't want to just take it with you?"

"You know the rules; every room must have armed staff on hand just in case. I will only be gone a few minutes, probably not even long enough for you to strap it on. You sure I can't bring you anything?" Brandy asked.

"No, shug, I think I am good." She said.

"Okay, I will hurry back." Brandy stretched, stood, and went out the doors.

The sunlight was blinding as she went outside, and she was pleased to feel the cool wind brush her skin. This late in the summer, the temperature was mild, but it still got warm inside the buildings. The power grid had gone down in the area a few days ago, and the army generators were only running lights and essential equipment, which almost everyone was dismayed to hear, included the buildings air conditioners.

"Ma'am," Said a voice to her left, "Your identification please?" she looked over and noticed a man standing rigidly by the doors she had just exited, she had forgotten all about the guard. She hadn't seen this one around before, his uniform was different than the others, instead of the typical green camo pattern, it was primarily a blue digital pattern. The name tag sewn to the front read Mueller and there was a white armband that read SP in black letters.

"Of course, I'm sorry." She fumbled in her pocket for the little card and held it out for him. "I haven't seen you here before, isn't that a navy uniform? I thought this was all army"

"Petty Officer 1st class Lee Mueller, United States Navy. This is a mixed unit now. I am required to remind you that identification must be worn at all times while on duty, by order of acting commander Lieutenant Colonel Murray." He checked her name against the clipboard he held. "I am showing you on duty for several more hours; please state your business and destination."

She was taken aback by his challenge, his brisk manner wasn't rude, just overly formal. "Coffee run, want anything?"

"No thank you, Ma'am." He handed her back her card and turned his attention back to the path approaching the library. She was obviously dismissed.

She clipped her card to her shirt collar and started towards the kitchens across the courtyard. The courtyard was lively at this time of day, groups of people milled about, talking animatedly and chatting in random clumps. Several people had started a pick-up football game and most people were watching and cheering for one side or the other. She knew that out there, outside these walls and perimeters, people were dying or running for their lives, but at least in here, it seemed like a normal day.

She had almost reached the kitchen doors when she heard someone calling her. She turned and saw Derek running towards her from one of the larger groups.

"Brandy!" He yelled one more time, and she waved to show she had heard him.

"Hey," he said as he reached her, "I tried to come see you today, but the sailor wouldn't let me in. He said I wasn't on that damn list."

"Language mister, if mom hears you talking like that..." she chided.

"Mom got called to the colonel's office, she's been in there all day, something about they found a hospital they think they can clear out of the infected. They want her to go because she knows what all that equipment they want looks like and they don't want to risk the doctors and nurses." Brandy could tell he didn't like the idea any more than she did. Their mother had overseen purchasing and supply for a large hospital back home, everything from supplies to equipment was in her expertise, but she wasn't a soldier.

"When?" Brandy demanded.

"I don't know," Derek said, "In a few days I think."

"I have to get back to the kids, but I get off in two hours. Maybe Mom will be out by then and we can find out what's going on." Brandy was wide awake now, coffee all but forgotten. "Why aren't you working today?"

"A bunch of us got sent away after breakfast, Military personnel only for some big meeting, everyone not on duty is in the cafeteria, that's why lunch was sandwiches, they even served it out here." He explained.

Brandy suddenly remembered that there had only been that Mueller guy on duty at the library when there had always been two before, and that she hadn't seen a guard at the edge of the courtyard like this morning.

"I don't think I like this, "brandy complained, "Something big is up."

"And that's not all, they moved all the buses and trucks to the student pick up area out front. Rumor is that they are about to evacuate us to somewhere. A couple of school buses showed up a few hours ago full of red cross people, about a dozen soldiers. Some people were taken to those portable buildings for quarantine that came in on a helicopter earlier."

"Were any of them bite?" brandy asked nervously. Everyone knew that a bite meant death, and death meant reanimation.

"No clue, but you know they don't quarantine everyone, just those who came close to the monsters, so they must have had a close call. You know that golfer guy? You know the one that's always asking for cigarettes?"

Brandy nodded, everyone knew that poor guy, smokes were not considered essential supplies, so the scavenge teams didn't bring them back.

"Well he saw the buses coming and headed out there, I guess hoping some of them would have a cigarette. They wouldn't let him get close, but he says the colonel was pissed. Apparently, Colonel Murray was expecting a lot more to come in. he says he heard the colonel say something about 500 people were supposed to be there. It's all second-hand stuff, but it looks bad."

Brandy took all this in, and added it to what she had heard from Chef Rob earlier today and felt a sinking feeling in her chest.

"Derek, go back to the gym and hang out there until I get there, or mom shows back up, I will come straight there. Quietly get all our stuff together and packed up, but don't make it obvious."

"Are we running away?" he asked nervously.

"No, But I think it's going to be better to be prepared to take off without much notice. Remember what dad taught us about bug out bags? Make us three, one apiece."

"Ok, I will keep mom there if she comes back by then and get things ready." He turned and darted off.

"Damn," Brandy said and went back to the children, she had already been gone longer than she should have been, and the kids would be waking up again soon. And she needed to think.

The sailor let her pass, and she entered the library, already some of the older kids were up and had been sent to the quiet area to read so as not to wake the smaller ones.

Linda looked up as the door closed loudly and started to scold brandy for letting it slam, but when she saw her face she stopped. She glanced cautiously around her to see if any of the kids were watching and mouthed silently "Everything Okay?"

Brandy forced herself to smile what she hoped at least a half convincing smile and gave the woman a thumb up. There was no point in worrying her; it was all just a gut feeling at this point. But still, she knew something was up.

The rest of her shift passed slowly, she kept looking at her watch, expecting hours to have gone by, but finding only minutes had elapsed. In a world where people died and then got up again to consume the living, a sense of security was an asset, and though she would rather be at home, this was probably the next best place. They had been here less than a week, but this place had already begun to feel like another home. Until this afternoon it had felt secure; high fences, armed guards and plenty of food had a way of relaxing you. She eyed the clock, less than an hour left on her shift, she could do that time.

# ~ 42 ~

## Immanuel

His feet ached, even in the cooling air of the afternoon; the blacktop remained hot and burned the soles of his feet. He prayed to find shoes repeatedly, his one remaining shoe having been left in the truck after the thing had stolen its mate. He wished that he had thought of this back at the road block, dozens of pairs of good strong combat boots laying around for the taking, but it was too late for that now.

He crested a hill and looked back over his shoulder at the horde that still followed, he had quickly outpaced them from the bridge, but at each hill now they seemed slightly closer. His mile lead was down to half that and they showed no sign of slowing down. He would have to think of something soon and the voice was still absent, drowned out by her.

He regretted helping her for a moment, but quickly pushed that feeling aside. He was here to help those who needed it, and even if that horde took him, it would be as god and THE voice intended. He weighed his options. He considered reapplying the foul camouflage he had washed off an hour ago in a small roadside pond, but had not seen another body or person since the bridge. He didn't want to seal himself inside one of these roadside buildings for fear that those behind him would trap him there. That left him only one option, keep going.

He walked, plodding along, step after step. He soon discarded the socks he had worn when they became saturated with blood and began to clump under his feet with each step. The road ahead of him was empty as far as the eye could see. He was in farm country and had started to see more and more houses spread out in front of him. He considered making a trip into one of these to find shoes, even simple flip-flops, but he could now hear the moans of those who followed. He didn't know how close they were, less than a quarter of a mile at most.

He stumbled and fell to his knees, the rough surface of the road cut mercilessly into the skin of his knees and even through the cloth of his pants; he knew blood was now flowing from new cuts and scrapes. He tried to rise, but all his strength had left him and on his second attempt, his arms collapsed, and he fell to his side on the hot roadway. He rolled onto his back and looked at the approaching crowd, there had to be a hundred of them. They would be on him in minutes.

"Dear Lord," he began aloud, shocked at how weak his voice seemed, "I am but your servant doing your work upon the wicked. I ask for your help to escape the demons that follow me so that I may continue your blessings upon those who have forsaken you. Please give me strength and the stamina to survive this, my greatest test from you, so that together we may cleanse this world of the sinners and remake it again in the image you created so long ago in the Garden of Eden before Eve forsake you and brought man down with her vile treachery. I pray this and nothing more in your name, amen."

He closed his eyes and tried to will his cramping legs to release so that he could rise, but it was no use. He could hear their approaching feet. He tried to look again, but his eyes themselves were failing him in his exhaustion.

The steady 'clop clop clop' of their steps grew louder as they approached, and he found himself surprised that they seemed to have started marching in synchronized steps with one another. It grew louder unbelievably quickly until the sound grew overpowering, they must be right on top of him, but still, the sound grew. He imagined the footsteps of God himself couldn't be this loud.

He struggled to open his eyes, to see his death approach, but what he saw wasn't death. A large black angel hovered over the road between him and the massed demons, as he watched, fire flew from the angel and a cacophony of gunfire exploded in his ears. He turned his face towards the road he had come from and saw the horde being ripped apart by some unseen force as pillars of flame erupted in their midst.

A second angel flew into view and landed on the road a dozen yards away, from it, three figures emerged from its sides, running towards him, they were yelling something at him, something he couldn't quite make out. They approached slowly, two holding rods... 'Could those be rifles?' he thought to himself perplexed, 'why do angels have rifles?"

"Are you bit?" the third was yelling, he was finally close enough to be heard. Immanuel looked at the man and his eyes found the large Red Cross painted on the man's helmet and finally understood. Not angels, but helicopters, God had sent angels of a different sort.

"No, I am not bit." He said as the other helicopter finally ceased its barrage upon his pursuers.

The medic looked back down the roadway towards the destruction, and then back down at the man lying on the ground. "Sergeant, I don't see any bites, let's get him on board and get the hell out of here, I'll triage in the air." One of the men hurried over and helped the medic lift him to his feet. It hurt severely as his cramps were stretched forcefully, but he ignored it as the pair dragged him towards the helicopter. The third man, he noticed, never took his gun off him the entire time.

They lifted him into the aircraft, and immediately he felt the weight of its take off. The medic put a headset on him and the din of the engine lessened. "What's your name?" a voice echoed in his ears, and for a second he thought the voice had finally quieted the new angel enough to be heard, but then he realized it was the medic speaking to him over the microphone in his helmet.

"Hey buddy, stay with me, what's your name?" the medic yelled again.

He could feel the jostling motion of the Blackhawk as it raced across the sky. He couldn't tell them his real name, it might be known by now, "Where are we going?" he asked feebly as he felt the sting of a needle go into his arm, they were starting an I.V.

The medic didn't answer, "Are you injured? Do you have any allergies or medical conditions I need to know about?" He felt a pressure surround his other arm and knew they were taking his blood pressure.

"No." Was all he could think to say; his head was starting to feel cloudy. He could feel his consciousness slipping away. He could hear the man start to ask him another question, but another voice came over the headset, cutting him off.

"Jim, we have been ordered back to base to refuel and provide air support for an evacuation of Naval Station Great Lakes, he stable?" the man speaking must be the pilot, but Immanuel couldn't see him from where he lay.

"10-4, I don't see anything serious yet, he has been through the ringer, but I think he will make it." replied the medic. "What kind of evacuation, Last briefing I heard was that was our fall back. Thirty thousand heavily armed sailors and more than the same number of refugees. I thought that place was too big to be in danger?"

"From what I can gather, fences are down and outer perimeter overrun. its sounds like they are surrounded; command is calling for a full strategic withdrawal.  Radio chatter suggests 2500 civilians and squid trying to break out. "

They continued talking, but Immanuel finally lost the battle with sleep and felt himself letting go. "Immanuel," he said, "my name is Immanuel." and allowed the darkness to take him.

***

*The pilot's buttocks ached from the many hours in the seat. He wasn't sure how long he had been flying today, but he knew it had to be coming up on twenty hours now. At any other time, he would have been grounded by regulation long ago, But these were not normal times.*

*The crew had been flying since the previous day, plucking people off roofs until they ran out of room and flying them somewhere safe and then going back for more. As the time had passed, the safe places to drop those they picked up had dropped from five, to one. It was a school out in a rural community south of Chicago, which is where they were headed now.*

*They had been shocked numb by the news of their base falling, and none of them relished the thought of seeing it overrun when they arrived. Then had dropped off the man they had picked up on the road in record time and launched again. They would be there in just a few minutes.*

*Ahead of them, they could already see streaks of smoke rising into the sky. Large sections of the base were aflame. The pilot's hands tightened on the stick and he subconsciously leaned forward as if willing the flying machine to move quicker.*

*He listened intensely for calls to come in over the headset, trying to make sense of the jumble of frantic calls for help of those on the ground. Their radio was not only picking up the official calls from the command center, but many others in isolated areas of the smoky battleground they approached.*

*"Get high! Get to the roof, we are one minute out!" The co-pilot was yelling into the radio. Neither of them knew if he was being heard over the clamor coming over the radio.*

*They arrived at the base and dropped to a hundred feet off the ground, searching for sign of survivors. They found plenty, scattered across the rooftops of the compound. The pilot selected the closest group and hovered down to them.*

*The mob stood on the flat roof of a four-story building, waving frantically. The pilot counted ten people needing rescue, which was two more than his Blackhawk was designed for, but he doubted and with him would object. The skids brushed the gravel scattered over the roof, and the survivors climbed aboard.*

*He throttled the engine and the bird lifted sluggishly back into the air. The added weight made flying harder, the controls bucked slightly in his hands and resisted his commands. As they gained altitude, his eyes scanned the roofs around him and did the math in his head. It would take more loads than they held fuel for.*

*"It's going to take too long to ferry between here and the school." He called into the microphone in front of his face. "We need another option!"*

*Everyone on board searched the horizon frantically, but none of them spotted anything. They were still searching when the radio cleared for a moment and one voice sounded out clear.*

*"U.S. army helicopter," called a heavily accented voice through the headset. "This is the Israeli Cargo Vessel ZIM Barcelona. We*

*are prepared to take on survivors. We are bound for Norfolk, do you copy?"*

*"We copy, Barcelona. Please provide your location!" Came the jubilant reply of the co-pilot. The ship was a mere ten miles off the shore.*

*They veered the helicopter off to the west and out over the water. Soon the vessel came into view. Its decks stacked high with steel containers. As the got closer, they saw three figures standing atop the containers painting a large white 'x'. The pilot aimed for it.*

*The ship was not equipped with a landing pad, but he touched it down lightly right in the center of the mark and held its weight off the ship until the passengers were off, then raced back into the air and back for more people.*

*They repeated this act more than a dozen times before they returned and were unable to find anyone else to save. The shapes of the infected were plentiful, raking their arms up at them fruitlessly. Dejectedly, they radio the Barcelona their thanks and turned back towards the school. By The pilot's estimate, they had dropped some one hundred and thirty off to safety on top of the cargo containers.*

*The pilot glanced at his watch, he had been in the air for 24 straight hours now. He encouraged himself with the idea that in another hour, if he was lucky, he would be asleep. He was just beginning to let himself relax when the airframe shuddered, and warning tones began to sound in time with the alarms.*

*"Come on Baby," He breathed as he fought with the controls, "just another couple of minutes..."*

*The computer indicated engine failure as the alarms continued their shrieking. The nose dipped, and they started to lose altitude. Ahead of them, the school appeared out of the canopy of trees. He urged the helicopter to stay in the air, but he knew it wasn't going to make it.*

*They cleared the tree line by only a few feet as he pulled the stick back, trying to pull the nose back up for a landing, but instead in speared into the ground with a thundering crash of metal. Around him, the spinning rotors struck the ground and splintered as they dug gouges into the turf. The helicopter rolled over onto its side and came to a rest.*

*The pilot looked above him to the co-pilot, who know hovered over him strapped into his seat, and called out to him. The man immediately turned and gave a hesitant thumb up.*

*From the back of them, a voice said calmly, "Well, I have seen better landings..."*

***

**Brandy**

Three o'clock came and went with no one showing up to relieve them.

"We all run late sometimes." consoled Linda. "Let's give them until three fifteen before we start raising hell, shall we?"

"I guess, I was just hoping to get out of here on time today..." Brandy complained.

"Got a hot date?" The other woman chided with an affectionate smile.

"You guessed it, with my cot." Brandy joked and smiled back. Just wanted to get out of here and talk to my mom."

"Sweetie, is there something you aren't telling me? You've been awfully tense since you came back from your coffee run with no coffee." The concern no longer concealed on her face. "What aren't you telling me?"

"Really, it's nothing I know for sure, just a feeling, something is up with the soldiers and rumor is they might be about to move us somewhere else." Brandy confided. "I heard they moved all the buses near the front doors, and a new group showed up today beaten up pretty badly."

"Do you think we are fixing to go somewhere else?" Linda asked, concern showing on her face, "They said this place was the safest place we could be!"

Behind them, the door slammed open, making both jump. They jerked their heads around to see three soldiers enter the room. She recognized the large hulking shape she called Shrek right away, but didn't recognize the other two in their helmets and sunglasses. Brandy was alarmed to see they were completely decked out in armor, packs and carried large menacing machine guns. The kids behind them fell silent, startled by the sudden noise and the severe appearance of the soldiers.

“it’s ok kids,” Brandy said over her shoulder, “they are on our side.” And then to the one in the lead, “What the hell do you think you are doing, you scared these kids’ half to death, you son of a bitch!”

“My apologies Ma’am, I am not used to doors opening that easy anymore,” The soldier said, removing her helmet to reveal red hair tied up into a bun, “and I can assure you I am nobodies son. I assume all is secure here?”

Brandy was taken aback for a moment, “Yes… sorry, um, yes Lt. Kelley, everything is fine here. What can we help you with?”

“We are here to relieve you of duty and advise you that all civilians are to report to the auditorium for a special meeting immediately. Attendance is mandatory by order of Colonel Murray.” She said as she removed her pack and placed it on a table near the door. “It’s ok, we have this under control, I Like kids in small doses and the meeting should be brief.”

“Sergeant,” the officer said as she relaxed into a chair by her pack, “Give me your firearms and go play with the kids, private, go help.”

Brandy turned to Linda; it was obvious they were dismissed. “Well, I guess we go to a meeting…” was all she could think to say as she removed the gun belt and handed it to the soldier.

The two men had wandered over towards the children, but looked lost as to what to do. As the door swung shut behind the leaving woman, the heard the lieutenant's voice yell, “hey kids, Shrek and Donkey Hide candy in their field packs that they think the rest of us don’t know about, you can keep whatever you take away from them!”

“I think the kids will be alright,” Linda remarked with a laugh as the children shrieked with joy.

The courtyard was empty. They could see the guards on the rooftop right where they should be, and the sentries stationed around the grounds looked alert. “We must be some of the last ones, I hope there are seats left, my feet are threatening to fall off”, Linda complained.

When they arrived at the double doors, two soldiers dressed in body armor reached out and opened the doors for them. Brandy again thought how odd it was to see the soldiers dressed fully for battle. She was used to the camouflage BDUs, they always wore, and those were bad enough for making the average person appear more intimidating, but the armor somehow made them seem less… human.

There weren't any seats left. The auditorium was so full that even the aisles were packed with people sitting and the walls were shoulder to shoulder with the crowd waiting to hear what was going on. So many people made the room seemed to suck the air out and the lack of air conditioning and windows did not help the smell.

She had to raise her voice over the roar of so many people having their own conversations to be heard by Linda. "Two weeks ago, a fire marshal would have had a stroke about this many people in here."

Linda nodded her agreement. "I was hoping to find Tom, so I could sit with him, but in this mess..." she waved a hand vaguely at the crowd.

"I am going to stay as close to this door as possible," Brandy asserted, "I would hate to be trapped behind this crowd when it's over."

Linda again nodded her agreement.

On stage, several soldiers were setting up a portable blackboard that had obviously been taken from one of the classrooms. On it they could just make out a large map. The room, while large, was still small enough that even here in the back she could still make it out as a map of the northeastern United States. She felt safe under the assumption that it was also pilfered from a classroom, as it showed the wear and tear of having been rolled and unrolled many times. She could also make out the faces of several of the officers that seemed to run the refugee center, and the two of the Red Cross workers who had been in charge before the army had arrived, their simple red vests looked almost unofficial next to the crisp dress uniforms the colonel and his staff had selected for the occasion. Brandy guessed the military wanted to make a good impression for this meeting.

"Hello, earth to Brandy... Yoo-hoo!" She was jolted from her thoughts by Linda's voice. "are you in there?"

"Sorry, lack of sleep. What's up?" Brandy said back, ashamed she had been lost so completely in thought.

"This very rude young man wants us to clear the doorway," Linda added huffily.

Brandy looked up and saw the sailor from earlier outside the library. "It was not my intention to sound rude ma'am, but orders are to keep the exits clear for safety. If you will step right over here, I believe some seats are about to open up."

The sailor stepped over to the nearest pair of men sitting at the end of the last row, and tapped them on the shoulder, they looked up and he leaned down and said something to them that Brandy couldn't make out. The men looked unhappy, but stood and yielded their seats.

“There you go,” He said to the women, and then to the men, “very chivalrous of you to allow these young ladies to take your seats.”

Linda leaned over and lightly pecked the sailor a kiss on his cheek. “I take back everything I said about you, cutie.” The young petty officers firm composure seemed to crack for the briefest second and brandy could swear he blushed, if only just a little.

They sat down heavily; glad to be off their feet, and when brandy looked to the doors, Mueller was again at his post, looking just as serious as ever.

A voice filled the auditorium at that moment and brandy snapped her eyes back to the front. The colonel stood at the podium tapping the microphone. The air conditioner may be unpowered, but the speakers along the walls were up and running.

“Corporal, I think this meeting will be more productive if the volume wasn’t set to eleven.” He said while looking stage left into the wings. “Let’s go about half that.” Chuckles lifted from the audience. “Testing …one…two… three.” Continued the older man, and as he spoke, the volume dropped in the room until the level was where he wanted, and he gave a thumbs up to the unseen soldiers.

I want to begin by apologizing for the suddenness of this meeting, and promise you that we will make it as short as possible as to allow you, good people, to get back to whatever activities we took you away from. As most of you know, I am

Lieutenant Colonel John "Mach" Murray of the united states army and acting commander of the military forces gathered here to secure and protect this location and the staff and refugees sheltering herein." he explained.

"Most of you know me and most of the men under my command, but early this morning we absorbed a mixed force made up of primarily naval and marine personnel from another camp like ours, as well as a small group of refugees from that same location. They have brought word that a group of the infected has escaped the quarantine and dispersed into the surrounding areas in large numbers."

Several people in the crowd gasped, and a barrage of question began to be hurled at the stage.

"Hold on, people…. Keep it down, let me finish…." He started, but when he saw that it had no effect, he brought his fist down on the desk, filling the room with a loud bang and yelled "QUIET!" The talkers suddenly fell silent, startled by the sudden bang. "Please hold it down," The man said; already back in his calm voice. "We are aware of the locations and movements of the groups via satellite and are in communication with command. We have been instructed by command to prepare to displace, that is, move to another, more secure location, and they have sent down a set of orders that we have all agreed is not only doable, but can be done quickly and efficiently. We will be joining other groups already in these locations." The Colonel turned back to the stage wings, "Lights please." He ordered, and the house lights dimmed as a spotlight illuminated the map board behind him.

"We are here, " He touched the map to indicate the position where the shelter stood. "We have been given three locations that all intelligence indicates will be good, defensible sites. Each of these will be more than sufficient to hole up in until our homes have once again been secured or a cure or vaccination is found." This statement again brought a few yells from the audience, but these quickly died out on their own. The commander simply waited as they faded. They had heard these promises for weeks as the situation grew worse, and many had given up on such hopes. Brandy herself was one of them. Most people no longer even liked the term "infected", seeing it as a dangerous underestimation.

"In the meantime, we will shelter in place at these locations, joining small groups of refugees already there. This plan does mean that of the almost two thousand of us here, we will have to split into three smaller groups, but every effort will be made to pick these groups intelligently and fairly. Families will stay together, friends will not be separated from friends where ever possible, and each group will take a proportionate amount of the available supplies and will have military protection during the entire journey and once they arrive at their destinations. I will not trouble you with too many specifics, but the first and largest group, "red group" will be traveling by helicopter to a nearby airbase for fixed-wing transport to a secure location here." He tapped an area several states away. "Blue group will head west to an isolated area in here" he jabbed his finger at a blank spot on the map. And the last group, dubbed White group, will be the smallest and will travel by military vehicle and bus to this location here, where it will meet up and travel with an armored unit bound for Tennessee." He paused to allow all of this to sink in, and the murmurs immediately rose to fill the silence as people leaned to neighbors and began hushed conversations.

"Why so far?" Linda asked into Brandy's ear, "it just seems like so far for them to move us when you said we may move, I guess I figured 20 or 30 miles, not halfway across the country!"

“There is something we don’t know yet, something they haven’t told us.” Brandy speculated.

The colonel began again, “Each of these locations was chosen for several specific reasons, primarily population density, defensibility, and range of available transport. None of these locations are within one hundred miles of a major city, and as such, the chances of random mobs of the infected running into them are lessened. Intelligence has informed us that the infected do not seem to coordinate their moves or head to a specific area, there seems to just be so many of them that they are everywhere, which is why the decision was made to relocate to less dense areas. The red group will land inside an established military facility, but one that is already well over capacity. Blue group will be established in an area where defenses can be easily created, and such perpetrations have already begun and will be completed shortly before arrival. White group is destined for an area protected by mountains with very few approaches on foot, and yet, we have no evidence the infected have retained the ability to operate vehicles.”

“I am not going to lie to you; this isn’t possible without some level of danger. I have been in the military long enough to know that nothing travels faster than scuttlebutt. So, I will address those rumors now, as it will all be known soon enough. Three days ago, there were more than fifty camps like this one set up here in Illinois and Wisconsin in addition to several military facilities acting as refugee stations in the same area. Per the regional commander, as of yesterday, the largest, naval station great lakes, fell to the infected. Of the sixty thousand people there, we know of only about a thousand that managed to escape in several small groups, one of which ended up here. Command has not been able to establish communication with any of the larger bases, though we know that all of them were under siege. Of the fifty-three smaller camps, only two, this one, and one outside of Beloit, Wisconsin are still on the air though we have no reason to believe it's anything but power failure that keeps us out of contact."

The room had fallen into a silence so deep brandy could almost hear the heartbeats of those around her. Several people, men, and women began to sob openly. It was worse than she could have imagined.

"Another rumor is that we no longer have enough personnel to keep our location secure. This rumor also is true. We have taken heavy losses on the patrols we sent out looking for survivors. As such, I have made the hard decision to abandon that goal. All available personnel must and will be used for defense and supply missions only." He looked around the room, trying to make eye contact with as many people as he could, trying to read the room. "I have been authorized by presidential order to enlist all available personnel into active service and use those individuals as I see fit."

A roar rose from the crowd as his words sank in. the crowd vented its fear into anger at the thought of being conscripted into danger. Brandy was on her feet with the crowd, not because she didn't see the necessity, but because the roiling mass of people could have crushed her had she stayed seated. She could still catch glimpses of the colonel between the furious waving arms of those in front of here. She watched as he banged his fist again and again to regain order, but she could hear nothing over the crowd noise.

She knew that their anger was driven more by fear than anything else, it was an off-gassing of the events and stress of the last week, but she knew enough about people to know that a riot was forming. She glanced at the doors and saw the petty officer was standing his ground as several people approached the door demanding to leave. This was going to get ugly very quickly.

A loud bang reverberated through the room, followed shortly by another. The room fell silent yet again, and brandy looked forward to see the colonel had drawn his sidearm and fired it into the ceiling. She admired the man's fortitude, the shots might have panicked the crowd into riot, but he had taken a chance and it paid off.

"EVERYONE SIT!" He yelled into the microphone. To her surprise, all most everyone did. A few yelled curses and threats at the man before settling down.

"As I was about to explain before I was interrupted," He said, spreading his glare around the room at the troublemakers. "This will not be a draft; no one will be forced into service. A volunteer group will be formed to provide support to our existing military structure, but will not be used for any offensive purposes. I will now ask anyone with any military background, be they retired, inactive, reserve, ROTC, auxiliary, law enforcement, security, or militia to please see Captain Bridges immediately after this meeting to register. There will be an evaluation process and those deemed able to serve will be equipped and given an assignment."

"As for the rest of you, see the Red Cross worker you were assigned to when you arrived to find out what team you will be attached to. The current plan is for all three groups to pull out of here in twenty-four hours. Until that time, no one will be allowed in or out of the perimeter, our best bet now is to keep a low profile until we are ready to go. As for now, get some rest."

As a special treat, dinner tonight will be large, as will breakfast in the morning. Your Red Cross workers have special information sheets concerning how to prepare for the move.

Read them carefully." With this, he turned and walked stiffly off the stage, his subordinates on his heels.

Brandy immediately stood and pulling Linda along behind her, rushed out the now open doors into the cooler air outside. They barely managed to beat the crowd.

"What's the rush sweetie?" Linda gasped as she was pulled along behind.

"It's my brother," Brandy said, too worried to explain fully, "He even brought his damn uniform to show it off to our grandparents..."

***

*Jack skipped the meeting and wheeled the trash bin out to the dumping area at the edge of the ball fields. With the breakdown of society, the dumpsters had quickly overflowed with the refuse the group made. The solution had been to haul it to the fence and dump it far enough away that the smell would reach the building.*

*He tipped the contents onto the edge of the growing pile as he fought the urge to gag. It was almost time turn burn the pile and the accumulation was a miasma of rot, maggots, and sludge.*

*Stepping far enough away for a breath of fresh air, Jack pulled the last of his cigarettes from the pack and lit it. As the smoke hit his lungs, he felt the nicotine start to kick in and smiled. He leaned against the fence and enjoyed the break.*

*Jack wasn't just sneaking out for a smoke, he was sneaking out. From here he could see the guards on their circuit, and even the ones on the roof. He took another drag and waited for the right time. When it came, he vaulted the four-foot-tall chain-link and rushed for the trees on the other side.*

*An hour later, he was moving through the trees beside the road wishing he had another smoke. The cravings and the long walk had been changing his mind and making him regret the decision to try this, but the break in the trees he saw on the side of the road kept his feet moving.*

*Ahead, he saw a collection of signs that indicated a strip mall or collection of small buildings. He could just make out that one of the signs displayed an image of a cartoon bee with smoke coming from its mouth. Jack was holding out hope for a smoke or cigar store, but even a head shop might have some tobacco. It turned out to be a shop selling electronic cigarettes.*

*"It's better than nothing," Jack said aloud as he used a rock to break out the front window.*

*To his relief, nothing moved inside at the sound. He walked carefully around the shop, making sure nothing was hiding before grabbing some of the bottles and some of the strange looking objects displayed in the cases. He took them into the store's office and sat down to figure them out. Luckily each box had good directions and he figured it out quickly.*

*Jack leaned back in the chair and kicked his feet up on the desk as he puffed. He was enjoying the buzz it gave him when keys hanging on the wall caught his attention. He could just make out the tag identifying them as "Van".*

*He found the vehicle parked outside by the rear doors. The same Cartoon bug decorated its white paint. Jack smiled and went back inside to start loading it with the things he found inside. He decided to take everything.*

*When he had loaded the last box, he glanced up at the falling sun and knew he wouldn't get back before dark. "Well Jack, it wouldn't be the first time you have slept in a van."*

***

**Derek**

Derek listened to the colonel's words, and as they sank he began to formulate his plan. They were getting split into three separate teams, red and blue teams were both heading west, away from home. Only the white team was heading in the right direction, and as luck would have it, almost halfway back to Florida. He didn't know how, but he would have to figure out how to make sure they could get assigned to white.

"We have to get all of us on White team," Derek mumbled.

"I guess it's as good as any, do you think we can just ask?" Chad answered.

Derek was confused for a minute, not realizing he had spoken aloud. "I don't know, maybe if I volunteer it will give me a little more pull. We can't go to the other camps; they are farther away from home for all of us."

Chad thought about this for a second. "Maybe we should both volunteer, I am sure it will be better than scrubbing pots and pans..."

"...or mixing egg glop." Derek added. "it looks like they are winding down, let's get out of here so we can be the first ones in line. Brandy is going to be quite pissed."

"But she is so pretty when she's angry." Chad chuckled, "meet you there."

**Immanuel**

He awoke in the dark, confused and then nervous. For a moment he thought he was back in the hospital and the past day had all been a dream. But then he concentrated and could just make out the sounds of voices, and further off, a truck was idling. The other voices were there also, his voices. His newest angels' sobs were the merest whisper, and it brought him joy to see her more accepting of the gift he had given her. He sat up and looked around; the faint glow of the night light gave shape to the room as his eyes adjusted. The space was just larger than the four beds and sparse medical equipment it contained. The door serving as the room's only entrance was at the foot of his bed, and on the other side of it was where the voices came from.

He threw back the thin blanket that still covered him and swung his feet to the floor. His head swam for a minute, but then cleared. He tried to stand, but when his feet touched the floor, lances of fire traveled up his legs, and he fell back to the bed crying out. His hand found thick padding wrapping his feet, and he remembered his long barefoot walk out of the city, at least it explained the pain. Cold wetness began to spread across his side, and he groped to feel it, and his hand came away holding a length of clear tubing. It was an IV he realized, he must have pulled it from his arm when he fell.

His startled scream must have alerted someone, because the door opened, and a soldier stepped in, flipping on the lights. "Hey man, glad to see you awake!" Said the smiling face, "You've been out so long some of those other guys were beginning to wonder if you would ever wake up."

The soldier stepped over and quickly shut off the man's IV, thankfully stopping the drips of fluid that was soaking his bed. "I need you to answer some questions for me Immanuel, you hurt anywhere?"

Immanuel's head had swum again with the sudden light, and now the man's words even seemed to be confusing, had the man called him Immanuel? Then it occurred to him, he had told the medic that was his name. "My... My feet feel like they are burning, and my knees ache." Speaking was a lot of effort now. "My head feels funny; I don't think whatever drugs you gave me have worn off."

"Well the heads the easy part, it will clear up soon. I'd feel a little loopy if I had just slept for two days also. We didn't give you anything, you just kind of crashed, we figured a bad case of exhaustion. Your knees are just a little banged up, I'd guess you took a pretty bad spill out there somewhere; we don't have an x-ray set up here so it's hard to tell for sure. As for your foot, that's another matter, you've got some major cuts and abrasions, not to mention one hell of a matched set of blisters. I don't know how far you walked, but it seems like it was lucky we found you when we did." As the man spoke, he efficiently bandaged the damage the needle on the Intravenous line had done when it pulled out and given Immanuel a thorough once over. "My name is John by the way. I am the medic that picked you up and now I am assigned here."

“Pleased to meet you John, where is ‘here’ if I might ask.” Immanuel Gingerly lowered his feet beside the bed again and found it wasn’t too uncomfortable

“You are in an old school about sixty miles south of Chicago.” John explained before continuing “or as we call it Fort Nowhere. Say, man, you feel up to eating something?”

“Thank you, I am starving. But I don’t think I can walk just yet.” Immanuel said.

“Not a problem, I can bring it in here, this is a full-service dump. Carlos, one of our guys shot a cow the other night when we were flying down, so we got steaks. Brady, our copilot is even pretty good with the gas grill out there so I will get him to fire you one up, how do you take it? Rare? Medium?

Josh didn’t like the idea of being carried, “Maybe just a little rare, thank you, and I would love something cold to drink.

“Your call dude, we got bottled water and canned soda, that’s all we have stocked for us here.”

“”is this a base or rescue center?” Immanuel asked, alarmed.

"This is some kind of rescue center. From what I understand, the Red Cross sat it up when stuff started to go bad, but then a National Guard unit moved in and kind of took over. We are in a building they have set up for newcomers, kind of quarantine. Rumor is that this has become a fall back point for all kinds of people. The army is here, some navy, even some air force. Not to mention a few cops and deputies. They have a good little set up going here." John explained with that same simple smile on his face, as if he was just bound and determined to be chipper, no matter what.

"What happened to your base? Wasn't there another helicopter? I think I remember that, but it's all hazy." Immanuel asked.

John's smile faltered, for the first time, "Yeah, there was, right after we picked you up, when had orders to drop our rescues at base, refuel and then go help with a big operation going on up north. But the time we got back to the post, it was overrun." The man sighed heavily, "The other helo was already super low on gas, so we circled and covered them while they dropped in to fill up, but there was just too many of them. It got overrun right away and we bugged out. They tried to get off the ground again, but those things had gotten inside when they were still on the pad, they got about twenty feet up and then just nosed over straight into the fuel truck. With that truck gone, we knew we weren't going to have enough gas to get where we were going, and ended up here. This was the closest place with the right kind of fuel and once here we were told to stay."

The medic stood suddenly, and that smiled returned to his face. "I'm going to go get you that food I promised, be back in a flash!" Before Immanuel could say anything, the man was gone.

Immanuel didn't know what to make of the situation, but knew he was stuck in it for now. His feet throbbed with the damage they had sustained. He would have to heal to regain a measure of his independence. He wasn't used to having to rely on others; in fact, the voice demanded he avoids the distractions of friends and had taught him independence.

He tuned out the sounds of the conversation in the next room and listened deep within himself. He could just barely make out the voice now, working to control the sobs of his newest angel. He knew from experience that it would not be long now before he had its full guidance back.

A cough brought him out of his concentration; he looked around at the other beds and saw a small shape in one of them that he hadn't noticed before. It was an elderly woman, her shock of white hair protruded from the blankets that hid the rest of her slight frame. She coughed again, a wet cough that told Immanuel that she was sick, quite sick.

He leaned closer, risking a little bit of pressure on his feet to get a better look at her. John's voice startled him from the doorway, "That's Mrs. Chen, we picked her up from the roof of this little gas station right outside Racine, nice old lady, they had her and her grandson trapped up there, completely surrounded."

Immanuel turned and saw the soldier had a tray in his hands, so he scooted back against the headboard. John carefully handed him the tray, "I've got to pull my shift on guard duty starting about 2 minutes ago, do you need anything?"

"No thank you, John, you have been most kind," Immanuel said politely, a little overwhelmed by the amount of food in front of him.

"No problem brother, "John flashed that smile again, "Glad to do it, one of the other guys said he would come check on you and Mrs. Chen in a few. Talk to you later."

Immanuel watched the man again leave the room, despite the smarminess, he liked the man. He looked back down at the plate in front of him; a large steak of some cut he wasn't familiar with covered the plate almost entirely. Obviously, this 'Carlos' who had hunted this particular cow was not a meat cutter, but it looked good enough. Its wafting smell made his stomach growl almost painfully, and he dug in.

As he ate, he pondered his next step; he had found people, which had been his goal, but how many? Listening to the voices in the next room, he didn't think more than a dozen, but how many people were in the nearby camp? It sounded like a large group, and that was good. The more people, the better, there was safety and concealment in numbers.

Already he could feel the need to return to his work. It was an urge to do the lords work that he often compared to the high he imagined some got from drugs or sex, but he knew this was better, because it wasn't a sin. It was a pure sensation that was a gift from the lord.

He finished eating and sat the plate beside him on the bed, to his surprise, he had found room for most of the steak, and had finished off the liter of water, which had more than satisfied his thirst. Soon another soldier came in and took away the tray. He was a skinny red-headed man with a southern drawl, but he didn't say much. He wasn't impolite, he just didn't seem like he wanted much to do with conversation, which was fine with Immanuel.

Immanuel had spent far more time in conversation lately than he liked. In the past he would go weeks isolated in his small house, speaking only muttered sentences to cashiers, or delivery people as he went about his observations and preparations for saving a soul. He had learned a long time ago, shortly after he had begun helping people was that getting close to anyone meant questions, and those questions normally meant even more questions.

Even Immanuel's father, who would often profess to his congregation about his own conversations with God, had started to ask questions. Immanuel's mother had believed in his father's lies about God. She had believed when his father had denied the rumors about other woman, even when the news showed pictures. She had believed his denials about the accusations of fraud even after the sports cars and fancy suits.

She even believed the 'healings and miracles' her husband performed on television, even he allowed the evil that had rooted in her grew unchecked.

The doctors had once said a malignancy was growing inside her, when a 10-year-old Immanuel happened to be within earshot, and it was one that was not in their power to remove. He had been a bright kid, mature for his age and frustrated that everything about his mother's condition was whispered or hidden when he was around, so he had gone to his dictionary and looked the word up. It meant 'the art of being malign, which he knew from his father sermons meant dark in nature, evil. His mother had an evil growing in her, and the doctors couldn't stop it.

Immanuel hadn't been worried, his father healed people with the power of the good lord almighty. No evil could have stood against that kind of power. But that healing touch was never given. His father had heard the news at the same time, but had merely thanked the doctor, and left the mother and child behind, off on another fund-raising trip. These trips became more frequent as Immanuel watched his mother become sicker and sicker, more and more pale and thin.

His father came home one day, taken one look at his wife lying in the bed, and left. He did not speak to her, or Immanuel or Immanuel's sister just shook his head and left. Immanuel had chased after him, but his father would not turn back when he called to him. His father had climbed into a waiting car and left.

His mother had died a few weeks later. His father had not returned to the house and was not at the funeral. Their nanny took care of them but always changed the subject when his little sister cried for daddy or mommy in the night. Immanuel waited for his father, confident that he would return. After all, He watched his father continue to preach on TV about the importance of family and giving money to god. Surely his father would be back soon to get them.

Immanuel had found a number written on a form from a lawyer on his mother bedside table. Lawyers had been bringing lots of forms, so this wasn't unusual, but this one had had his father's name on it as well, and written directly underneath the name was a phone number.

When Immanuel couldn't wait any longer, he had dialed the number. His father answered on the third ring.

"Daddy, can you come get us?" Immanuel had asked.

A pause on the other end, then "You shouldn't have called me here Immanuel… I ..I can't come get you."

"Why not daddy, we will be good, we watch you on TV and have tried to send you money like you say, but the nanny won't let us, we just want to come be with you."

“I’m sorry Immanuel, but I’m with someone new now,” his father explained hesitantly, “And she doesn’t want kids around… I have made sure you have good people to take care of you. I also made sure that neither you nor your sister will ever need money… but I’m sorry… Please don’t call here again.” There was a click and the line went quiet.

That was the night the archangel had spoken to him the first time. Its voice, THE voice had gifted Immanuel with many treasures that night. It had taught him the truth about his father being the false prophet who had placed the evil in his mother. It had gifted him with the sight to see the evil, and what it meant. But mostly, it had taught him his true mission to purify the malignancies from the innocent.

The gifts had come with a cost, Immanuel had wanted to be a scientist and build rocket ships. But the voice told him those were the dreams of childhood, and that he must serve God in everything. He knew the way ahead would be rough, as the lives of those given a mission from above usually were, but he would persevere.

He could still remember the day, just a few months later, that he had been given his first angel. The voice had been proud of him for helping his sister so bravely, and though she had not survived, he thanked the Lord every day that he could still hear her voice singing to him after all these years.

A rough, gasping noise brought him back to the dimly lit room in the present, and he glanced over towards the old woman lying in the next bed. Her breathing had roughened while he had been lost in his thoughts and was now a wet sounding rattle. She seemed to be trying to cough, to clear her throat, but was too weak to accomplish it.

"This will not do Mrs. Chen, I have a lot of thinking to do and that noise is very distracting," Immanuel said in a whisper he was confident would not carry to the next room.  He opened his sight upon her, and felt a mixture of relief and sadness when she showed the same grayish glow as most of the people he encountered. The old woman was not for him to purify.

"oh well," Immanuel said with a sigh as he reached across and rolled the ancient woman on to her side, causing her breathing to ease, "I guess you get to make it through this night anyway."

# ~ 76 ~

**Brandy**

"What in the hell do you think you are doing?" Brandy demanded as soon as she saw the camouflage uniform laid out on the bed.

"I don't need this brandy. I know what I am doing." Derek replied quickly, he had obviously been expecting her to have exactly the reaction she did.

"You are barely sixteen years old; you aren't old enough to be running around with a gun. You are going to blow your own foot off." Brandy declared.

"I am only two years younger than you, and I know a lot more about guns than you do. Besides, I have had military training, which I might add you have not. I have seen you with that gun on your hip in the library. At least this way I can help." Derek protested.

"Civil Air Patrol does not qualify you for armed combat." She declared, stabbing at the blue patch sewn to the front of the camouflage shirt with her finger.

"Look, Brandy, I know I am not a soldier, I know I don't even have a driver's license yet. I talked to mom before the meeting;

she is going on that hospital raid." Derek paused in lacing his boots to look up at his older sister. "I also know that that same raid leaves in one hour and mom has already gone back to the final planning meeting. They want to get it done and be back before helicopters start landing to evacuate people, because all that noise will draw those things from miles around. It is also common sense that the more people they have on the walls here, means more professional soldiers they can send on the raid, and the more badasses that go with her, the more likely she will come back. And right now, I don't care if that makes you angry, or if I get in trouble for it with mom when she comes back or dad if he is still alive, but I am doing it."

He stood and grabbed his shirt, she was between him and the door and he met her eyes and held contact. She stared back for a single breath, and then stepped aside.

He started to walk past, but then stopped, "Want to walk me over there?"

She started to refuse, but then reconsidered, he was right. Everything he said made sense and for the first time in her life she looked at her younger brother and didn't see a kid anymore. "Sure, let's go."

"What's the trick?" He asked, glancing sideways at her, "last time you gave up that easy on an argument was when you let me climb on to the roof when I was seven and then threw rocks at me."

Brandy laughed and held up her hands, "See? No rocks. I just agree with you is all, you sold me on the idea. I think I may join up also." She admitted.

They started walking, and after a few paces, Derek said: "I think that would be a bad idea."

"Why the hell do you say that? I am just as good as you!" Brandy felt the flush of anger rising into her cheeks.

"I don't doubt that, but those kids need you. No offense, but you work with a bunch of airheads in that nursery. If you leave to go sit a guard post, who is going to keep the kids safe? Julie? We both know that most of the kids are smarter than her and twice as dedicated." Derek put his hand on her shoulder as the continued walking. If you join this F troop they are starting, you will be another grunt, in the nursery, you can make a difference."

Brandy considered his words, yet again struck by the maturity of it, and had to agree. He seemed to be becoming older by the minute. "Yeah, you are probably right, but isn't that what you will be? Just another grunt?"

Derek smiled "Nah babe, you forget I got the mad skills." He quipped and flashed a grin. "I am willing to bet they will put me on a radio since I was a communications officer back home. And

I am okay with that, I was working up to flight crew, but I doubt they have much need for a half-trained pilot nowadays."

"Probably not," she agreed sadly "Do you think it will ever... ever get back to normal?" It wasn't something she had worked up the nerve to discuss with anyone yet.

"I don't see how it could," Derek confessed. "Even if all this... whatever it is... stopped right now, a lot of people are dead, millions, entire cities are gone, even the damn united states military is retreating from this thing. And we barely know what's happening twenty or thirty miles away, much less around the world. There could be billions of dead by now, especially in more crowded areas, and areas that couldn't respond as fast as we could. There could be billions of those things out there."

"So, what do we do?" she asked.

Derek looked up and saw that they had arrived at the sign-up location. This is where they would be separated until after they had assigned him some new duty.

"Whatever we have to do to live another day, every day." And with that, he pushed open the door and went inside the captains' office.

Brandy stood staring at the door. It was hard to believe that just a few weeks ago, her biggest concern in life was what to wear or what college classes to register for. “And now everyone in the family is wearing guns.” She finished the thought out loud. She went back to the gym to her cot to lie down and try to sleep.

**Derek**

The last few hours had been periods of intense activity, followed by long stretches of waiting. The t man who interviewed him, Captain Bridges, had listened patiently while he explained his need for everyone to be on the white team and said he would do what he could to arrange it. He had answered a few questions in the captains and then been whisked away to the clinic. From there he had been rushed with some of the others to a staff lounge in the school where they were told to sit tight until someone came to get them. It was only then that he had realized that he hadn't received a promise about being assigned to white team; just a vague 'will try'.

He looked around the room; he was the youngest by several years. Chad had still been seated in the waiting room when Derek had been escorted directly to the clinic for his medical evaluation. The group of men now surrounding him was composed of all fit, lean figures that had a distinct military bearing on them. He was just starting to wonder if they had put him in the wrong group when the door swung open and the largest man he had ever seen strolled in, Derek recognized the one Brandy called 'Shrek' immediately, but he saw a couple of the others show a moment's surprise before going back to their carefully cultivated bored look.

"Hello and thank you for volunteering to give us a hand. Welcome to the United States Army, I am Sergeant Hansen, and I will oversee you fine gentleman until such time as the current emergency passes. You will be considered active duty military with all rights and responsibilities due to a member of the

United States military. Do you have any questions?" The gruff-voiced man finished.

"No sergeant!" the others barked in unison, and Derek suddenly felt very out of place.

The large man looked at the teen and asked, "Do you have a question?"

"No sir," Derek answered, and was rewarded with a scowl.

"You must be Hobbs, is that correct?" Sergeant Hansen asked as he flipped through the clipboard he carried. Before Derek could answer, he added "I see here you are fifteen and come to us from the Air Force auxiliary, but you have no active duty experience. Someone explain his mistake to him."

One of the others, a man of about 25 with large scars covering his left arm and left sides of his face answered loudly, "The FNG referred to the staff sergeant as a 'sir' obviously confusing him with someone who does not work for a living." the gathered men laughed, and Derek felt heat creep into his cheeks.

"Now listen up people. Tonight, we have our first mission, as promised you will not be used for direct combat with the infected, but you will be armed in case you meet them. Make no mistake; these are the evilest most determined sons of bitches you will ever come up against. Do not hesitate when confronted by one of these things to fire upon it." Sgt. Hansen began.

"This location will be overrun by a few thousand of those things in just over twenty-four hours. As you just found out, we will be hauling ass before they get here, but to accomplish that, we must pick up a few things we are short of, namely food, medical supplies, and a few comfort items." The giant explained "This facility will be reorganized into three distinct units, and tonight's mission will provide most the supplies for two of them. The target is a large hospital about thirty miles from here."

"That's bullshit," one of the men exclaimed, "Hospitals are the last place we want to go, we all watched the news when all this started going down, we know they are nothing but slaughterhouses since day one. Why don't we hit grocery stores and pharmacies?"

Hansen let him finish, then explained. "We have been supplying over a thousand people in this thrown together shelter for over a week. There isn't a standing grocery, pharmacy, gas station, discount store, or neighborhood we haven't essentially looted. This hospital is going to be a tough nut to crack, but it seems to have gone down quickly, so it should still be fully stocked. "He lifted a large hand and started raising fingers as he spoke, "This means antibiotics, sterile dressings, painkillers, equipment, food,

Blankets, fuel from its generators, and who knows what else. But don't worry your pretty little heads; none of you will be going into the actual building. We are a support squad, we will hold a position nearby and provide security for the staging area the real soldiers will use when getting in and out."

Derek let all this information sink in, this must have been what Jack was talking about earlier, the reason there wouldn't be very many people walking the fence line. An operation like this would require almost all the soldiers stationed here.

They had listened to the stories on the radio driving up from Florida about the trouble with hospitals. In fact, the first reports of reanimation were from hospitals across the country, people had arrived at emergency rooms critically injured or passed quietly on one of the floors and the next thing you knew you had a building full of infected chasing the living. In fact, it had been the presidents warning to avoid hospitals that had caused him to first realize how bad things truly were.

"All of you, head down to the cafeteria where you will get equipped and a more detailed briefing from the LT." the big man ordered. "Hobbs, a word please before you head down."

Derek waited as the others filed out and down the hall. The man placed a dinner plate sized hand on his shoulder, "Son, I know this is probably a lot more than you bargained for when you signed up, and it should show you how desperate the situation is if they are issuing automatic rifles to kids who can't even drive cars. But don't worry, stick with me and I will watch out for you."

"Thank you, sir... sergeant," Derek answered, feeling heat rise into his cheeks yet again.

The soldier chuckled and steered the younger man out into the hallway.

**Immanuel**

Sleep did not come that night. Between the sounds of helicopters and the old lady's snores and coughs, he spent a restless night on the uncomfortable cot. John came and checked on them just after three in the morning. His chipper persona, damped by his obvious lack of sleep, still tried to peak through the dark circles under his eyes and his perpetual smile was drooped at the edges.

"I hope the old lady didn't keep you up too late, has she been breathing like that for very long?" asked the medico.

"just for the last few hours," Immanuel admitted. "It was very difficult to sleep."

"Sorry about that buddy, she doesn't have long now." The medic sighed, "Nothing we can really do for her. She needs a team of doctors and a fully equipped intensive care unit but I doubt very seriously there is a hospital within a thousand miles that wasn't overrun on day one."

John sighed his weary sound again, and then his smile forced its way back out to the front. "We are almost cleared to move into the compound, just a few more hours. They have better facilities in there, man I would fight a bear for a warm shower right about now!"

“I assume they are waiting to clear us until they see what happens to her?” Immanuel asks, nodding towards the old lady.

“That’s my guess. The medical briefing, I went to told us that those that got infected only lasted 24 hours, tops, so I don’t think they are waiting for us to be cleared. I think they don’t want one of them to come back inside the center if they can avoid it.” John explained. “I don’t think she has very long, but sometimes people can hang on for days like this. And from what we were told last night they are about to bug out, I don’t know what that means for us yet, they have already cleared the pilots and bird for active duty, it’s the rest of us they aren’t sure about.”

“You aren’t implying that they would leave us, are you?” Immanuel asked startled.

“A lot of panic in the world right now, but no, I don’t think they would. “John said as if trying to convince himself. “We have until tomorrow from what the rumors tell me, we will be fine. “

“Will she come back… as one of those things?” Immanuel inquired, finally voicing something that had lingered in the back of his mind.

“You don’t watch the news much do you,” John asked incredulously, “We will all come back as those things when we die, nobody is quite sure why, but whether you get bit or not, if you die, you will come back. It may take a few minutes or a few hours, but you will. This guy from USAMRIID, sorry, the army's medical gurus on diseases, says he thinks it's some kind of an airborne prion that went wild and spread really quickly. It doesn't kill you itself, but just kind of hides out in your brain and waits for you to die of something else. This guy says the way the bites kill you is either by making you bleed out or of whatever disease the one that got you had and caught from the one that got him and so on down the line. Of course, we all thought he was full of crap since even he says there isn't any evidence or tests to confirm what he says."

Immanuel sifted uncomfortably in his cot and stared at the women across the room. 'I know the truth, it's not a disease, it's possession. The body and mind become weak and something from hell moves in and takes over." But he kept this thought to himself. John stood before him as a man of science, secure in his own beliefs, and Immanuel knew he wouldn't be able to convince him otherwise, and trying might endanger his mission, better to fit in. "Is there a priest for the old lady, someone to pray with her in her final time?" was all Immanuel could think to ask.

"Nah, her grandson says she is a Buddhist and there really isn't anything she would want to be done. He came in yesterday while you were still out and sat with her for a while and said his goodbyes. They have already cleared him to go into the compound. "John sighed. "Only a few of us left here in the building as of about an hour ago."

"You look tired, you should go sleep," Immanuel urged, "I can sit here with her for a while."

"Thanks, Gabe, I am dead beat on my feet," John said standing and flashing that huge smile again. "I will be in the next room if you need me, just give me a holler, I have always been a light sleeper." He patted Immanuel on the shoulder and left the room.

Immanuel sat up and tried putting weight on his injured feet. He found he could almost stand; it would be good enough for now. He waited for the sounds of sleep from the next room. "Even the man's snoring sounds overly happy." He thought to himself as he listened.

"Mrs. Chen, I don't know if you can hear me, but I hope you can. I am very sorry for what I must do, but judgment must be hastened upon you. You have a clean soul, but your death will free me to continue my mission, and your continued life may hinder it. I pray for your entrance into heaven, despite your heathen nature."

He reached behind him and picked up his pillow before lifting himself to take the painful step to sit on the edge of her bed. From his robe he withdrew the steak knife that he had kept from dinner earlier and placed in on her bedside table. He looked down into her closed eyes, "May the warm arms of the lord almighty comfort you."

He placed the pillow across her face and used his hands to force it tight over her mouth and nose. She didn't struggle, after a minute she made a barely audible series of gasps and then laid still. Immanuel kept his hands in place and applied his steady pressure for a slow count of two hundred, before removing the pillow and tossing it back to his bed.

Her eyes were open but sightless. He took her pulse and listened to her heart. She was gone from this world. He closed her eyes and kissed each lid before straightening and reaching for the knife he had saved from last night's meal.

He watched her and said prayers, hoping that she would be spared the turning, the corruption that seemed to be taking over the world. His prayers were not answered. As he watched, her eyes opened again, and her head slowly turned towards him.

He was ready for this and acted quickly. The malignancy had her now; he drove the steak knife into her temple with a quick powerful thrust and twisted the blade. She fell very still again.

Immanuel Made the painful move back to his own bed, exhausted. He knew he should call for the medic, but he knew he was tired as well. Besides, the voice offered to wake him up in an hour.

**Brandy**

The noise of the helicopters startled her from her sleep. She sat up and looked around the room, trying to shake the fog of sleep from her exhausted mind. Around the gym, others were doing the same. The clock on the wall showed it to be after one, and the darkened windows showed it to be the middle of the night.

She hurriedly put on her shoes, and made her way across the crowded gym towards the courtyard. The cacophony grew louder as she exited the doors. The large clearing in front of her held two helicopters, both were being loaded with assorted cases by lines of men in fatigues as two more helicopters circled overhead. Across the courtyard, she could just make out the colonel standing in a small group of men, and he did not look happy.

Brandy knew that all this noise would be upsetting the children, so she made her way around the courtyard, giving the spinning blades a wide berth. The wind and noise they made were enormous. The surrounding walls seemed to echo and amplify the sound.  “I bet you could hear these thirty miles away,” Brandy said aloud “It’s going to draw every one of those things straight at us!”

She rushed to the doors to the library and burst in. Julie for once was awake, comforting a small group of kids obviously awakened and scared by the noise.

“What’s going on out there?” the woman demanded. Luckily the brick walls of the building muffled most of the sounds and despite the ringing, it had left in her ears, brandy could understand her.

“I have no clue,” Brandy admitted, “A bunch of helicopters just showed up and some landed in the courtyard. They were loading a bunch of stuff in them.”

As brandy spoke, the pitch of the idling helicopters changed and then diminished as one after another they lifted off and flew away. Less than a minute later, another set moved in and landed. “I think they are moving stuff out in preparation for the evacuations.” Brandy theorized out loud.

“At one o’clock in the morning?” Julie demanded incredulously. “Did the guards tell you anything about what was going on?”

It was then that Brandy realized that she hadn’t been challenged before entering the library. There had always been a guard before. Without saying a word, she turned and walked back out to the courtyard. The floodlights were on, brandy assumed to make it easier for the helicopters and loading crews, but she couldn’t see any soldiers at their normal guard posts, either on the roof or outside of the few doors that were guarded.

She noticed the Cafeteria lit brightly and made her way quickly to the door marked staff only. This door was always left open to allow the heat from the stoves and ovens to vent to the outside. Chef Rob was there, hastily organizing supplies and equipment into large flat green case.

"Chef," brandy called out, catching his attention for the first time, "What is going on?"

"No time to talk sweetie, but you best go pack your things and get ready to get the hell out of here." the man responded in a hurried tone.

"I thought we weren't leaving until late tonight. Please, Rob, tell me something." She pleaded.

The large man stopped pacing and sighed. "Not surprisingly, someone in intelligence screwed up. The built our evac plan around some damn chart the military built about rate of enemy march, never once considering that these damn things don't need 15-minute breaks or to stop to nap. A whole damn horde of them will be here this morning, and we haven't even begun to move people out. To make it worse, the buses were supposed to move out long before these damn helicopters started showing up because the helicopters noise will draw them like flies."

"Have you seen Derek or my mother?" brandy asked desperately. "I have got to warn them."

"Not yet, the hospital raid hasn't come back yet." The chef consoled. "But they both looked fine when I saw them getting onto the trucks."

"You saw them both getting onto the trucks?" Brandy asked, not believing. "Derek is only fifteen Chef, why was he getting onto the trucks? He wasn't supposed to go!" She felt her disbelief sliding into anger.

"I am sorry brandy, but I don't know. A few of us were supposed to go and ended up being told at the last minute that we had been replaced, but look around, almost everybody else went. Hell, I bet there aren't a dozen damn soldiers left to run this place and coordinate this evacuation. Now I am sorry, but I must get back to work, kitchen is low priority anyway and I doubt they are going to give me any extra time." The cook turned his attention to the two civilians he was assigned and began to shout instructions, indicating what needed to go on the trucks.

Brandy, realizing she was dismissed, turned and stepped out into the courtyard in time to see the two helicopters lift into the sky. She watched while two more glided in and softly touched down in the yard, amazed that they both managed to fit in an area not much bigger than the blurred discs of the spinning rotors.

She noticed the group of officers supervising the loading of supplies and made straight for them. "Colonel, I need to speak with you!" she demanded.

The man, whose back was towards her, turned and snapped, "What the hell is it now?" and then looked abashed when he saw the young girl he had just snapped at. "I am sorry miss, but we are very busy now, please be brief."

"You sent my mother and brother on some stupid supply run, and I want to know what's going on!" she demanded.

"You are the young lady who works with the children, Brenda?" he asked, giving his politicians smile. She knew he was a good man in a difficult spot, but she was mad. Furthermore, he was charming, and that made her madder because she didn't want to like this man right now.

"Brandy, my name is Brandy, my mother is Annie Hobbs, and my brother is Derek, neither is a soldier and you sent them off to fight ghouls at an overrun hospital, can you remember that?" she snapped, irritated.

"Trust me, young lady...Brandy, I assure you I have not sent your mother into combat, she is to be very well protected. Her knowledge of equipment is extremely valuable to us. I regret that I don't know your brother, Derek?" The older man rubbed his jaw thoughtfully and then turned to a man standing nearby. "Captain Bridges, look up this Derek Hobbs on your list and see if we can help this young lady."

The shorter man consulted a clipboard that he fought to control against the winds of the helicopter blades and then pointed at something for his superior.

“Aw yes, the air patrol kid, He went as radioman since he knew the equipment. I assure you, Miss Hobbs, both are more than safe and were to be kept out of harm’s way during this mission. Now if you will excuse me.” And he turned to walk away.

“Colonel, what about the children in the library?” she asked, unable to think of how to respond to what she had just learned, but feeling the need to say something.

The gray-haired man leaned down and whispered to his aide, who turned towards brandy and then nodded to his superior.

“My name is Captain Bridges, I oversee organizing things and can answer all of your questions.” He explained. “The orphaned personnel are assigned to blue group and will be going out in the first convoy. How long will it take you to prepare them for the move?”

“We have been teaching them fire drills, I can have them ready in just a few minutes.” Brandy said proudly.

“Most impressive Miss Hobbs, but that kind of haste won’t be necessary, we should have everything ready to roll at right about eight in the morning. We will have rations waiting on the bus for them to eat, so you shouldn't even have to worry about breakfast." He consulted his clipboard again. "I see you are assigned to white group, your caravan will leave at the same time. Will you be able to prepare your own possessions for travel by then?"

"I am not going with the children?" Brandy was shocked. "Who will take care of them?"

"We have put most of the Red Cross on that group as well as most of the families with children since it will be going to the safest area, I assure they will be well provided for. Now, about your possessions, will you need assistance? What about the rest of your families things? Will you require assistance preparing the children to travel? I can assign someone to aid you..."

Brandy considered, "No, I will get the other people that work there and we will all go over. I will get our stuff together, where do I put it?"

"Just pack it up and leave it on your cot, I will send someone to collect it." offered the captain. "Thank you for your service ma'am, and feel free to come to me with any concerns, be safe." He said and then walked back to the other officers watching the helicopters being loaded. For the first time, she noticed civilians gathering, this was obviously the group that would be flying out.

She wished that she had remembered to check with the Red Cross like they had advised everyone to do, then she would know more about how this was all going to work, but it was too late now. Not sure what else to do, she headed off to wake Linda and the others.

**Derek**

The truck bench was certainly not comfortable as it bounced down the road, nor was the heavy gear they had given him to put on. At six feet four but only one hundred and fifty pounds, Derek had always been hard to fit and the body armor he now wore was evidence to that fact. Only the helmet fit him well. The pack at his feet was full of things he didn't know how to use and many that he didn't even know what were. The sergeant had given him a run down on how to use the night vision goggles that they had all been issued, before finding out that they didn't have batteries to supply them with power. Many of the other guys had laughed at this and made comments about how nothing had changed.

One thing they were well supplied with was weapons. Each man had received a rifle, a pistol, a combat knife and enough ammo to start a war. The heavy feel of the rifle made Derek feel better, even though he had never fired an M-16 before, he felt confident that he could handle it.

The lieutenant, a tough looking woman named Kelley had been yelling final instructions at them for the last few minutes as they neared the staging area. Derek had listened intently, and it all seemed to break down to jump out of the truck, run to where they were told, and wait there until someone told them to do something different.

The truck lurched to a stop and they all jumped out, Giving Derek his first look at the area. They were in a large parking lot in front of an abandoned grocery store; Derek guessed someone had been refurbishing it since all around him was bulldozers, cranes and construction equipment. The lot was surrounded by a tall chain-link fence.  Several other squads of men were rushing in different directions setting to the tasks they had been assigned, and this reminded Derek that he should be running somewhere himself. He looked for his crew and saw them already forty yards away and moving at a run, so he hurried off after them, the cumbersome pack and rifle slowing him down.

He caught them at the gate they had been assigned and Sgt. Hansen was already growling out commands. "Rodriguez, Michaels, grab some of that junk and set a defensible barricade to the left. Palmer, Porter, to the right side. The rest of you, I want a sweep of those trees and out 50 yards. Not you Hobbs, you are with me, on my six and never more than Five feet away. Get on the radio and call us on mission and digging in. Tell them the gate is open."

Derek cocked his head to the side to hear the shoulder microphone of the radio, one of the few available, and listened to other units' radio in their situations. When there was a break, he pressed the button and spoke the codes they had taught him, feeling a little silly, "Kansas, Kansas, Bravo three on mission and digging in, red gate is open, I repeat, red gate is open. Over"

"Roger bravo three on mission, red gate open. Maintain position and secure area. Raiders ready to roll in one minute. Over." Came the woman's voice over the speaker.

Derek turned to look back at the trucks and saw the crates they had brought with them were being handed down from the backs. Already other teams were opening them and setting up their temporary base. Large lights were being erected as other teams used the bulldozers to clear away the construction debris to open the area up.

"Kansas says raiders ready to go in one." He shouted over all the noise to his leader, who nodded and went back to yelling instructions.

A series of shots rang out from the store and Derek ducked involuntarily. They had been warned that the area was not secured, but for the first time, the situation became real to him. The shots meant they had found infected. He gripped his gun a little tighter.

"First time out in it?" the sergeant asked, and continued after Derek nodded his head, "I can't say you get used to it, but it gets easier, just keep your guard up and your wits about you. These things aren't smart, they aren't fast, and if you don't let them corner you somewhere you will be okay, out here in the open isn't so bad, it's those poor bastards clearing the store earning their pay right now."

"Yes, sergeant," Derek answered. His radio clicked again, and the lieutenant's voice came through.

"The Raiders are rolling. Gates standby to secure after they leave." He heard and relayed it to the squad as the powerful engines behind him start to rev. They watched as about twenty vehicles rushed out the gate and disappeared into the night. Half of them were trucks he noted, and half of them armored personnel carriers, alternating one then the other. He remembered in the briefing they had explained that each truck would have an armored vehicle protecting it.

He watched them go, knowing that one of those trucks carried his mother, and he said a silent prayer for her. He hadn't seen her at the briefing or when they were loading up. He wondered if she even knew he was out here, but then realized it didn't matter. He would do his best to be here when she got back, though he knew she would probably not be happy about him joining up.

He heard his name and looked away from the receding tail lights. "Stay with me, Hobbs." He realized he had become lost in thought and had not seen the sergeant move away from him, he rushed back to stand behind him. The rest of the squad had retreated into the gate and the expanse was being shut. Now all there was to do was watch and wait.

“Raiders clear of the Alamo, red gate closed and secured. Bravo three out” he called and stood watching the night, He wished that he could hear the reports come in from the vehicles, but all of their communication would come in on a different channel.

“Hey, Sarge,” one of the other men called out almost an hour later, “movement dead ahead.”

Derek looked up and saw two shapes coming down the road, he couldn’t see more than their general outlines as far away from the powerful lights behind him lights.

Hansen looked up and watched the pair. “Infected.” Was all he said about the two. “Let them get closer. It’s easier to take them out at short range.”

“How do you know they are infected?” Derek asked.

“The way they move, watch them, see how they seem almost drunk? They all move like that.” He explained. “Watch them as they come closer.”

Derek watched the duo shamble, and the man was right, it was very distinct. As they came closer, he could make out their details. It was a man and a woman, both in their twenties. She wore jeans and a white blouse, and her entire chest was covered with a crusty black stain that he recognized as dried blood. The man wore a shirt and tie that looked like it was freshly dry cleaned. Derek could just make out that a large portion of the woman’s face was missing; exposing white bones and red black strings of what he assumed was muscle shreds hung down.

They continued moving forward until they were a few dozen yards from the gate. One of the men raised his rifle. “Do I shoot them?” he asked.

“Standard operating procedure is to issue a challenge unless you are under imminent threat of violence.” Explained the big black man. “Halt!” he called at the pair.

When the two didn’t respond, “Stop where you are, or we will be forced to open fire!” He bellowed. Again, the pair proceeded, not acknowledging the soldier’s words.

“Rodriguez, take the man, porter, take the woman.” He ordered, “Fire.”

The twin gunshots sounded almost like one, momentarily drowning out the noise of the generators behind him, and made Derek jump. The woman fell to the roadway like a rag doll. Something that looked like a rose suddenly blossomed on the man’s shirt and he staggered, but quickly recovered and took another step before another gunshot rang out and a second rose appeared beside the first.

“Damn it Rodriguez, headshots,” The squad’s leader scolded, “Nothing but headshots!”

The Hispanic man apologized and quickly sighted down his rifle again. The next shot made the top of the man’s head fly off like a cork from a champagne bottle and he crumpled.

Derek felt a wave of shock pass over him but immediately forced it back down. The sergeant was already at the gate, opening it a wide enough for him to slip out. “Porter, Hobbs, with me, stay alert.”

They moved outside the compound, weapons raised and approached the prone figures lying on the road. When they were ten feet away, the sergeant motioned for them to stop. He raised his rifle and fired twice, once into each of the prone figures heads before explaining. “It’s always better to be sure; you can never tell if these damn things are truly dead.”

Derek looked down at the bodies. Now that they were closer, Derek could see the extent of the woman’s injuries, most of her face was missing, and the wound was caked with a mixture of dried blood, grass and Mud. She had a small hole in her forehead just above the left eye where the soldier’s bullet had finally ended her walking. The man didn’t appear to have a mark on him except for the recent bullet wounds.

“How did he get infected? Heisn't bit.” Derek asked the other two men.

The one named porter answered, “You don’t have to be the bite,” He explained as they donned gloves to pull the body from the roadway, “I saw this back when all of this started. My neighbor, an old man named Walker, died at home, he was a hospice patient, cancer or something. His wife was good friends with mine and she came over to sit with us while the coroner came to take away the body. Next thing we knew we heard all this yelling and then a gunshot. Mr. Walker came back when they were putting him in the body bag and attacked the guy they sent to pick him up. The deputy that was there shot him when he wouldn’t stop. That’s when I knew something big was up and we started getting ready to get the hell out of there.”

Derek took all this in. the news had said this was just a disease and referred to the victims as infected, but he had known there was more to it. This just confirmed it. He looked down at the dead man again as thick black blood oozed from the wounds in his chest. His father was a mortician, and Derek had helped him at work before. He knew what blood looked like after it had clotted inside a dead body, and that was it. Confirming this made him feel better about having watched these two be gunned down.

They had just dragged the bodies clear of the road when Derek heard a noise in the distance. He considered the blackness. “Did you guys hear that?” he asked aloud.

The sergeant stepped to the middle of the road and squinted into the darkness; he reached to his helmet and lowered the night vision device, the only one the squad had been issued, over his eyes. He watched for a moment and then stiffened.

“Get back inside the gate!” the barked and then started backing away. “Hurry!” he reinforced the order.

They ran for the opening as Derek again heard the noise behind them, this time he realized it was moaning. The made it inside and the gate swung closed, closing with a rattle as the chain link vibrated from the force.

The sergeant reached to Derek’s shoulder and unclipped the mic. “Alamo, Alamo, this is red gate!” he yelled “Santa Ana alert, repeat, Santa Ana alert ,a large group of hostiles inbound to this location, request back up, repeat, request back up.”

Derek looked back down the road and saw the shadows now as they got closer to the range of the pole lights.

“Red Gate, message received, Bravo one move to assist. Hansen, how many?” the voice asked.

Sgt. Hansen looked back down the roadway, and then back at the microphone in his hand. “L.T. I don’t think a single squad is going to be enough.” He dropped the microphone back into Derek’s hands.

He turned to the squad that had gathered around him. " Everybody pick your targets. Remember anything that isn't in the head is a waste of ammo. Fire at will!"

Derek's squad ran to the fence and stuck their barrels through the links. Already Derek could see dozens of the enemy had moved into the lights. He was brushed aside as another squad arrived, and could hear the footfalls of another as they ran to take position along the fence.

From behind them, a pop was heard, and a second later a flare burst into life overhead, its parachute slowing its return to earth. Its brightness illuminated several hundred yards of a roadway covered in a surging mass of infected.

"Holy crap!" Derek exclaimed and lifted his rifle.

**Immanuel**

Immanuel was called to wakefulness just as the first rays of the sun sent fingers of brightness through the small window sat high on the wall. He looked towards Mrs. Chen and found her just as he had left her. Her sightless eyes stared straight up, and the previous night's beginnings of a snarl had settled into what could almost be called an expression of peaceful contentedness, despite the knife handle protruding from the side of her head. Immanuel smiled to himself; pleased that he had given her rest. Birds were greeting the sun outside and he listened for a few minutes, imagining they were listening together.

His thoughts were interrupted by the sounds of the door being flung open, "Damn it, Sorry I overslept dude!" exclaimed John as he rushed in, he only made it a few steps into the room before he took in the scene.

"Holy shit! Are you Okay Gabe? Did she bite you? Scratch you?" John demanded, the permanent smile gone in his panic.

"No John, everything is good. She passed peacefully and gave me no trouble. I assure everything is fine, and she is at rest now." Immanuel said calmly, his mood greatly improved by a few hours' sleep.

"Aw man, I still feel like crap for not being here, you could have been infected or killed. I am sorry man. I will make it up to you." John swore.

“Get me out of here and into that hot shower, and all will be forgiven.” Immanuel smiled at the medic. Try as much as he might to distance himself, he liked the man despite his overly happy demeanor.

“Now I truly feel like shit, there is no time. We got the order just a few minutes ago, we have to pull out right now, can you walk? The buses pull out in fifteen minutes with or without us on them. A big herd of those things is heading this way and will be here any minute.” John explained, his frenetic movements and speech shocked Immanuel.

“I guess I had better be able to then,” Immanuel said, again smiling to pacify the alarmed medic. “I assume you will be flying out with your crew?”

John looked at him for a second and then sat heavily on the bed next to him. “They clipped my wings, those bastards. They reassigned me off the bird and back onto ground pounding.”

Immanuel was confused but then he translated it, his new friend was a helicopter medic, and now the powers that be had, for whatever reason, taken that away from him. “Why did they do that?”

“Some damn Logistics officer decided transport was more important than Medevac, so they took the pilots and the helicopters and put the rest of us on foot. I guess the thought of being out there on the ground freaks me out a little. I and my crew have spent this entire thing looking down on it from the sky."

"I see..." was all he could think to say to the soldier.

They sat quietly for a few seconds before John suddenly stood and turned to Immanuel, the smile back on his face. "Well, let's get you up and out of here, if you can't walk, I will be happy to carry you." He said cheerfully.

Immanuel found that he could walk, if slowly and with his arm around the other man. Together they made their way out of the room, then building and out into the morning sunlight. The brightness hurt Immanuel's eyes, so he stopped for a minute rather than trip over something he wouldn't be able to see. As his vision cleared he could make out a line of buses a few hundred feet away.

"That's our target, can you make it?" asked John.

Before Immanuel could reply, a series of gunshots sounded in the distance. Immanuel looked down the long road and could see two figures firing guns across the top of a police car. Further down the road, he could just make out a large dark shape that he knew from experience was a mass of the monsters. "I think we had better hurry," he said to the man beside him, and together they doubled their speed.

**Derek**

Several hours later, Derek looked to the west again, trying to decide if the sky was truly getting lighter, or if it was his imagination. He had been thinking this for a while, disappointed each time when the sun failed to rise. He had no watch and no way of knowing what time it was, but he knew dawn had to be coming. This had been the longest night of his life.

All around him the still bodies lay. People from all walks of life, of every race and description, had been gunned down. He had become numb to it after he had fired the first clip of ammunition dry. Sarge had told him that he had done a good job, and complimented his accuracy, but Derek had been too exhausted, both emotionally and physically, to feel any pride in that.

He needed a shower and a good night's sleep, but until that was possible he decided and occupied his mind with trying to decide which order the two should be done.

"Hobbs!" the sergeant called.

"Yes, sergeant," Derek answered automatically.

"Get on the horn and call for a dozer, it's too many to move by hand and we have to keep this roadway clear." He ordered.

Derek realized what the man meant and made the necessary call. "Hey Sarge?" he asked after reattaching the radio to his epilate, "How many do you think?"

"A few hundred, give or take, almost had us back there, but we pulled through."

The infected had made it to the fence despite the punishment the gathered men with rifles had doled out. Their combined mass had managed to bend the fence down and some had even made it through that breach, walking across the first ranks until they had spilled over the reduced barrier into the compound. That was thankfully when more backup had arrived and turned the tide, but the fight, one-sided as it was had still lasted almost an hour. Derek's shoulder ached from the recoils and his arms burned from holding the gun up that long.

"And how many are heading at the shelter?" Derek asked, truly wanting to understand the situation.

"The last estimate I heard was around ten thousand give or take. That's why we have to get all this done, get somewhere safe, where these big groups are less likely to wander, it's like a tidal wave, big enough group and nothing short of a nuke could stop them." He took a deep breath, obviously exhausted.

They stood and watched as the bulldozer arrived and the massed bodies into heaps beside the road. "Are more going to come like that soon?" Derek asked, indicating the growing pile.

"Probably, all this noise, all this light, and movement, it will attract them. When haven't done an operation this big since the shit hit the fan, but even our small operations would attract groups of them, luckily, this was a small community before the epidemic, so we would encounter groups of fifty to a hundred, but they have steadily been getting bigger as more and more get here from the larger cities. It doesn't help the way they seem to gather together, different small groups walking along and then they find another group and start walking with it, soon you have giant masses of them moving together. I read a report a few days ago from Los Angeles, before we lost contact with California, about a group they thought had a hundred thousand in it, all walking down the interstate going god knows where."

Derek pondered that for a minute. And imagined what places like Miami and New York must be like, the implications blew his mind. “Can we win?” he asked.

“Win? Depends on what you mean by win. Things can never be like they were. If you ask me, being alive in a month would be a win. Being alive in a year will be a major damn victory.” The sergeant lamented. “Some say I am a pessimist, and I guess they are right, but there isn’t any way to know until it happens.”

“That’s kind of bleak,” Derek responded.

“Yeah, I know, I am in kind of a bleak mood today I guess. It’s been a tough week.” He responded, rubbing his head with his baseball mitt sized hands.

“It has been for everyone,” Derek responded as he looked back down the long road. Where were the trucks and A.P.C.’s? They had said they would be returning by dawn, and the sky was growing a lighter blue, Derek decided. For a moment he considered asking the squad leader, but knew any answer from him would be a guess, Derek had the only radio, and as such all information would come to him first.

The rapid series of gunshots rang out from the far side of the compound, shattering the relative peacefulness of the pre-dawn still. The radio was suddenly a tangled skein of voices, ranging from the calm voices of command to the panicked voice of someone where the shooting was.

A hundred yards away, in the area, they had begun referring to as the headquarters, sat the only motor vehicle that had stayed when the rest had gone out of the gate last night bound for the hospital. Derek watched as several men jumped into it now and drove away, towards the area the shots were coming from. Seconds after it drove out of sight, Derek hear the vehicles large mounted machine guns join add its voice to the battle.

“Should we go help?” asked one of the nearby men.

“Stay put, and stay alert, sounds like another big herd, we could get some stragglers from it.” The sergeant answered.

Derek glanced back at the area of combat, though the contours of the land hid any action from sight. A bright light caught his eyes and he turned to face it. The sun was finally rising.

## Brandy

Brandy handed the big brown rabbit to the little boy and watched the Red Cross lady walk him towards the waiting buses. He was the last of them, and the stillness that had taken over the library was overwhelming. She looked around the room, taking in the chaos. An hour ago, cots covered in sleeping children had filled this room, now it seemed way too big for comfort.

Even the quiet seemed oppressive after the chaos of getting the kids ready to leave and all the activities of the evacuation. Here in the library, she couldn't even hear the buses, just the occasional pop or bang that she wasn't even sure what was.

She considered going out to the courtyard and demanding another update on her mother and Derek, but she knew all she would get was yet another explanation about how they had no indications that anything was wrong, and that the mission was still on schedule. She knew that they were supposed to meet them at the first night's camp, about forty miles south of here. Brandy was not happy about the prospect of not knowing what was going on for the next twelve hours.

She looked up at the clock on the wall, fifteen till eight. She still had time to put together some books to send with the kids on the bus. Maybe Linda or one of the others would read to them. She grabbed a box from the library storage area and searched the walls until she had collected several dozen appropriate books. She sat the heavy box down on the desk and gathered her belongings. She didn't have much in here, a few odds and ends. A few candy bars chef had snuck her one day, a Bottle she filled with water, and of course the extra clips and ammo for the pistol the nursery staff wore.

Brandy still wore the pistol, no one had asked her for it, and she hadn't volunteered. The way she saw it, in the world the way it was, a gun was a good thing to have. She gathered her meager belongings into her backpack, slung it over her shoulder, lifted the box of books, and looked back up at the clock. Its hands showed seven forty-five.

It had taken her at least ten minutes to gather everything up, she knew it had, how can the clock not have changed?

Then it hit her, all the people and equipment were due to be gone by eight in the morning, including the generators. The clocks must have stopped when they disconnected the power. She ran out into the courtyard, and then to the loading area. There was no one in sight, and all of the vehicles were gone. At the far side of the lot, just starting to file in the open gate, were the dead.

Brandy felt a tear begin to sting her eye and quickly wiped it away. There was no time for this, in less than a minute the corpses would be all over her. She dropped the books and ran back into the compound. She could lock herself inside one of the room or buildings, but she quickly ruled that out, she knew that if she did that she would be trapped there, and even if someone came back to look for her they wouldn't be able to get in through all the dead. There had been thousands in the herd, so many that the army had been ready to retreat rather than try to make a stand, the cavalry wasn't coming.

Brandy ran through the empty courtyard and out onto the athletic fields behind the school. There were woods there that she may be able to hide in. she had to get away from the infected she was sure had to have seen her. She could see the tree line a few hundred yards ahead, and she urged her legs to pump faster.

She was halfway across the fields when she spotted movement up ahead; alone shape had just emerged from the wood line and was making its way slowly towards her. She knew it was too far away for the pistol, but she drew the weapon and fired, hoping that luck was with her.

She was surprised to see the figure stop suddenly and then dive face first onto the ground. She kept running, the sound of the shot ringing in her ears. If it wasn't dead when she got closer she would fire again if it rose to come after her.

When she was twenty feet from the prone figure, she lifted the barrel again and sighted in. its head lifted to follow her progress and she started to pull the trigger.

"Don't shoot!" the man screamed from the ground, covering his head with his hands.

Brandy was so surprised that she lost her stride and almost fell. It had spoken, and the infected don't do that. "Are you one of them?" She challenged the figure, gun still at the ready.

"God no, I just wanted a pack of Winston's!" it yelled back, and that's when Brandy recognized the man.

"Jack?" she asked incredulously.

"Yes! Yes! Don't shoot!" he yelled again. "What's the hell is going on?!"

"That!" Brandy yelled, pointing to the school. The horde had made its way through the courtyard and was just emerging onto the fields. She grabbed the man's arm and helped him to his feet. "We have to run!"

He looked at where she pointed and swore softly. Brandy again grabbed his arm and started pulling him away; breaking his surprise at what he had seen. the two began to run towards the concealment of the woods.

They made it to the tree line and paused to catch their breath. Behind them, the dead continued to lurch across the fields, but the pair had a few minutes lead.

“What are you doing out here?” she asked, breathing heavily.

“I snuck into town when everyone else was in that meeting to find some cigarettes, I had to walk a long way to find a vehicle and I am just now making it back. What’s happened at the school?” he inquired back, gasping from the exertion.

“They pulled out about half an hour ago, everyone is gone because those things were coming.” She explained as she watched the approaching mass. “I lost track of time and got left behind, then those things showed up.”

“Great, so what do we do now?” he demanded. “How could they just leave us like that?”

“I don’t guess any of That matters right now, we have to get out of here.” She answered. “You said something about finding a vehicle, do you have one?”

“Yes,” he answered proudly and held up a set of keys, “a van, it’s about a quarter of a mile from here parked on a back road.” He explained.

Brandy jogged off into the woods in the direction he pointed, and Jack took off after her. Before long, the dense woods opened onto a roadway, and a few hundred feet away, brandy spotted the large cargo van. It was bright yellow with red letters proclaiming, “Agape Vapes – A healthy alternative”.

Brandy saw Jack run past her, keys in hand, and ran to the passenger side and climbed into the cab. “What the hell is all this stuff?" Brandy wondered aloud, staring at the boxes behind her.

Jack looked into the back briefly. "Flavored nicotine juice and electronic cigarettes." he said, "First time I ever smoked peanut butter!" he said with a laugh. "It's not cigarettes, but its close enough."

Brandy looked up as movement caught her eye, the infected were coming into view deep in the woods, but closing none the less. Let's get out of here, she said and hit the door lock button. Jack started the engine and turned the vehicle around, heading away from the undead.

"Where are we going?" He asked, taking another drag.

She thought for a moment, again wishing she had made time to learn more about the evacuation. "South, I know the convoy was heading south. We have to find them and then we should be safe." She explained.

"Sounds like a plan, "Jack agreed, " which way is south?"

"I have no idea." Brandy said with a sigh.

***

*Heroes.*

*"Screw this, I'm out of here," the officer to their right muttered as he backed away from the barricade, "there are just too damn many of them." A few seconds later he was back in his patrol car, and he wasn't alone. Five officers had been all that was available to guard the approach to the emergency shelter, and three of them were now leaving.*

*The two remaining officers glanced back at them, and one started to protest. "Let them go," said the other, "I am surprised they stayed this long."*

*"Damn cowards, there are eight hundred women and children in that shelter, see if you can raise the army again." He lifted off his hat and ran his fingers through his black hair, before settling his rifle back of the cruiser into a shooting position.*

*The other officer, a reached for the microphone clipped to his collar, "Dispatch this is 438, any ETA on National Guard to my location? Over."*

*"That's a negative 438, all available military units currently occupied. Whats your situation?" Asked the female voice over the radio.*

*The officer looked over the roof of his patrol car at the crowd of approaching infected, and back at the school building at the people being herded into buses. He met his partner's eyes for a second and then keyed the mic again," The situation is not good, estimate five hundred plus infected two hundred yards and closing. Only 535 and I remain, I don't see how we can hold this position. Get on the horn with that Red Cross lady and tell her she has five minutes to get everyone out of there."*

*"Understood..." came the reply over the radio, then after a moment, "Godspeed 438 and 535, dispatch out."*

*"Well partner, looks like it's just you and me on this one, "said the larger officer, "all we can do is try to hold them as long as we can."*

*"Yeah," said the thinner man," as long as we can...", His resigned tone almost chilling as he sighted down the barrel.*

*"We aren't dead yet." Replied his partner, joining him, rifle laid across the car. "Remember what they said in the briefing, only headshots, so let's let them get a little closer."*

*"I will fire when you do." He said as he chambered a round, "Bill, we've been friends for a long time, I want you to know...."*

*"I know, norm, I know." His partner said is squeezed off his first shot.*

*The child jumped when he heard the shooting start and almost dropped the stuffed brown rabbit he was carrying. He clung to it tighter; it was the only thing he had left of his home before the monsters came. The lady in the red vest put her hand on his shoulder and guided him towards the waiting buses, "It's ok, that's just the police keeping us safe while we get on the buses." Even at four, the boy could tell her smile was strained, but it still made him feel better."*

*She escorted him onto the bus and he took a seat in the very back next to a girl his own age who was quietly crying. As the bus began its roll away, he looked out the back window, and could just make out the two figures standing on the police car. He could see them swinging what he thought were rifles at the things surrounding them.*

*He turned back to the girl next to him and hugged her, "it's OK sandy, everywhere there are monsters, there are heroes here to save us."*

***

**Immanuel**

The bus was crowded and very noisy. Immanuel could feel a head ache coming on, he remembered why he didn't like crowds. He had made the mistake of using his gift on those around him and had instantly regretted it. Dozens of the people he rode with were corrupted; he was literally surrounded by them and locked into this small space.

"Dude, you okay?" asked the man next to him in a whisper.

Immanuel looked towards the medic, who was leaning towards him, waiting for his to answer. "There are just so many people... It's making my claustrophobia act up is all." Immanuel instantly felt bad for lying to the John and this surprised him. Immanuel regretted the attachment he had formed with the soldier, and knew that it could cause trouble down the road for him.

John nodded at his friend's words, accepting what he was told as the truth. "Try not to fret it. We will be at the rendezvous shortly and will be able get out and walk around while we wait on the other groups to show up. "

"And what will we do then?" Immanuel asked, "Did they tell you in your briefing where we are going from there?"

"All I know is that we are heading to some fair grounds right now where they will set up a temporary camp for the night, and then in the morning all these," the medic indicated the odd assortment of school buses, military transports and commercial buses, will split into two groups, one heading south-east and one going southwest. I couldn't find out which one we are going with, I have to find some captain at the camp, he is supposed to give me my orders. You can go with me and he should know where you are heading too."

Immanuel thought for a moment, remembering the trail of angels he had left in his travels from California. He had done the lords work to the west already, He should go east, and in fact he felt the hands of the lord beckoning him in that direction. If he could do anything about it, that's the way he would go. He thought for a moment that it would be nice if John went that direction as well, but then instantly chastised himself. The two going in different directions would be a blessing, freeing him of the emotional attachment that could hinder his mission.

"I am going to try to nap." He informed his friend, and laid his head back against the corner of the seat and window. He closed his eyes and listened to the voices guidance.

"This is for you to decide" came the disembodied voice inside his head, from somewhere further back, he heard a woman's voice hissing for blood, and another, maybe his sister's sweet voice calling for mercy. Immanuel felt himself frown. It was like this sometimes, he couldn't always count on the total agreement in his choir; after all, he had given up long ago on trying to count the voices he heard. Not even angels, it seemed, could agree on everything.

Johns aura glowed brighter than all but a few Immanuel had witnessed. Maybe the man could become his disciple. Surely if he explained the situation, the calling that Immanuel had been chosen for, the man could be made to believe. This was the work of none other than the lord almighty. John was an intelligent man; he would be a good person to have on his side.

But then again, if he couldn't convince John if he couldn't get him to see reason, John could be his downfall. If the man told others, they would arrest Immanuel and put an end to his works, probably by execution since martial law had been declared. Immanuel contemplated that and wasn't happy. He knew he would one day sit at the right hand of God for the work he did, but knew he hadn’t yet done enough to be finished. There were still out there needing purification.

The seat shifted slightly, and Immanuel opened his eyes. John was still seated next to him but was leaned over playing with a toddler seated across from them. The two were playing peek a boo, and each time the soldier uncovered his face, the child would have cried out in joy and let slip a long string of giggles.

Immanuel knew then what he had to do. John probably wasn’t going to be convinced. In many ways, he was as innocent as the child bubbling its mirth at the simple game. He wouldn’t be able to see the auras, and might not accept the truth that the real world that lay beneath the façade of this one.

Immanuel knew that very soon he would have to return to the Lord's work. It would be nice to have help.

**Derek**

They had watched the empty road leading to their gate, waiting for the dead to arrive, but so far none had. Behind them, they could hear the number of shots intensify until it sounded like all-out war, and then the radio had gone wild again.

"Sarge," Derek called out, "Fence is down over there, way too many people yelling to know what's going on, but it sounds bad."

The huge man came over and listened to the voices emanating from the small device clipped to Derek's shoulder. He listened for a minute and then looked up in the direction of the gunshots, which were beginning to lessen. "oh, shit!" he eventually mumbled to himself, and then to the gathered men under his command, "Fix bayonets, check your armor and make sure you have your weapons fully loaded and ready to go."

The gathered soldiers stood with shocked looks for a moment, but then began to prepare. Derek did as he was told, but was confused. He couldn't see any infected, and the shooting over the hill had stopped. "What is going on?" he asked the Sarge.

"The radio, nobody from the gate was talking; all that comm. chatter is other units demanding to know what's going on." He responded.

Derek tilted his ear towards the radio and listened, the Sarge was right. Now that he knew what to listen for, he couldn't hear any real information, just people demanding to know what was happening.

A scream split the air from the command area, Derek raised his head and looked, several shapes were stumbling around the command tent. As Derek watched, several of them grabbed another and forced it to the ground. They fell to their knees around the now prone and struggling form and even at this distance Derek could tell they were beginning to feed on it, bloody hands rising to gore covered faces. Derek felt nausea rise in him but fought it down.

“Bravo Three,” their leader bellowed, let’s go, and stay close. We must make it across the lot to the store; we can hold up there until the column gets back. Shoot anything that gets close!” with this said, he started out at a fast trot towards the looming structure a few hundred yards away.

Derek looked at the block building and could make out several shapes on the roof, each firing down into the area of the parking lot they could not see from here, the building seemed miles away. They moved out, forming a clump as they waded into the horde.

The crowded command tent was set up between them and safety, so the sergeant led them in a curve around it. Fifty of those things surrounded it, and Derek hoped they would pass by unnoticed, but luck was not on their side.   About the time they had made it halfway there, the gathered dead saw them and let out a collective moan that raised the hair on his neck, and then started shambling across the lot.

As one, the troopers lifted their weapons and fired, dropping the front rank in its tracks, but as quickly as they fell, others moved forward to take the place of the dead in front of them. Derek realized that they were close enough to see the gate that had fallen and brought on this mess, he quickly looked in that direction and instantly regretted it

The fence was not only down at the gate, but the massed creatures were jamming the opening, and an almost unbelievable amount of the infected was already inside. He estimated quickly in his head, maybe a thousand were already inside the perimeter, with twice that many still coming in. They would have to fight their way through that mob to get to the entrance to the store.

He forced his mind back to the closer ones and fired again, missing the one he aimed for, but was rewarded when the one behind it fell, half its face ripped away by the bullet. "There's too many of them, we will never make it!" He yelled to the sergeant, his words pulled from him by the cold fingers of the panic he felt in his chest.

"No time for shit like that Hobbs, stiffen up, keep shooting!" Putnam yelled from nearby.

Hansen fired several quick bursts, and then slapped another clip into his gun, "Everyone makes for that front-end loader, we will ride in style!" he ordered, indicating a large bright yellow machine a few dozen yards away. The squad changed its slow advance into an all-out run towards the vehicle.

They reached the vehicle. "Porter!" yelled the sergeant, get this thing started, everyone else, climb on!"

The soldier named porter climbed to the cab and whooped with joy, "The keys are still in the damn thing! He yelled, and the engine roared to life. The others climbed onto every available surface and the machine lurched forward.  A few of the creature that had been pursuing them wandered in front and Porter swerved the vehicle slightly and they disappeared underneath, Derek heard a sickening series of pops and crackles and watched the turning tread resurface red and caked with offal.

The big machine lurched into the massed dead between them and the structure they were headed for. Derek noticed that the creatures were completely oblivious to the losses they were taking or the danger the big vehicle posed to their fragile bodies. Dozens of the things were crushed by its treads as it made its way through the crowd.

Derek looked again at the building, this time noticing that the large entrance was open and scores of the creature were entering. “Sarge! The building isn’t safe, they are inside!”

The others looked up and Derek heard them swear, but the large black man just set his face and yelled, “They aren’t on the roof, that’s our goal, these things can’t use ladders!” He pointed and for the first time, Derek noticed the figures on the roof were unrolling rope ladders down the building’s exterior to small groups of men huddled at its base. “We just have to pull up to one of those.”

The noise of the big machine was drawing the attention of the hordes and the infected were swarming in their direction. They were completely surrounded.

Porter pulled the big machine up against the wall and its sudden jolt announced that he had misjudged the location on the left tread and the wall. A section of brick came crashing down. Crushing several of the nearby creatures and pelting the men riding the machine. The men wore helmets and body armor, but most of the gathered ghouls did not. Derek looked up to see he had gotten them right under one of these rope ladders.

“Everybody up!” Hansen yelled, and Derek felt pushed towards the dangling escape. He looked up the twenty-foot climb and saw a helmeted figure staring down, urging him to climb.

He reached up and grabbed a rung, pulling himself hand over hand, the climb seemed to take forever, the weight of his pack pulled down on him and the thing swayed every time he moved. Below him he heard gunfire; he risked a peek and saw several men standing on the cab of the loader, firing as the dead scrambled on to the machine in an effort to reach the feast gathered there. Two others were on the ladder below him, but he couldn’t tell who they were.

Derek looked up and saw the helmeted figure was much closer now, he could make out the man's features as he reached down, encouraging him to climb faster. "Get the lead out private!" the man yelled.

Five more rungs and Derek was over the edge, lying on his back where he had landed when hands had yanked him over on to the roof. He could still hear the rifles occasional reports below. He looked around him and took in the people gathered on the roof, about ten in all. Another figure landed beside him, Putnam had been lifted off the ladder like he had.

Derek stood and rushed to the low wall that marked the edge of the roof and looked down. Below him, the big machine was almost obscured in the bodies of the dead as they crawled over ever surface. The roof of the cab was the only bright yellow area not covered in their rotting flesh. On it, two figures stood, he could make out that one of them was much larger than the other, It had to be the Sarge. They were swinging their rifles like clubs at the creatures reaching for them.

Derek raised his rifle and fired down into the massed enemy, but knew he couldn't make a dent in their overwhelming numbers. The ladder swung over the back of the large tractor, a few feet from the cab of the roof. He saw the larger man point to the ropes and say something, but his words were lost in the cacophony of the dead. The smaller figure turned and jumped for the ladder, his fingers found it in midair and he grabbed on, his hands reaching for the next rungs as a dozen other hands reached for him. They caught his legs and began to pull down. The man screamed, and Derek watched as he fell from the ladder, disappearing as if being swallowed up by the sea of the dead that surrounded him.

The larger living figure below watched the man sink into the reaching hands and then looked at the figures above. The ladder swung just out of his arms reach. He took a step back, feeling the fingers of the dead pull at his pants legs and then lunged forward and up, arms extended to grab the rungs as high as he could. He grabbed a rung and started to climb, but like the man before him, decaying fingers locked on and began to pull him towards their hungry mouths.

"Pull him up!" Yelled Derek, grabbing the rope and straining, the friction against the edge of the roof, the sergeant's weight and the grip of the undead seemed to be an insurmountable burden. More hands joined him and the rope began to respond to their combined efforts. They gave a yank, and Derek felt the burden lessen, they had won the tug of war with the grasping hands below. He couldn't see Sgt. Hansen anymore, but he knew they were dragging up a weight.

"Please god, don't let him be bitten, he muttered to himself, and then screamed to the man below, "Hold on! We have you!" They had dragged the rope back several yards when he saw a gloved hand reach over and grab the ledge, followed by another. He let go of the rope and rushed over, helping the man over and onto his back.

"Did they bite you?" he half screamed at the prone figure.

"On the foot, but I don't think they got through the leather." The man explained and pulled off his boot, examining a bruise forming there against his dark skin. Derek could see the outline of teeth marks in the black leather.

"There are more soldiers out there, get to the edge and provide them some covering fire." He ordered and the survivors from the squad quickly obeyed.

Derek looked across the parking lot, several two clusters of soldiers were out there, fighting their way across the crowd of gnashing teeth and grasping fingers. As he watched, one group was overrun where they stood, trapped in the shifting waves of walking corpses. He knew immediately that they were beyond hope.

The other group of about ten, the closest, was less than fifty yards away, near the Humvee. The vehicle had attempted to drive through the thickest group of the dead, and Derek could tell from here that it was high centered on a mound of moving corpses. They were fighting their way towards an excavator parked a few dozen yards away. Derek fired his rifle several times, taking down as many as he could, but know the group wouldn't all fit on the vehicle the way his squad had, there just wasn't room.

The group reached the side of the machine, and one figure climbed in. The big machine roared to life, the huge mechanical arm twitched as the soldier took the controls. The heavy bucket swung out, catching several of the infected in its swing, crushing them like a foot might crush roaches. The arm extended and swung again, cutting a swath through the ghouls approaching them. The rest of the soldiers fell in behind it as it advanced towards the wall, rolling forward as its giant arm crushed and knocked them aside. It cleared a section of the wall, and its massive bucket reached down. Several soldiers crawled onto it, and they were raised to the edge of the wall, where they scrambled up and over. The bucket dipped again, repeating the action.

Derek fired several more times as a wave of creature closed in on the loud machine, watching as another group of men was raised to the roof. All that was left was the driver. The bucket swung out again, crushing lines of the undead and then lurched up. The building shook under Derek's feet as the bucket crashed into the edge of the roof and hung there. Below them the noise of the machine cut out, revealing the moans of the massed dead below them.

The driver exited the cab and gracefully scaled the boom, before stepping nonchalantly onto the roof and looking around. "Sgt. Hansen!" a woman's voice bellowed, "Situation report please?"

"Just getting to that L.T." he responded. "twenty-four of us made the roof, including the group you brought. The fence is down in three places and enemy numbers are between a thousand and fifteen hundred. We have five men injured, of which two are bit, one has an injury of unknown cause, might be a cut, but looking at the gore on his uniform, he is probably infected." He finished and waited for her as she thought over his report.

"Not enough ammunition or soldiers to fight off this herd. Issue orders to the men to target only those infected in fatigues should only be about sixty of them. Gather grenades from whoever has them. Bind our infected and give them the choice. Set guards and put someone on the radio we had brought up here earlier. We need to get in touch with the convoys. I don't know about you, but I have things to do and would rather not be stuck up here." She finished, and walked off along the edge of the roof, surveying the scene below.

The sergeant started barking orders, and Derek didn't have to wait long before his came in. He was familiar with this type of radio, so he set about getting it set up. As he worked, he listened to occasional gunfire as a soldier on the roof picked off their infected counterparts down below. He looked over to the three men sequestered by themselves in a far corner, these were the three that had been injured and infected when the shit had hit the fan, he could see the sergeant and lieutenant talking to them, one man was in tears. As Derek watched, he nodded, and the officer drew her gun. He looked away, and ignored the following series of three shots.

## Brandy

Brandy and Jack stood staring into the darkened windows of the run-down country store. The tinted windows didn't show much of what was inside, but from what they could see it didn't look like the building had been looted, and the intact door lent credence to that fact.

Beside her, jack puffed nervously on one of the little electronic things, filling the air with the faint smell of cinnamon. Brandy drew the pistol from its holster, holding it down by her side. She tossed a pebble against the glass with her other hand and waited.

"Are you sure we want to do this?" the man asked as he scanned the area around them for movement.

"Want to? No. Have to? Yes." She answered, and then explained, "We don't really know where we are, or how to get where we are going. Inside there should be maps, not to mention food and bottled water to make it a happier trip."

"Inside there could be a dozen of those things also." He retorted.

Brandy tossed another rock and listened to the satisfying 'plink' noise it made as it struck the glass. "Maybe, but I don't think so, nothing is moving to check out the noise." With this, she tossed her third stone, this one much bigger than the other two. The result was a loud crack, and the window shattered but held together. She counted to twenty silently, and then said: "Well, I guess nothing is in there, let's go check it out."

“Easy to say when you are the one with the gun!” Jack joked, but stepped forward towards the buildings glass door. He peered in for a second, and then announced, “I don’t see anything.”

“You open the door, and I will call out. If anything comes out, I can shoot it.” She shifted into a shooter's stance and waited.

Jack reached out and grabbed the door handle, “On three!” he said, “One...two...THREE!” he yelled and yanked on the handle. The door gave a great rattling sound and shook in its frame, but stayed shut. Jack stared at it. “It's locked!” he exclaimed, and then yanked again, harder. The glass cracked as the frame twisted, but the door stayed closed.

Brandy took a deep breath and looked towards the crouching man, still jiggling the door. “The other push.” She said, indicating the sticker on the door.

Jack looked at it, confusion on his face before it dawned on him. He pushed the door lightly and it swung easily on its well-oiled hinges. Brandy stepped forward into the opening and scanned the room. It wasn’t a very big store, but her eyes instantly fell on the display of maps next to the register.

She felt Jack step in behind her. “We have to clear the store before we load up.” She instructed and began to search the aisles.

Together they crept across the store, watching for any movement. The store was clear, a drink cooler lined one wall, but it was not the walk-in kind. That only left the small stock room, and the twin bathrooms.

Brandy approached stock room warily, it had no door, and just an old shower curtain separated it from the main customer area. She used the barrel of the handgun to slide the divider aside, revealing an area not much bigger than a closet. Nothing moved inside. Both bathrooms proved to be clear as well.

"Let's load up what we need," Brandy said, picking up and empty box from the stock room and filling it with snack cakes and nuts from an end cap, "Check behind the counter, see if they left any kind of weapon."

Jack moved to the large counter and started to search the cluttered shelves beneath it. "I wonder where they all went?" he said aloud.

"Who?" asked brandy, distracted as she picked items off the shelves.

"The person that was working here, the owner, or whoever, where did they go? The store was open; somebody must have been working here when whatever happened." He wondered.

" A-Ha" he cried triumphantly and raised a sawed-off shotgun from below the counter. The amount taken off the barrel and the guns pistol grip made it look grim and menacing.

"Good, did you find any shells for it?" Brandy called as she started to fill another box with water and soda from the cooler.

Jack reached under the counter and produced two small boxes. "About a hundred rounds of twenty-gauge buckshot."

"Awesome!" Brandy agreed and set the box of water down with the first she had packed beside the door. "Think we should pack some more?" she asked as he checked the load in the gun and put the boxes of ammunition into one of the paper bags by the register.

"Do you think we will need it? Aren't we planning on hooking back up with the guys in green in just a few hours?" he asked.

“That’s the plan, but you never can be sure, especially nowadays, let's fill up one more box of each, make sure to grab some maps.

Ten minutes later they had loaded their pilfered goods into the back of the van and stood with a map spread across its hood. They had traveled about 20 miles before finding the store and it had unfortunately been mostly in the wrong direction. Brandy was pretty sure the first nights staging area was about fifty miles away.

The made it less than a mile before they found the first major obstruction. The road was completely blocked by fire trucks and they knew at a glance that they would not be able to squeeze around them because the shoulders of the road dropped away abruptly into deep culverts. No less than a dozen figures wandered around the roadblock, but brandy could see that none of them were living.

“I saw a dirt road a little way back.” Jack offered, and backed the van into a wide turn. “maybe we will get lucky and find a way around.

The van was not made for the kind of roads they were taking, but it seemed to be handling the dirt ruts well enough. By mid-day they were locked to these back roads trying to find a way around the multiple traffic jams and road obstructions for over an hour, finding one after another congested to the point of being impassable. The only good news was that the vans fuel tank was almost full.

“I am guessing we should be coming up on this county road any minute now,” Jake stated, looking at the map they had gotten at the store, “But I don’t know if this dirt road isn’t marked or if this map isn’t even of this part of the state.”

“We will find a way through,” Brandy consoled the man as he maneuvered the vehicle around another soft spot in the road, spinning the wheels to keep them from getting bogged down. They had almost gotten stuck several times now.

Ahead of them, a paved road appeared, revealed by the thinning trees. “Alright!” exclaimed the older man and gunned the engine up the embankment and onto the shoulder of the roadway. The road ahead appeared clear.

“So, you think we are here?” Brandy asked, looking at the map.

“Maybe,” responded the man, taking another drag from the electronic device he held, filling the cab with the smell of cinnamon.” It’s hard to tell until we find a landmark or a road sign. I wasn’t sure where we were to begin with, much less after driving in circles in the woods for half the morning.”

“Let’s just go that way,” brandy hooked her thumb towards the passenger window, “I guess it’s as good a way as any!”

“Your call.” He agreed and started the vehicle down the road. The road was long and straight here, stretching for what seemed like endless miles ahead of them.

Brandy studied the map as he drove. “They were going to stop at a fairground somewhere around here, she pointed to the map. They were going to stay the night and then head out first thing in the morning. I know it’s about an hour from the school, but I have no idea where they were going after that. We have to get there by sundown if we want to have any chance of catching them.” she explained.

“We don’t even know where we are, what do we do if we don’t find them by then?” He asked nervously

“I don’t know.” Was all she could think to say, she hadn’t planned anything further than being with the convoy when the sun came up.

They rode in silence for several more miles before they came across a marked intersection and found themselves on the map. Jack had been very close to his guess of their location. “It looks like it will be just over sixty miles.” She complained. “That could take all day!”

“I wish we knew what route they took, I am sure they knew what ways were open.” He added.

They had come to a stop in the intersection amid the wreckage of what brandy could only assume was a failed roadblock. A large S.U.V. was nearby, resting on its roof, the sheriff's badge decal on its door still recognizable despite the massive damage done to it. A nearby Highway patrol car set seemingly untouched, and on the far side of that, buried halfway into a stand of trees was the twisted skeleton of a large pickup truck. It appeared to have rammed the S.U.V. at high speed and ended up in the woods. She looked, but couldn’t find any people nearby, either living, dead, or undead. Around the intersection, a few dark stains marked the pavement.

“This is creepy,” Brandy complained, “something doesn’t feel right about this place.”

Jack glanced up from the map and took in the scene around him for the first time in detail. “That looks like one hell of a wreck.” He commented. “We need to check out those vehicles, they probably have some guns and ammo in them.” He put the vehicle in park and reached for his door handle.

“Yeah, but let’s make it quick.” Brandy said as she opened her own door and stepped onto the pavement.

They approached the patrol car, and even from twenty feet away could see the shotgun attached to the dashboard. She got down on her knees and looked under the vehicle, then carefully through the windows before trying the door. It was unlocked and opened easily to her pull. She noticed blood on the passenger's seat as she reached across and tugged on the twelve gauges barrel. It wouldn't budge.

She felt for the car's ignition and was relieved to find the keys still in it. She used one of the smaller keys and it unlocked the weapon. "Ammunition is probably in the trunk," she said as she backed out of the car and tossed the keys to jack.

He caught the keys and opened the trunk. She heard him give a low whistle as the lid raised between them. When she stepped around, she saw why. The lid had a built-in rack that held three long guns, one of which looked just like the automatics the soldiers had carried back at the shelter, one was another shotgun, and the third was a wicked looking thing that brandy recognized from several movies, an MP-5 she remembered. "Derek would be in love." She breathed.

"It's a pretty bad ass little setup, let's take them all." Jack said as he lifted them from the vehicle, "No point leaving them for somebody else."

Brandy nodded her agreement and rummaged through the contents before coming up with two bags full of boxes and magazines of ammunition, which she carried to the waiting van where Jack was organizing the rifles amongst the boxes already there.

"What about the pickup and the S.U.V.?" she asked, indicating the two wrecked vehicles.

“There isn’t much left of the pickup,” he answered thoughtfully, “maybe the S.U.V.? but don’t we have enough stuff? We only have to survive a day on our own.”

“Better safe than sorry.” She responded.

The S.U.V. had been hurled from the road by the force of the impact of the truck, and set twenty yards away. Its large back window was angled towards them, reflecting the sun towards their eyes. Brandy reached that window and put her face against it, peering in. her eyes caught movement and the vehicle shifted slightly as if something inside it had moved. She took a step back and tripped as she brought her pistol up. She fell onto her butt and accidentally pulled the trigger, the bullet exploded the glass covering the rear of the vehicle.

The thing that had waited within launched itself from the cargo area, catching her in the chest and Brandy screamed.

***

*Officer Dunhill spun the wheel of his vehicle as he took the corner, the Pickup ahead of him had not handled it so well and was closer now. The ruts in the grass showed where it had drifted off the road as it careened to wide on the turn.*

*Behind him, his partner was barking excitedly at the action. The thrill of the chase and the sirens always got him excited. Some canine cops would yell at their animals for barking, but Dunhill didn't like to discourage Bruiser.*

*The brake lights of the vehicle ahead flashed on again, and he braced for them to make another reckless turn to try to lose the pursuit. Sure enough, they took the next crossroad. The pickup managed to keep all four wheels on pavement this time.*

*The officer had been following them for miles. He had rolled up on the men as they unloaded the belongings from a families' minivan when he first saw them. When they had seen him, they had dropped what they held and run for the truck. Only as he got closer had he seen the bodies inside the minivan. Their panicked flight had told him all he needed to know what they had been doing.*

*Bruisers barking provided the beat for the drive and the sirens the music as he pursued. The radio in the car announced that other units were in the area, but only one was available, and it was almost to them.*

*The red lights of the truck flashed again, and it started its turn at a speed that should have flipped the truck, but its wheels held grip with the asphalt. Dunhill saw his chance and accelerated to nudge the truck as it turned. That was when the other car appeared.*

*None of the drivers had time to act as the third car appeared around the blind turn. It smashed into the truck and the rears of both vehicles lifted from the force as their noses were driven down into the pavement. Dunhill's S.U.V. struck a fraction of a second later.*

*None of the people from the cars survived more than a few minutes, But eventually, they all crawled from the wreckage and walked away.*

***

**Immanuel**

Immanuel stepped off the bus and looked around. He was glad they wouldn't be here for very long, the field that stretched before him offered little in the way of obvious comforts, work area, and privacy. At the far side of the lot, he could see a series of long buildings, and the people stepping off the buses were being directed in towards them. He could see that the three closest buildings had their doors flung wide, and people were already entering the milling crowd had pressed against him as it was herded in that direction, pushing him along with it. He looked around for his friend, but the medic was not in sight.

As the mass of people he was entwined with grew closer, he began to hear a voice, and for a second he thought it was one of his. He listened closer and soon realized that it wasn't one of his angels, but a soldier on a bullhorn directing people to specific buildings based on their group. Immanuel was confused, John had said something about different groups, but he didn't know which one he would be in.

He made his way to the edge of the crowd and stepped up to one of the soldiers standing and watching the people pass. Immanuel studied the man, both with his eyes and his sight, before speaking. "Excuse me, Airman, can you help me? I was in quarantine until right before the buses left and don't know where to go."

"That's sailor, sir," the man snapped back stiffly, "but I will be happy to help you. What's your name?"

Immanuel almost gave his true name, but caught himself in time, "Immanuel… Immanuel McNeil." The sailor started moving his finger down the list and Immanuel felt foolish. He knew it would not be possible to find a name he had just made up, and in not finding a name, it would draw attention. The voice chastised him for his stupidity. He should have just found John.

The sailor glanced up at him, and then back at the list, "Sir, I am not showing you on my list. If you will please follow me, I can take you to the people that can straighten this out for you."

Immanuel shrugged, he doubted they would ask him for identification, and he knew they would be too busy for background checks. This wouldn't jeopardize his mission he decided and followed the man.

Together they walked towards the first building and stepped inside. The inside area of the building was fifty-foot-wide by two hundred feet long and the air carried the smell of animals. Immanuel recognized it as a livestock pavilion. Already he could see people claiming small areas of the massive floor as their own.

The man took him to a small table with a bored looking officer seated at it. "How can I help you, Mueller." asked the man.

"Lieutenant Anderson, this man is Immanuel McNeil, and he doesn't seem to have a group assignment." The sailor explained.

The soldier scanned his own list as he beckoned Immanuel to sit. "No sweat, we will get you set up in a jiffy. When did you arrive at the shelter?"

"A couple of days ago, I was brought in on a med-evac helicopter and was in quarantine until this morning. I wasn't released until the buses were loading."

"Aw, that explains it, no problem though. Mind if I ask you a couple of questions to see which group to put you in?" the soldier flipped to another page of his clipboard as he talked and continued without waiting for his answer. Do you have any family, significant others or close friends currently in this shelter?"

Immanuel shook his head and the man continued. "Any special knowledge, skills or training, or college that might prove useful?" brought another shake of the head.

"Any military or paramilitary experience or training, weapons training, expertise in the manufacture and maintenance of weapons, ammunition, explosives or vehicle repair?" the man asked.

When Immanuel had indicated no to all three questions, the man had set back and asked simply, "which color do you like better, White or Blue?"

"White." Immanuel had said without thought. White was the color of angels, the voice, and purity.

**Derek**

The sun had only been up for a few hours, the roof was growing hot and the tar sticky underfoot. Below them, the dead moaned a chorus that Derek knew would drive him mad. He thought back to the movies he had watched on late night television where people boarded themselves up in houses and sheds to escape the zombies outside. The one thing they never truly captured in those films was the sounds, it was the worst thing about being trapped.

"That sound is going to drive me nuts!" A nearby soldier said. Derek looked at the man; he wasn't much older, maybe eighteen or nineteen. "It's also the damn smell, why didn't anybody tell us about the damn smell!"

Derek understood the man's frustrations; the smell of the wandering corpses below as they heated up was growing very unpleasant. "Look, it's not that bad," Derek said, "We got in touch with the convoy and they are on their way back. In a few minutes, we will be on the move again."

The other made a disgusted face and grunted. Several of the survivors were in a bad mood, displacing grief for their fallen comrades with anger. Derek stared off towards the road, wondering what had happened at the hospital. He had been there when the lieutenant, the only officer to survive the night, had called the raiding team. They had been finalizing the loading of supplies, and reported that they had taken casualties as well, but did not elaborate as to numbers. They also didn't say if all the civilians were okay. Derek had wanted to grab the radio and scream into it, demanding information about his mother, but had held back. They would know soon enough when the armored vehicles rolled in to clear the dead out below them.

He spotted the first vehicle coming down the road a short time later. It was one of the Bradley's, the armored machine stopped at the crest of a hill a few hundred yards from the gate. Derek could just make out a figure as it stood up atop the machine and waved, and then the radio crackled behind him.

"Wayward son calling Kansas, Wayward son calling Kansas." The voice came through tinny, even at this relatively short distance. Derek looked at the distant figure again, even at a few hundred yards he could make out the growl of the engine of the vehicle.

The lieutenant picked up the handset. "Good to see you there, Mind giving us a lift?"

"Certainly, gorgeous!" the voice responded with a chuckle. "Looks kind of thick down there, any way you can clear that out for us?"

"We are just waiting for the word colonel."

"Consider the word given; we will be down there in about Three minutes. The paint on this thing is relatively new, can you have the fireworks over before we get down there?" The distant man asked.

"Starting now," she said and nodded and Sergeant Hansen.

The second in command bellowed out "Get ready… one… two…toss them!"

The survivors drew the gathered grenades and began to toss them into the milling crowd below. As one they took several steps back from the edge, bringing the building between themselves and the imminent destruction down below.

Derek closed his eyes and covered his ears, but was surprised when the grenades went off softer than he had always imagined they would be. He stepped to the edge again and looked down, the things below were already closing the holes the explosions had made in their ranks, pushing into the side of the building.

"Again ... one... two... now."

The explosives arced into the air again and disappeared into the crowd. Derek took a few steps back, but this time kept his eyes open and aimed towards the edge. The hand grenades went off, and he saw chunks of bodies fly into view before falling back out of sight.

He stepped forward and took in the damage. They had had forty-one fragmentation grenades when they had been gathered up, and they had used them all. The horde below them was in shambles, about a quarter of its number where on the ground, but sadly a lot of them were still moving. Lost legs, arms, and unidentifiable pieces littered the area. Derek saw one severed head still working its jaw as if trying to moan its miserable sound at him.

"It didn't work." He said aloud to no one in particular, but the lieutenant answered, startling him.

"Yes, it did soldier, these things are hard to kill when they are grouped up like that." She said and glanced up at the sound of the approaching engine changed. The combat vehicle burst through the trees and knocked down a section of fence as the mounted gun fired several dozen rounds in short order, shredding swaths of the gathered dead.

The ghouls turned as one towards the distraction the vehicle offered and began walking in that direction. The A.P.C. slowly backed away, leading the herd like a puppy before making a tight turn and slowly exiting the parking lot the way it had entered.

Derek watched in shock as the milling crowd of walking dead marched away, the men on the roof forgotten.

The woman patted him on the shoulder, “See young man, we thin them out and he marches them away.” She walked away, speaking a rapid series of orders to the sergeant who followed behind, listening and writing in a notebook.

**Brandy**

The wind was taken out of her as the weight of the thing crushed her to the pavement, cutting her scream off abruptly. She looked up into a toothy mouth as it descended towards her face. She thought frantically of her gun but felt her fingers twitch on empty space.

Brandy brought her other hand up and tried to shove the thing back, but its skin was loose, and it easily stretched past her grip, moving towards her face. All of this happened in an instant, but her panicked mind stretched it to an hour. The jaws came together as it reached her nose and she tried to scream again, but her lungs were empty, she closed her eyes and tensed for the attack. That's when the long pink tongue slid up her face and the whining filled her ears.

Brandy opened her eyes and found a dog sitting astride her, its dark nose against her face as it frantically licked her cheek. She pushed the animal off and rose up on to her elbows, the beast moved to her feet, studying her intently with soulful brown eyes and continuing that sad whine.

"You dumb dog," she yelled "you scared the shit out of me!" the dog looked down at her and yawned slowly.

Brandy looked at Jack, who stood nearby with his gun raised and saw that he was fighting to control a powerful burst of laughter. She stood and reached a tentative hand towards the dog, letting it sniff her. Jack gave up his inward struggle and guffawed, Brandy, shot him a dirty look.

"Well I am sorry," he said between fits, "that was just about the funniest thing I've ever seen! Scared the crap out of me when that thing jumped out... but you... but you looked like..." but his laughing took the ending from him.

"It's not funny!" Brandy protested but then had to fight a smile herself. She disguised her own mirth by kneeling beside the dog.

The dog was a large German shepherd, the largest she had ever seen. It wore a black harness with a golden star affixed to the front of it. She glanced into the now missing back window of the S.U.V. and saw that it was set up as a kennel; the large padded cage had probably saved the animal when the truck had attempted to break through the roadblock. The remains of a dog food bag were shredded around the cage, and she could see small drops of blood on one wall.

She rubbed the dog down, looking for an injury, and was impressed with how calm he stayed. Brandy found a small cut behind the dog's ear, but it didn't seem serious.

Jack finally won the battle with the giggles and disappeared into the truck, he returned a few seconds later with a bottle of water and a plastic clamshell he had salvaged from the stock inside to serve as a bowl. They watered the dog and watched him drink.

Brandy looked around the nearby woods, wondering what had become of the officer, "It takes a lot to make a K9 officer leave his dog behind like that. He must be nearby, one way or the other."

"He probably became infected, wandered off," Jack ventured, "and left poor Bruiser behind."

"Bruiser?" Brandy asked.

Jack pointed to the side of the truck, under the now broken glass in a stylized script, the words 'Deputy Bruiser' was stenciled in a shiny gold script.

"Bruiser," Brandy repeated, "Good name."

“Yeah, but what do we do with him?” Jack asked, running his finger through his hair.

“What do you mean? He is going with us.” Brandy added defensively, grabbing the back of the dog’s collar.

“That’s what I figured, I just meant about food for him, and what will the army guys say when we get there?”

“We will cross that road when we get to it, food should be easy to find.” Brandy looked around them, scanning the tree line. “This couldn’t have happened too long ago, it rained the other night and none of the papers lying around are wet, so whoever was here probably hasn’t gone very far. We should get out of here.”

“I am all for that.” Jack agreed, heading towards the van.

Brandy opened the back doors and Bruiser hopped in, making himself comfortable amongst the boxes. She scanned the area again, and something glinted down the road, she strained her eyes and could make out several figures walking towards them, but they were too far away to make out.”

“Let’s get out of here,” She said as she climbed in, “something is coming.”

**Immanuel**

The officer had directed him to the building marked "white barracks", and he had found them and joined his new team members inside. The building was large and open inside, like a warehouse. The smell of animals filled the air, and he could see holes in the floor where cattle gates could be installed when needed.

Several hundred people were settling in and the room was crowded and stuffy. Immanuel looked around and saw people claiming cots by setting bags of possessions on them. He realized that he hadn't had the opportunity to grab his things, and wasn't even sure if they had been brought on the helicopter when he had been picked up.

He selected a section of cots in a dark corner that people seemed to be avoiding and sat down in the one farthest from the mass of people. He let out a sigh and laid back on the cot, with no pillow and no blanket, he was cold and uncomfortable. He stared up at the exposed beams of the ceiling and felt himself start to drift off to sleep despite the dull roar of the mass of people milling about when he heard someone approaching.

"Hey mister, your foot is bleeding." Said a voice near his cot. When Immanuel turned his head, he found a small boy standing there. He was around seven or eight years old, had a dirty face and a pale mop of hair on his head. He looked down at his feet and realized that he still had no shoes, and that one of the bandages was saturated with blood, the wound has reopened.

"Thank you, young man, I appreciate the heads up, you wouldn't happen to know where I can get a pair of shoes, would you?" Immanuel asked the child hopefully.

“The army men have lots of stuff in a truck outside, clothes and hat and some shoes. You should go get some, you left some bloody footprints when you walked by our beds and scared a few people. They thought one of those things was in here,” the boy explained, “I followed you down here to finish you off before I realized that you weren’t one of them.” The boy held up a toy rifle proudly, a wide smile dividing his face.” My Daddy told me to be brave, so I am!”

“Wow, you are a big strong man,” Immanuel said kindly, “But don’t you think you should hurry back to your parents and protect them? In case more of those things come?”

“I ain’t got no parents anymore, just my aunt,” his smile faded as he spoke, “Daddy and Mommy got hurt by one of those things and made me go away with Aunt Claire because they were getting sick and didn’t want to make me sick.”

Immanuel absorbed the Childs words and felt sadness in his heart for him. ‘Damn the dark powers that had brought this evil onto the world’ he thought to himself.

“I am sure he would be very proud of you,” Immanuel reassured the boy, “but I do think you should go find Aunt Claire and stay with her, you and the soldiers outside have your work cut out for you.”

A young woman appeared, calling to the boy. “Ethan, what are you doing bothering this nice man for!?” she exclaimed. “I am very sorry he bothered you.”

“No bother,” Immanuel said truthfully, “I like kids and young Ethan here was telling me about how brave he was.”

The woman’s smile faded as she looked down towards his feet. “Oh, my goodness!” she exclaimed. “What happened to you?”

she asked as she kneeled beside his foot and started to examine his bandages.

He sat up and started to protest, but she had already removed the tape and started to unroll the gauze. “Ethan, get me my big orange bag.”

Ethan nodded and rushed off, returning a minute later and dropping a big canvas bag with a blue EMS patch sewn onto the top. Claire had finished removing his bandages and withdrew a bottle of water and some gauze to clean his foot.

“This looks really bad,” she said as she worked, “How did this happen?”

“Escaping the city, I had to walk out and one of those things got my shoe in the process.” He explained.

“Did it bite you,” she asked suddenly, a startled look freezing her face, “did your wounds come in contact with any of its bodily fluids.”

Several people had gathered around and now were taking steps back, fear in their eyes. It struck him that he was not doing a good job of maintaining a low profile.

“No, No, nothing like that, my feet were injured long after I was near those things.” He said, trying to ease their minds, “I assure you, I am not infected!”

Claire seemed to relax at this, and those nearby seem assured and wandered off, back to whatever they were doing before. “We can’t be too careful,” she explained as she went back to cleaning his foot, “It only takes one.”

“I understand. I have seen what those things can do.” Immanuel winced as she dabbed at the wound.

"Sorry about that, almost done... there, that should do it." She exclaimed. She used her free hand to rummage around in the big bag again and withdrew several rolls of gauze and tape. "I think the sutures look good, but I can wrap it up for you, but you need to stay off it and keep it clean for two to four weeks until it heals, you can't risk an infection. It's going to be one hell of a scar."

Immanuel smiled at her, "Better a scar on that sole than the other." He joked.

She nodded halfheartedly at his jest as she finished wrapping the tape around his foot, the stark whiteness of the wrap contrasting sharply against the filth that was his pant leg. "We need to get you some crutches and clean clothes. Do you need something to eat or drink? How is the pain?" She asked.

"It is much better now, thank you, Claire." Immanuel sat back up and looked around. "Ethan tells me there is a truck nearby with spare clothing?"

"Yes," she responded, "it's a bunch of luggage they held onto from people who did not make it, they decided to keep it around for people like you, let's find a way to keep that foot clean and dry and we will help you get out there."

She lifted his arm over her shoulder and helped him stand. He knew he could have walked, but she seemed very insistent about him taking it easy, so he accepted the close contact with her despite his dislike of touching anyone that wasn't his angel.

**Derek**

Derek dropped into the hatch of the vehicle and quickly stepped aside to avoid the next person coming down the rope ladder. The interior of the A.P.C. was small and cramped and reeked of fuel, cordite, and sweat. Even over the rumble of the engine, he could hear the remaining dead outside banging their fists against the sides, trying vainly to get in at the living that had escaped them.

"Kind of makes you feel like a sardine doesn't it?" said a familiar voice.

Derek looked over and found Chad sitting with another man in the back corner of the vehicle. He moved over and sat down beside him. "What are you doing here?" Derek demanded.

Chad laughed, "Did you think I was going to let you have all the fun? They wanted me to stand in a parking lot and patrol the buses all night, so I snuck into one of these things before they rolled out." He explained. Before adding. "They made me stay in here when they found me, but it was still better than nothing."

Derek sighed. "I would happily have stayed back at the camp and guarded busses." He said sadly.

"I could hear what was going on over the radio," Chad nodded to the cab of the vehicle they rode in, "It sounded rough."

"What happened at the hospital?" Derek changed the subject, seeking information about his mother.

Chad hung his head before speaking. "It was pretty bad, they lost lots of people, mostly soldiers but a few of the civilians that came along." He answered, and then quickly added: "Your Mom is okay though, I saw her getting into one of the trucks when they left."

"Good," Derek said, relieved, "Do you know where she is now?"

"No man," Chad answered, "We were all in a convoy and then they got you guys call for help. The general or whatever he is told the trucks to keep going and directed these bad boys to come help."

The two boys felt the vehicle lurch to a start as it began pulling away from the side of the building. The driver up front turned and yelled to those in the back, "Next stop is the rally point at the fairgrounds. There are cases of M.R.E.'s stowed under your benches and some cases of water up front. Help yourself, but do not attempt to heat the food inside my vehicle."

At the mention of food, Derek's stomach rumbled, and it occurred to him that he had not eaten much in the last twenty-four hours. He found the heavy cardboard case under his seat and slide it out, grabbing one of the drab green pouches for himself and sliding the case down to the next man with his foot.

Sarge staggered over, his gate unsteady, due to the bumping of the vehicle, and passed out several bottles of water. Derek took two and settled back into the seat to eat. The emotional draining events of the day were finally taking their toll, and he ate his food quickly, barely tasting it. Despite the noise, heat, and crowding of the military vehicle, Derek quickly fell asleep.

***

*Annie rode in the back of the truck staring down at the man sprawled in the aisle. Two others were working on the man's wounds, trying frantically to stop the ooze of blood that now puddled around him.*

*The soldier had been bitten on the chest and right arm deep enough to severe the muscles which now hung down in tattered strips where they had been ripped from the teeth of the ones that had him. The ones now working on him were the ones who had wrestled him away from his attackers and were trying to save him again.*

*She could tell by the man's coarse sporadic breaths that it was already too late. If she had been in a trauma center, with full access to its equipment and blood banks, he might have had a chance. She had gotten out of the others way to let them figure it out themselves.*

*Annie waited for them to accept what she already had, and it only took a few more minutes.*

*"We have to take care of him." She said softly as the two men abandoned their efforts. "He will come back soon, and we can't have him do that in here."*

*One of the soldiers looked up in horror. "That's Hal, he enlisted with me!" he protested, shocked at the idea of what must be done.*

*"I am sorry for your friend," Annie said as earnestly as she could, "but you know what happens next." As she spoke, she pulled the handgun she carried from her belt.*

*The soldiers glared at her with a mixture of anger and sadness, pausing several seconds before nodding gravely. He grabbed one of the arms of his friend and helped drag him to the end of the truck. The soldier helped the others remove the equipment the corpse still wore before stepping out of the way.*

*Annie moved into the space that had just been occupied by the prone figures friend and took aim. As she squeezed the trigger, the things eyes opened. The shot filled the cargo area and hit the ears each of the living like a sledgehammer.*

*She slides down the bench to make room for the others to do what came next and ended up beside the man's buddy. She placed a comforting hand on his shoulder. They watched together as the body was slid out of the truck to tumble to a stop as they drop on.*

*As she felt him sob next to her, Annie cursed the world for what it had become, and what it had made them all into.*

***

**Brandy**

The road stretched out before them long and straight. From the driver's seat, Jack puffed nervously on his electronic cigarette as Brandy glanced up from the map to watch the trees blur by. The van was traveling well over the speed limit, and for a moment she considered urging the older man to slow down but decided against it, figuring the chances of another car being on the road were slim.

The dog stood in the space between the seats, gazing intently out the front window. Brandy absentmindedly reached over and scratched the animal between the ears before glancing down at the map. She had a good idea of where they were now, having compared the passing road signs to the markings on the map.

Thanks to the confusion of their escape and having to work their way around obstructions on the road, they had ended up twenty miles north of the school. The fairgrounds that the rest of their group was supposed to spend the night was almost a hundred miles south of them now, and they needed to hurry if they had any chance of catching up to them before they pulled out in the morning.

"I have been looking at the map," She began, "and it looks like I have found a way to get us where we need to be. The question is, do we want to avoid the bigger roads and towns where we can? We can do it, but it will take us way out of our way, and add a lot of distance to the trek."

Jack took another long puff and sighed contentedly before speaking: "I don't know, we will need gas again soon and I would like to get some before we run out of daylight. I feel better about the back roads personally after that" He glanced over to the animal. "And a gas station will have some food for the officer here."

Brandy studied the map again, trying to guess where a secluded gas station would be. This area was mostly rural, with few main highways, but there were a few. She found a promising looking set of crossed lines on the map just a few miles ahead. "A few miles ahead is highway 45, We need to turn there anyway. Maybe there will be something there."

Jack nodded, Returning his full attention to the road ahead of them. Brandy reached over and scratched the dog's ears again. Bruiser whined softly once before shooting out his tongue and giving her an affectionate lick.

She was still caressing the animal a few minutes later when the intersection came into view. They had been seeing the plume of smoke for the last mile or so, and as the small complex of buildings came into view, their hearts sank. The smoldering remains of a gas station stood as one of the several burned buildings. Several squat shells of cinder block stood on each of the four corners where the roads met, and only the slightly fewer charred signs by the road gave clue to what they had once been.

"So, what now?" Brandy wondered aloud.

Beside her, Jack glanced at the fuel gauge. "We are under an eight of a tank, we may be walking very soon."

She felt tears begin to well up in her eyes. Tears of frustration, exhaustion, and anger. She fought them back, something she suddenly realized she had been doing too much lately. Her dark sense of humor kicked in and she started mentally wondering where she could find a shrink after the zombie apocalypse.

"If we don't get to the fairgrounds by dawn, I am not sure we will ever find them." She added, stating the obvious. They knew about the fairgrounds only because they had heard it mentioned by one of the soldiers, and neither of them knew what the next stopping point would be.

Jack brought the vehicle to a stop in the middle of the intersection and turned the ignition off before opening the door and stepping out. Brandy followed his lead, climbing outdoor and stretching the stiffness out of her legs while the dog clambered over the seat and jumping to the pavement.

The two humans stood silently as the dog padded off to investigate the area. Brandy turned slowly, looking for anything she might have missed that might be useful. Even the cars she could see had burned, so there was no chance of siphoning some gas from the tanks.

“How much further do you think we can get?” She asked finally.

“Twenty miles?” He answered dejectedly. “Maybe thirty?”

“Maybe we will find another station.” She said hopefully.

“The bitch of it is that the gas in the tanks is below ground, so should be fine.” He said, his words touched with frustration, “I just can’t for the life of me figure out how to get any out. I was hoping there would be somewhere we could find a hand pump or something, but nothing here survived.” He said as he gestured to the destroyed buildings.

Brandy glanced to the west and saw the sun starting to touch the top of the trees on the horizon. She figured they had maybe half an hour of light left. “Well, all we can do is keep going. Maybe we will get lucky.” She said, trying to make her voice sound encouraging.

Brandy called the dog, and he rushed over and leaped into the van. Jack and brandy followed him in and they started driving again. Nobody spoke, and the only noise was the purr of the engine. Even Bruiser sat in silence, not even letting out his occasional whine as Brandy stroked his head distractedly.

From her seat, she could just see the low fuel light go from its steady glow to an urgent flashing. She felt those same frustrated tears try to fight their way up again, but couldn't stop them this time.

**Immanuel**

Immanuel opened his eyes and slowly turned his head to look around the room. He noticed that several small clusters of people still littered the room, yammering away.

He had spent the last hour or so feigning sleep to avoid conversations with those around him. The large barn-like room they were in was crowded and devoid of any entertainment, so people had been trying to alleviate the boredom with the only real entertainment available to them, conversation.

He had been unfortunate enough to be the new face in the group. All the others had at least known each other a little bit from their time together at the shelter, but being the new guy, he had been singled out as a prime target for their inane interest.

Immanuel wondered why people felt the need to chatter incessantly to one another when they could devote that time to speaking to god. He knew they didn't all have the special advantage he had, being able to hear the voice answer him.

'On second thought,' he said to himself, 'I am glad they don't pester the lord with such foolishness.'

The door to the building was firmly shut, and he could see the sky darkening beyond the triangular window set high in the wall above it. From where he lay, he was happy to see several people had already taken to their beds. The coming darkness would signal the move to sleep for most of the people still milling about.

They had been warned earlier that electricity would be in short supply, so only a few lights would be allowed. For the entire building. Immanuel assumed that the soldiers didn't want to fire up the big truck-sized generators for just the one night.

He watched silently as the few remaining clumps of talkers broke up into smaller and smaller groups as they worked their way to their beds. He was happy to see no one had taken the cots closed to him, thankful that he had picked the darkest corner.

Within an hour most people had made their way to beds, mostly towards the middle of the building. The building was lit only by a single strand of lights mounted atop a tall metal pole pointed towards the sliding doors that spanned the front of the building and the single table that sat there.

His eyes were drawn to the figure sitting there. She was dressed in jeans and one of those red smocks he had seen many of the Red Cross workers with. She was a brunette, slender and pretty, who looked to be in her early twenties. She was leaned back in the chair with her feet on the table, staring intently at the ratty old paperback cradled in her lap.

Immanuel could see the darkness shrouding her despite the glaring brightness of the power bulbs shining down on her from the lights. It was one of the darkest he had ever seen, seeming to suck the very energy from the bulbs and shine with its own glossy iridescence.

He quietly slid his feet off the cot and quickly found his new shoes, a pair of flip-flops. Pulling them on, they felt snug over his heavily wrapped feet. He knew he would need new ones when the bandages were removed. The swelling and wraps had increased his shoe size by four. He said a silent prayer of thanks that there had been so many to choose from in the truck outside.

Limping across the room, he willed himself to be unnoticed by the people sleeping and talking around himself. He was gratified to notice that the timber of those murmuring around him did not seem to change as he moved the few hundred feet to the front of the structure.

He approached the desk and leaned on it to take some of the weight off his aching feet. The girl looked up and smiled at him. He imagined that her smile would have tempted a lesser man. To Immanuel, it just seemed false and calculating: Another tool the darkness had given her to corrupt mortal men. He concentrated his will to avoid showing disgust.

"Excuse me." He said with calculated shyness in his voice. "Where is the bathroom?"

Her smile cracked a little bit. "I'm sorry, the only bathrooms are out in the courtyard. No one is allowed out of the buildings unattended. The soldiers are making patrols but the should be by soon and the can escort you." She explained.

Immanuel remembered hearing this when they had been brought in, but he had to do what he could to get the girl alone. "I can't wait, can you go with me?"

The brunettes face changed, her half smile becoming and unsure frown. "I can't leave my post, I am the only one here. The patrols should be here every hour or so. Can you wait?" She asked.

Immanuel forced his face into what he hoped was a look of pain. "I just don't think I can!" he protested, going for urgency in his words. "It's these meds they gave me for my feet." He said as he pointed down at the bandages. He didn't know if the medications he had been given would make him need to urinate more frequently, and hoped she wouldn't either.

The woman glanced under the table at his bandages and sighed before looking around the room at the mostly still figures she was charged with watching. “Okay, but you have to be quick.” She said firmly as she stood.

Immanuel said a silent prayer of thanks to the one above and followed her to the door as quickly as his feet would let him. He said another as he saw the knife clipped to her belt. ‘Fortune was smiling on him’ he thought as she undid the lock on the door and looked carefully outside before exiting.

“What is your name, my angel?” Immanuel asked her as they stepped out into the darkness.

**Derek**

The Shrill squeal of the brakes and lurching of the stop brought Derek out of his sleep with a jump. He scanned the cargo area in alarm but relaxed as a realization came to him that the others packed in around him were calm, with a few still sleeping despite the cessation of motion.

Looking towards the front of the vehicle, he could see the hulking shape of Sarge leaning into the driver's area, talking to the man at the wheel. He could not make out what they were saying to one another.

"The bridge is out," Chad said beside him, answering the question Derek had bouncing around his head. "They are trying to figure out what route to take."

"What happened to the bridge?" Derek asked the other boy.

"No clue, that's just what he yelled to the big man there when the called him up to the radio," Chad explained.

Derek rotated his neck from shoulder to shoulder, trying to relieve the stiffness in his upper back from the uncomfortable wooden bench. "How long was I asleep?"

Chad held up his empty wrist, "I am not sure, no watch, maybe an hour?"

"Do you have any Idea where we are?" Derek wondered as he did he best to stretch in the cramped confines of the armored vehicle. All the firing slots were closed tightly, and the only light was a pale-yellow glow from the lights set in the ceiling. He couldn't even see much into the operator's area because of the sergeant's bulk blocking his view.

Derek considered getting up and moving to the front to see what he could find out, but looking at the compartment crowded with sleeping people, he decided against it. Every Seat was taken, and a good deal of the floor space was covered in huddled people. He realized he was lucky to have a seat at all.

Sarge's Voice Brought him out of his observations. "LISTEN UP!" He bellowed, bringing the remaining sleepers awake and all eyes on him as his hunched form turned to address the passengers. Derek realized how uncomfortable the man must be in the low roofed vehicle. He was a foot taller than the average man, and even they would have to constantly duck in here.

"It looks like some fly-boys have taken out some of the bridges around here to try to stop the flow of this herd," Sarge continued, Irritation tinged his words, "But no one bothered to tell us about it. The Colonel Is trying to find us another route to the rendezvous, but that's going to take a little while."

A collective groan resounded through the crowd punctuated by a few swear words. They were all ready for this trip to be over.

"When I tell you, we are going to get out of this box and establish a perimeter. When that is done, we will set a guard and some of you can get some rest. Get your kit together and lock and load."

Derek felt the deep rumble of the engine starting up, and then the sensation of movement. In the distance, he could hear at least one other engine growling.

"As soon as the vehicles are in place we go." The big man said as he checked his own rifle.

Derek Realized he was one of the closest to the door and a wave of dread draped over him at the realization that he would have to be one of the first ones out. He began to shake when he realized that he had no idea what to do when he was out there. He nervously checked over his own rifle and waited.

All too soon, the armored personnel carrier came to stop, and the engine died. Derek took a deep breathed and readied himself as best as he could.

“READY!” Sarge hollered, making Derek jump a little. “STEADY!.GO!” He yelled as the rear door dropped, forming a ramp to the ground.

Derek willed himself quickly to his feet and pushed towards the opening, determined to do his best. Chad was the only one between him and the door, and it occurred to Derek that the other boy was not armed, but would be pushed out in the rush of troops. Already he could feel the man behind him pushing him towards the outside.

Derek placed his left hand on Chad's shoulder and guided him off the side of the ramp, out of the way of those coming up front behind and swung his rifle around to cover the way ahead of him. He steered the boy to the side of the vehicle. “GET DOWN CHAD!” He yelled as he put a downward pressure on Chad's shoulder, urging him to kneel by the heavy wheels.

Chad dropped to a ball on the ground and Derek stood over him, scanning the area in front of him. He could hear the others moving around behind him, but could not see what they were doing. He was relieved that none of the dead were in sight. He was tense with the expectation of the shooting to begin, but as the seconds ticked by, all he heard were the boots of the others and the occasional barked command.

Derek felt someone walk up beside him, and risked a glance over to see the redheaded Lieutenant standing beside him staring at the figure on the ground. “Good instincts Hobbs.” She said and patted him on the shoulder. “This area Is secure for the moment; you can stand down get your friend up off the ground."

"Yes Ma'am" Derek answered, but she was already moving off towards a group of soldiers that had gathered around Sarge as he pointed and gave orders.

Slinging his rifle over his shoulder, he reached out a hand and pulled Chad to his feet. "I guess they weren't kidding about the bridge." He said as the other boy dusted himself off.

The road stretched behind them for roughly a hundred yards back before it dropped off suddenly into a gap cut across the countryside. Derek guessed it was a river, but couldn't see the bottom as the rising wispy smoke rose from below.

The three APC's were parked at angles across the area where the road met the bridge, effectively forming a wall with only a dozen feet between each, But allowing room for all the trucks to get away without the others having to be moved.

All around them soldiers dressed in a hodgepodge of assorted camouflage and civilian clothing were busily scurrying like ants, and Derek felt uneasy at standing there but wasn't sure what he should be doing. He was startled when he heard a gravelly voice yell out from close behind him.

"Hobbs!" the voice barked, "Get the lead out of your ass and grab a bag of magazines out of that truck and start passing it out to everyone, make sure everybody has ten minimum and then get a list of what each of the three LPOP will need for the night and make sure you get it to them."

Derek looked at him confused, "What's a l.p/o.p.?"

The dark face scrunched in anger, but a hint of a smile cracked up at the corner of the lips. "Listening Post, Observation Post, son." He pointed down the road where soldiers we busily stacking debris into a shelter. "They are also putting one in each direction to the sides of the road."

"Right away Sargent!" Derek answered, proud of himself for remembering not to say 'Sir'.

The Big man tuned to Chad, "Have you ever loaded a magazine before?"

Clearly uncomfortable with the direct attention, chad stammered, "Um, no, not really, just seen it on tv."

"Well good news," Shrek said is he patted the young man on the shoulder, "by the time you are done with the job I have for you, you are going to be an expert."

As the Sargent steered Chad away, Derek set to work. He grabbed the large duffle from the truck, surprised by the weight of it, and rushed off to set to work.

He quickly realized that there weren't very many people holding firearms, and that worried him. When they were preparing to set out from the school, there had been more than a hundred armed people, now he could see no more than forty.

He felt his mind wandering to his mother who had been on one of the trucks that went on the hospital raid, and that one had been even larger, but forced his mind onto the task at hand, and wiped the beginnings of wetness from his eyes as he began to hand out the ammunition. Each soldier handed him back any empty magazines they had, but he was passing five to everyone he was handed. He would have to make a note to not drop his anymore when he removed it. They were going to run out quickly at this rate.

Derek ran supplies and helped build the security until almost dark before he was finally finished. They only bright spot in the drudgery had been when one old man, obviously a recent volunteer like himself, had let him help set up the explosives and devices they had strung around the makeshift camp. He was still a teenage boy after all.

As he staggered back onto the bridge where they real camp was set up, he could see a thin trail of smoke rising from near the end, someone had started a fire and he could see people sitting around it on crates and whatever they could find. He could also smell food cooking, and his stomach growled.

He staggered into the ring of people and saw a pot hanging over the fire, he walked close and peeked into it, he could see beans boils merrily along and felt his mouth water.

As he stood there watching hungrily, he heard a familiar voice behind him say, "It won't be ready for another few minutes, and you don't get a bite until you wash your hands!' it scolded.

Derek spun in surprise, hunger, and fatigue forgotten. "MOM!" he cried out in surprise and rushed to her and pulled her into a hug.

**Brandy**

The van was dark and the temperature outside was dropping, giving the scenario a foreboding feeling of coming discomfort. She had begged Jack to wait until morning, but he had insisted on walking off to find gas right after the had run out. He had sworn he knew a gas station was only a mile or so down the road and he could be there in back in an hour. But as she glanced at her watch, she saw that it was after midnight. It had been several hours.

Brandy absent-mindedly stroked the dog's side as it laid in the seat beside her. She had decided earlier that she envied the animal and its seeming complete lack of stress under their present situation. She could just make out its slow steady snore.

The light from her watch timed out, plunging her into almost complete darkness, she could just make out the shadows that she knew were the edges of the windshield, but the other side of the glass was an impenetrable mass of black.  The clouds covered the moon and stars in such a thick layer that she couldn't even make out the line between the trees and sky.

Even when she strained her ears and ignored the canine, she couldn't hear anything outside, it seemed even the birds and animals in the night had decided the end was near and given up their calls for the coming end of the world.

Brandy leaned her head back and closed her eyes. Trying to force her ears to pick up any sounds that may come. She was listening intently when her exhausted mind pulled her into sleep.

Her dreams followed her real situation so closely that she wasn't aware that it was happening. She found herself sitting in the van, staring out the window, amazed that the day had come suddenly as she blinked her eyes into the bright sunshine.

Brandy listened to the birds happily chirping and remembered the times she had gone fishing with her father and he had told her which birds made which calls.

As she watched, his figure walked out of the woods and waved cheerfully to her. She reached for the door handle to get out and run to him, but the smooth interior showed no handle. She searched frantically for it, as she yelled his name.

She looked up to see him getting closer, only a few feet from the door, now, and felt her blood run cold. His face was ripped and dripped large viscous red drops from the dangling shreds of flesh. His ruined features pressed against the glass as he peered in at her, leaving smears of ichor on the glass as the head moved back and forth. "DADDY!" she shrieked in horror.

The face in the glass didn't answer, just swayed back and forth, its eyes locked on hers. She could see the mouth open slightly as if to speak, but the noise that came out was low and steady. The realization that it was a growled jerked her back to wakefulness, and back into the cold dark van.

She glanced down at her watch, hitting the button on the side to illuminate it. The glow hurt her eyes for a moment as they adjusted: almost three in the morning.

As she shook off the sleep gathered fog in her brain she realized the growling remained, low and threatening. She placed her hand on the dog by memory and found his position had changed, He was now sitting up in the seat, with his back towards Brandy. She could feel the vibrations of the growl through his body.

"What is it?" She asked as she felt fear begin to rise in her.

As soon as the words escaped her mouth, she heard it herself. The sounds of feet hitting the pavement behind the van, and it sounded like a lot of feet. The stead tread loud in the quiet night.

“Shhhhh!” she urged the dog in a whispered plead. “Be quiet,” she begged him and felt her heart lift as he instantly went quiet.

The feet kept coming, and she felt Bruiser’s hair bristle under her hand. That was when the first of the things bumped into the rear of the van in the dark. Brandy Barely stifled the involuntary scream that tried to escape her throat.

The vehicle shook with another impact, the thudding sound becoming a rubbing sound as whatever had walked into the back of the vehicle now dragged itself along the side as it continued its mindless trek towards whatever drove it forward.

Brandy clutched the dog close to her chest, barely aware of the low growl it was making, the low guttural grumble barely audible of the sound of her heart beating its frantic staccato. She scrunched low in the seat, willing herself invisible.

Outside of the animated carrion of humanity proceeded their drudge towards the horizon, searching only for flesh. The battered forms were countless shapes in the dark outside the windows stretching far back into the gloom.

Brandy felt tears burn cooling trails down her face as the fear of her situation overcame the adrenaline of the surprise. She listened to the roar of falling feet outside as they blended into one another creating an almost continuous tattoo.

***

*The Herd that now passed had begun its movements to follow the retreating form of a deer that had run through the area they had been standing dormant. The animal had quickly run out of sight and hide in the woods. The mindless group now moved only because the other members did. Their own movement spurred on by itself.*

*In the following days, other groups had been encountered and joined. The numbers had grown from a few dozen to hundreds. The day before, they had crossed the path of another heard as it came up a side road. When the first of that group had run into the others, it had been bumped into, turned and continued in the new direction. The ones behind them had simply followed.*

*The encounter with the white van was one of many the herd had had that day. The milky eyes of the infected had not been able to see the obstruction in the darkness. When the head of the column had run into it, the functioning portions of its brain had not recognized it as edible.*

*Its lack of reaction had quickly spread through the shambling figures behind it, and they paid it no attention. They proceeded on into the night, searching, but oblivious to the girl cowering inside the metal shell.*

***

## Immanuel

Immanuel sat in the darkness of the concession stand looking down at his work. She was laid bare before him, he had done everything he could, but again, success had eluded him. He had viewed the find of the building being empty and unlocked as god smiling down on him, after all, it held all the tools he would need and even had a drain in the floor to keep things from getting too messy.

He idly toyed with her brown locks as he thought of how to proceed. He had checked everywhere for the darkness he had seen in her with no results. He had been sad to see her blood stop its flow before he could finish his search, but at least he had tried to save her.

Glancing up, he could see the sky lightening thru the cracks in the window and he knew his time with her was coming to an end. Placing his hand gingerly on her cool forehead, he said a prayer for her, and closed her eyes.

He stood carefully, stretching the stiffness from his body and moved to the sink to wash the blood from his arms and chest. I had stripped down to the waist, conscious of the need to keep his clothes clean because of the close quarters he was confined to.

As he redressed, he pondered how to get back into bed unnoticed and decided on his plan. He regretted not having a mirror, to check his appearance, but he would have to trust that the powers above had guided his hands in cleaning himself.

Immanuel opened the door slightly and peeked outside, he saw no one moving about. “Goodbye and godspeed to your soul my cherub.” He said to the still form on the floor, as he moved outside.

The morning was clear and there was a slight nip in the air. Immanuel found himself grateful for that as he moved towards the trailer parked nearby. He knew it contained a variety of things everyone would need and the desire for a sweater would be a perfect excuse to be up and about on a morning like this.

He could see the tall chain link fence securing the fairground in the distance, several hundred yards away, and the men walking along it, but all their attention was focused outward. Immanuel couldn't find anyone else nearby.

Crossing the distance casually, he stepped up the stairs and into the truck. It was a mess of open and spilled boxes. Assorted clothing and personal items covered the floor. "Such messy people!" he said aloud, before sparing a glance back out into the grounds. No one seemed to have noticed him.

Contented, he began his search for clothing and anything he could use. He quickly located a windbreaker that would work for his purposes and stepped down from the truck. All he had to do now was wander back to his cot and hopefully get a few hours' sleep.

The building was quiet as he entered, with no one even appearing to be awake. He made his way to the darkened back corner where his cot sat in midst of several others that where not being used. He said a silent thanks to his lord for this as he gingerly lowered himself into his bed, and another as it did not squeak or rattle under his weight.

He quickly fell asleep amid the snores and noises of the others in the room continued without interruption. The sound of the sleepers was loud enough that no one in the building heard the door to the concession stand being banged open and then slamming closed as his newest angel exited, driven by its need to feed.

***

*Her body twitched once, then once again and opened its eyes. The floor beneath her was cold and damp, but those feelings did not register in the small section of her brain that still held activity.*

*As she rose to her feet, the Incision he had made in her abdomen slipped open and the things once held inside by the skin spilled out. Most of them hung awkwardly down her front, but the fluid that spilled from her coated her feet and she slipped. Her shoulder smashed into the stainless-steel table as she fell, but the nerves that would have fired off their signals of pain found only dead tissue at the other end of their communications.*

*Driven by primal instincts to feed, she rose to her feet again. The process drove a jagged splinter of her shattered collarbone through the skin and spilled a black viscous liquid down over her breast, dripping in thick drops from her nipple with each step.*

*The swinging door moved easily out of her way as she walked into it and stepped out into the cool morning. In the distance, she sensed what she needed and walked towards it.*

*She encountered her first meal as it came around the corner of the metal buildings. The soldier had not been paying attention and bumped into her. She had wrapped her arms around him and bitten into his lips in such a way as to stifle his scream. The blood poured down his throat and filled the lungs he would need to try any further warning to the others.*

*She had fed on him until he reanimated, and losing interest, she had moved off to find another meal. He followed. The pair walked up behind the guards at the gate, who had unfortunately fallen asleep in their chairs. She had grabbed hers and bitten into his exposed neck before pulling her teeth back to rip free the flesh for chewing. Her companion grabbed the other and his teeth cracked on the helmet the man wore.*

*The man jumped up, screaming and her companion moved forward. She held her struggling screaming meal, and had no interest in the other while hers still lived.*

*The living man backed into the gate in his efforts to escape, and in his panic fumbled for the keys to the padlock. He sprang the lock and pulled the chain just as her companion reached him, this time his bite found the soft flesh it wanted, and the screaming resumed.*

*He was chewing his first mouthful when the gate swung open under its own weight.*

***

**Derek**

Derek was ripped from his restless sleep by a hand on his shoulder shaking him. He sat suddenly looking around in alarm. The brightness of the rising sun blinded him to the person kneeling beside him, but before his eyes could adjust the voice identified who it was.

"It's just me." Came the gruff voice of Sarge. "It is time to get up and get moving."

The air carried the smell of wood smoke and something cooking as Derek stretched and felt the stiffness in his back from sleeping on the rigid concrete that had been his bed. He made a mental note to find something to put under his sleeping bag, even handfuls of leaves would have helped.

His eyes finally let him see the giant above him, all be it thru a squint. "Up and at 'em, start breaking down camp, we are on the road in 30." He said as he stood and moved over to the next sleeper.

Derek worked himself out of his sleeping bag and began to roll it up. All around him where people were rising and doing the same. He looked over to where his mother had fallen asleep the night before and saw that her space was empty. Her pack was already rolled up and ready to go.

They had sat up around the fire very late talking about the situation and sharing stories about what they had been through. To his surprise, she did not scold him about volunteering the way he had, but he knew it would come. He knew the look in her eyes well.

Looking around as he fastened the elastic of his rolled-up bed to his backpack, he spotted her standing at the back of one of the trucks, clipboard in hand talking to a soldier that was shifting the supplies inside. Derek shouldered his rifle and lifted his pack before he made his way over to her.

"Move the equipment to the front of the truck and leave the meds and other stuff towards the back so we can grab it easily if we need it." She explained to the man inside. "We are more likely to need gauze and analgesics than one of the I.V. machines."

"Good morning," Derek said to get her attention.

"Good morning sweetie." She answered without looking up from the clipboard. "Did you get something to eat yet?"

Derek was close enough to see the clipboard she was holding contained a handwritten list of supplies. He recognized her handwriting and could see she had obviously been busy. The list was already several pages long and she was still making notes.

"Not yet, I just woke up." He answered, "How long have you been up?"

"A couple of hours, I couldn't sleep." She Explained. "I figured it was better to stay busy with all that was going on.

Derek Knew what she meant, even though they had now come together, His thoughts were still full of concerns for his sister and father and sister. He knew his sister was safe where ever the rest of the shelter had gone, but his father was two thousand miles away and he had no clue if he was still alive or not. His mother must be trying to stay busy to keep the thoughts at bay.

"Did you stop long enough to eat yet," Derek asked, knowing that she had not. His mother had a history of skipping meals when there was working to be done.

"I tell you what," She said by way of answer, "let go have breakfast together." She laid the clipboard down on the bumper of the truck and part her arm around his shoulder and began to lead him towards the fire.

The meal being prepared was oatmeal, one of their favorites. However, whoever had looted the containers of oatmeal on some supply raid had neglected to grab any sugar or dairy. To make matter worse, they had to eat the clumpy meal from paper plates, and the only utensils available where plastic forks. Derek made a mental note to keep the spoons from his next M.R.E. for just such an occasion.

"They say hunger is the best seasoning." His mother joked as they finished the meal, "I guess I am not that hungry yet."

Derek laughed as he swallowed the last gloopy forkful. "Well, I am not sure we could get hungry enough for that to taste good.

His mother rewarded him with a smile and took his now empty plate from him, tossing it into the fire that was serving as a combination cooking station and camp trash can. Derek watched it curl up from the heat and then burst into flames.

"I was speaking to that lady Lieutenant, the redhead?" She said suddenly. And continued when Derek nodded that he understood who she meant. "she says we should be at the fairgrounds by noon. That's where Brandy is."

"That will be good," Derek said. He thought back to the last time the three of them had all been together. It had been a few days at least. As he tried to remember, it felt like weeks ago. The last 48 hours seemed like a week on its own. Had it only been three days since they had all sat at the picnic tables having dinner together?

He was drawn from his contemplation of time by the sudden blare of the loudspeakers on one of the armored vehicles. "Attention, Attention, everyone mount up!" an amplified voice announced. Derek recognized the voice as the woman his mother had just spoken about. "We have just received a mayday from the rally point, they are under attack. Military personnel will depart in one minute, civilian to follow in ten."

Derek Leaped to his feet, gathering his things. Around him, people had jumped up and were running for vehicles as the engines roared to life with plumes of black smoke. The relative silence of the camp shattered by the sudden burst of motion.

Behind him, he heard his Mother yell, "Derek!? Where are you going?" she called desperately.

He turned his head to catch of here standing there staring wide-eyed. "Brandy!" he yelled as his feet found the ramp leading into the back of the armored vehicle, "That's where they sent her group!"

He claimed a seat and watched her as the ramp lifted into place. He lost sight of her as it clanged into place. The Vehicle Lurched forward and was away. He looked around him at the concerned faces seated with him and could tell he wasn't the only one with relatives and friends in danger. The din of the engines was incredibly loud with the speed they were traveling, but his mind screamed for them to go faster.

Derek Checked and rechecked his rifle, and counted the magazine in the pouches on the vest they had given him, and the bag that hung from his belt. The speakers hanging in the corners played the desperate radio calls they were receiving and he had to fight back tears as they swung his mood from despair to anger and back again.

"… one of them got inside somehow! Attacked the guards at the gate as a herd of them were approaching it. By the time we got more people there they were pushing down the fence… must be a thousand of them. They have gotten into two of the buildings, we have lost hundreds of refugees and most of the soldiers. They have this building surrounded, I can hear them pounding on the walls, can't hold out for long!" The tinny voiced was saying in a carefully controlled tone, but everyone could hear the growing panic behind it.

From the cockpit, the Lieutenant answered. "How many survivors? How many buildings are still secure?" She yelled into the handset.

"Two buildings, this one and the one in the middle, about fifty in each plus about a dozen soldiers scattered around. We need help! How long?" the man answered. The sound of the things outside almost drowned out the reply.

From his seat, Derek saw the woman glance down at the map she held folded in her lap. "fifteen minutes. Hold out, we are coming!" She said desperately in reply.

"Fuck!" the voiced answered. "the door is giving in, they are almost inside!" The panic now taking over the voice.

Derek felt the surge as the vehicle accelerated even more. It had to be traveling at its top speed now. The engines rumble had a whine that told him it was being pushed hard. He realized his hand was clamped tensely on the grip of his gun, and he forced his hand to relax so that it would not be frozen up on him.

Ahead of him, he saw the lieutenant point out the window, and yell something about a van. The APC lurched to the left violently. Derek had a sudden fear the vehicle would roll over, but it steadied itself quickly and continued its path right side up.

"Rally Point, report!" she demanded into the radio.

Several seconds of static issued from the speakers before a frenzied voice answered. "They are inside!" it screamed into the microphone over a cacophony of gunfire. Everyone in the vehicle could hear the screams coming through with the gunshots, but they could also hear the moans of the dead.

They sound hit Derek's heart like a bullet of ice and stuck there. He felt anger fill him as he listened. Anger at the situation, anger at the things killing people on the other end of the radio and anger at his own helplessness.

Around him, the sound of the radio devolved into unintelligible gibberish as the guns slowly fell silent and the screams took over. The other end of the microphone seemed to be locked open, and they listened as even the screams began to die.

They listened in silence, no one wanting to interrupt the slim thread of hope that the sounds would change to something positive. It was still playing when the officer turned and began to shout orders. They had arrived, and it was time to work.

**Brandy**

The roar of the Military vehicle snatched Brandy from her sleep. She looked out the window to see an army vehicle scream past her. It was soon followed by another, and then another as she watched them shrink into the distance. Her first thought was amazement that they could move so quickly. It that dawned on her that vehicles meant people, and she quickly opened the door and stepped outside, waving madly at them to get them to come back for her.

As the disappeared over a distant hill, she sullenly gave up her waving. They had either not seen here, or had decided not to stop. She felt something against the side of her leg and looked down to see Bruiser looking up at her desperately.

"Yes," she said, understanding the dogs need and watched as he rushed off to the side of the road to do his business.

As she watched him, the memories of the night before rushed back to her, and the same feeling of panic returned. She looked around urgently, trying to see if any of the things that had passed in the night had hung around. She didn't see any, but she forced herself to remain calm as she walked slowly around the van to make sure.

Here and there on the ground, evidence of the herds passing lay like leaves after a storm. Parts of shoes, clothing and what she was horrified to see were actual body parts littered the graffiti of footprints made from blood and other fluids she didn't want to think about. It even emitted a smell that she was alarmed to realize she was starting to get used to.

She looked back in the direction the vehicles had just gone and realized it was the same direction the things had been going last night, and that Jack had gone. As she looked, she realized something was moving in that direction. She could just make out a lone figure ambling down the side of the road, heading towards her.

"Bruiser!" she called in a hushed tone, wanting the comfort of the dog beside her.

The animal slinked over to her and sensing where she was looking, gazed in the same direction. She felt the animal tense against her, and know he had seen it too. They watched together, unsure of what to do.

Brandy was trying to decide whether she should hide in the van until it passed, or if she should run into the woods. The van would keep her safe, but the woods would give her a chance to escape. As she stared at the approaching figure, she debated with herself.

As she watched, a whitish could of haze emitted from the thing on the road, and her heart lifted in joy. The cloud of vapor could only mean one thing, it was Jack. From as far away as he was it would take him at least fifteen minutes to get here, and she was just able to make out the red shape in his hand that had to be a gas can.

She again checked in all directions for any threats and busied herself with putting out food and water for the dog. As well as setting out something for the two of them to eat. She knew the man would be tired and sore from how far he must have walked. By the time she was done, he was within shouting distance.

"Brandy!" He yelled. "You okay?"

She answered with a thumb up and walked out to meet him, handing him a bottle of water. It was not cold, but he drained it in all the same and gave a satisfied sigh.

"I wasn't sure if you were going to come back," she told him, "a bunch of those things came by last night, thousands of them, and they were going the same way you had gone! I thought they would get you for sure." He could tell she was relieved to see him.

"Yeah," He answered as they made their way back to the vehicle. "I got lucky on that one, I saw them coming from the top of a hill and got into the woods before they saw me. I hid in there until they had marched past. Did you see those Military things zip passed? They almost ran me down coming around a corner!" He complained.

"Yes," she complained back, "I tried to wave them down, but I don't think they saw me."

"Well, they definitely saw me!" he answered. "swerved around me and kept going!"

They reached the van and Jack started to pour the gas into it. "All I could get was two gallons. But the station is only five miles up, so we can refill completely there. It has the above ground tanks, so it's easy to get the gas out.

Brandy handed him another bottle of water as he opened the back doors of the van and sat down and pulled his shoes off. "These loafers need to go!" he exclaimed, and she was alarmed to see the bottom of his socks crusted with the fluid of the blisters they must be hiding.

"I walked some pretty big blisters on my feet!" he explained. "these are good shoes for the mall, but I need to find something better.

Bruiser, who had just finished wolfing down his food wandered over for and let Jack scratch his head. Mid scratch, the dog suddenly looked down the road, staring intently. It was several seconds before the humans heard it also.

The low thrum of engines approaching from the way they had, and it sounded like several of them. The vehicles weren't yet in sight. Jack snatched up his shoes from the pavement and hurriedly pulled them back on, grunting at the pain it caused, but determined. "It sounds like more big vehicles, maybe more military, let's get ready to follow them. Can you drive?" He asked Brandy, Indicating his sore feet.

"Yes!" she exclaimed urgently and the three of them loaded into the van.

Brandy turned the key, afraid it would not start, and the engine failed to turn over on the first try. 'Please..." she thought to herself, and then tried again. The engine roared to life to the relief of the humans on board. Behind them, the dog barked. She could see him in the rearview mirror. He was looking out the back window, and further back, she could see several large trucks, all painted flat mixtures of green, black and brown.

"It is the army!" she announced to the vehicle and put the truck into drive, turning it out of the way, and onto the shoulder so they could pass. She remembered how much the van had rocked when the first column had passed and wanted to give plenty of room.

Brandy noticed the vehicles were slowing down as they approached. The lead vehicle coasted to a stop just fifty feet behind them and stood there. She could make out the slight vibration of its motor and just make out its dull grumble.

"Should I get out?" She asked Jack, who was leaned back over the seat, watching out the window.

"I don't know..." he answered meekly.

Together they watched in indecision. A full minute passed before the large truck began to crawl forward. It inched forward slowly until it was right beside them. Brandy leaned towards the glass and looked up to see the large black circle of a gun barrel pointed at her. Instinctively she raised her hands and gasped.

Even through the rolled-up window, she could hear the man holding the gun yelling at her to not move. She had a fleeting thought of jamming her foot down on the gas pedal, but before she could, she heard a pounding on the other side of the truck, and another voice yelling something she couldn't make out.

She looked over as the door was yanked open and a man dressed in camouflage filled the opening.

"NOBODY MOVE!" the man yelled.

Even in the fear of the moment, Brandy admired the strategy. While they had been watching the truck, men must have jumped out of the back and swung around the other side to surprise them, brilliant.

"ARE YOU INFECTED?!" the soldier yelled over the pistol he held pointed at Jack.

Brandy heard the growl, and her fear deepened as she saw the blur of fur move from the back of the van. She reached out with her hand, grabbing for the dog as it launched itself across Jack. She missed, and the animal struck the soldier in a complete surprise, knocking him to the ground in a pile.

"BRUISER!" she yelled urgently. "NO!"

To the credit of whoever had trained him, bruiser immediately let go of the soldier, though he stood over him menacingly. Brandy looked at the soldiers laying on the ground, and yelled again, "Mueller!" Only now did she recognize the man.

The man looked up in surprise. “Ms. Brandy.” He finally said in recognition. “What are you doing out here?” he asked as he waved at the men in the truck.

She glanced to her left and saw the barrel of the gun recede from view and be replaced by the face of a man she had seen at the school a few times. Turning back to the sailor, she said, “We got left behind. We have been trying to find everybody.” She explained.

Jack finally found his tongue and answered the question he had been asked. “No, we are not infected, we have been lucky.”

Mueller nodded his understanding and spoke into the microphone pinned to his shoulder as he stood up and glared unhappily at the dog. “All clear. Some people that got separated during the evac, no infection. Two civilians and one mean ass dog.”

He turned his attention back to the two seated before him. “When we pull out, get in line behind us and keep up. There is trouble up ahead. Stop when we stop.” After he said this, he rushed back to the truck and climbed in. the truck started rolling before he had even closed the door. The other trucks started rolling at the same time.

“Well…” Said Jack, “I guess we do what he said…”

“I guess so.” Brandy answered and called jack back inside. Once he was safely seated in the back, she pulled out in line with the convoy.

The truck in front of them had a canvas cover, but the back flap was rolled up. They could see stacks of boxes held down with larges camouflage nets and a few people seated on one side. Brandy almost lost control of the vehicle in shock when she realized who she was seeing. She rolled down her window and yelled into the wind as loud as she could…

“MOM!”

**Immanuel**

He had slept through the beginning, as the screams had blended seamlessly into his dreams. His newest angel had not yet come to terms with the change. It was always screaming in the beginning. It was the gunshots that had stolen the sleep.

Immanuel set up abruptly, looking around at the dim room. All around him people were panicking. Small groups of people were huddled together crying or praying, or both. Another group was stacking things in front of the large double door as others frantically worked to keep it closed against whatever was pounding on it from the outside. He rose gingerly to his damaged feet and was surprised how much better they felt. He was also amazed at his level of fear compared to those around him, but then again, he had the lord on his side he thought to himself.

He approached the closest group of people to find they were ripping one of the metal cots apart, pulling off legs to make makeshift weapons. Towards the front of the building, he saw a small group of about 6 soldiers readying their guns and looking nervously at the now bowing doorway.

Through the thin sheet metal of the walls, he could hear another layer of sounds. Yells, screams, and gunshots reverberated from the next building over. Even further away he could hear another grouping of shots and terror. All the buildings in the compound must be in the same situation.

Immanuel listened, but couldn't hear any engines. "This could be bad." He said aloud to no one. But to his surprise, some answered him.

"The army is coming." Said a young voice beside him.

Immanuel looked down to see the young boy that had brought him clothes last night. The child was standing with his toy gun and exuding a confidence greater than his age.

"How do you know?" Immanuel asked calmly.

"One of the army guys," he pointed at the group of soldiers standing in a line watching the door, "I heard someone talking on the radio he has. They were calling for help. Some lady answered and said they were coming.

Immanuel considered this for a second. "I see." Was all he could think to say.

They stood side by side for another minute, watching the door slowly bend inside under the weight of the massed bodies outside. Even from this distance, Immanuel noted that the upper right hinge was separating from the wall.

"Well," He added finally, "they good lord helps those that help themselves." Josh reached down to the pile of scrap that had once been the cot and lifted a long L-shaped piece of metal that had been the side rail. The others had left it because it was almost six feet long and they were looking for clubs, but it fitted Immanuel's plans to a tee.

He approached the door just as it opened a few inches under the strain from outside. Immanuel held the length of metal and jabbed it forward into the first face he saw. The end pierced the flesh and bone with a wet crunching sound. He pulled the spear back sharply and thrust it into another face revealed as the first fell.

The gap was slowly widening, the small group of resistors being slide across the concrete by the force of the combined dead. Immanuel thrust his weapon thru the opening again, withdrew it, and thrust again. Each thrust rewarded by the sound of breaking bones and spurting fluids. Each time a falling body becoming something for the ones behind it to slip or stumble on.

He thrust the point forward again before turning to the timid one standing behind him, watching. “You four, grab that desk and put it up against the doors!” He ordered. When they didn’t move he added “NOW”. He was rewarded with them starting to move.

Immanuel thrust again, scoring a direct hit into the eye of an Asian lady he had seen on the bus yesterday. He twisted the rail and withdrew it, watching her drop into the growing pile. He was satisfied her falling corpse knock down another two that were moving forward to take her place. It was working.

The desk arrived, and he jabbed again, killing one that was dressing like one of the soldiers. He stepped back and let the ones carrying it to slide it against the door. He leaned his hip into it and employed the rail again, dropping another one. “Now, everyone over here, press against the desk!”

He knew of the fifty people in the room, only a few would obey, but that’s all there was room for. Several rushed forwards and shoved, the desk rammed the doors closed, breaking the arms that had been reaching through. Immanuel used the jagged edge of his spear as a club, severing the limbs that dangled thru, satisfied when the door finally snapped shut the last few inches. Then he jammed it thru the handles of the door to hold it shut. He finished it off by cinching his belt around them to arrest any wiggle.

He looked back at the group gathered around him. They were all looking at him expectantly. He looked back. Not sure what to do. When one of them finally spoke up, “what do we do now?”

Immanuel looked back at the speaker, one of the soldiers. He was a tall lanky man dressed in the blue digital pattern associated with the Navy. He realized that by getting the door closed, he had become the de facto leader. The thought made him unhappy, he needed to fade back out of sight. Attention was to be avoided, it interfered with his mission from God.

"Who is in charge here?" Immanuel asked the crowd. And stood to wait for anyone to step up. The only sound was the things outside.

"Who is the leader here, who was put in charge? He asked again.

Finally, someone answered. Claire, the boy's mother who had helped him last night stepped forward. "well," she began, "it was the brown-haired lady at the desk. But she isn't here anymore. I guess it's you now..." she said, trailing off on the last word.

Finally accepting the inevitable, Immanuel hung his head and picked three of the largest men to come forward and help brace the desk against the door the rest he directed to take the beds apart to make more weapons. He was pleased that this time, the longer pieces like his weren't left on the floor, they were learning.

He was aware of a change in the group. They had gone from panic to a cautious optimism. They were psyching themselves up for a fight, and though he dreaded the attention, he found himself enjoying the feeling of power.

He scanned the crowd moving about the various tasks he had given them, a few showed the dark auras, but the majority shined with the light. It struck him suddenly, this group was a reward for his works. God had given a flock. He could show them the way.

'They will be yours' the voice whispered in his head, 'you must save them.'

"I will!" he said aloud, and one young lady turned to him and gave him a nervous smile, then went back to work.

Outside, several explosions sounded...

**Derek**

Derek felt the Personnel carrier lurch to a stop and immediately the gate at the back dropped, letting the blinding sun spill into the cabin. The rushed out and to the driver's side of the vehicle as the other pulled in a few yards away and disgorged its contents of armed men who joined them between the two vehicles. The third pulled in, forming a box with heavy vehicles on three sides and the chain link fence on the other. The last vehicles men filled the gaps between the trucks watching the rear.

Derek took his position, kneeling along the fence, so close that the barrel of his rifle was almost inside the links of chain. He knew that another line of men was rushing up to stand over him. A hundred yards away, he would see the sheet metal buildings, surrounded by the infected.

They beat their fists against the door, but it didn't appear they had gotten into the closest building, but he could see the other buildings door gaping open like a wound. They things were wandering out of them slowly, and most of them looked fresh and familiar.

"No one fires until I give word." A commanding voice exclaims. The red-headed officer, Derek knew. It was all part of the plan they had gone through. "Sarge, launch enticements, and start the music." She ordered.

Loud thumps rang out from the tops of the A.P.C.s followed by loud bangs. Derek risked a glance up and saw what looked like fireworks going off overhead. As soon as that sound faded, the speakers blared to life. Despite the situation, he felt himself smile as the beginning of 'thriller' by Michael Jackson filled the air.

In the distance, the effect was immediate, the massed shapes began to turn and make their way towards the sound. The milling crowd was large enough that it was hard to get a count, but Derek estimated there must be hundreds, if not thousands. The sound and lights in the sky had made most of the things forget about the people inside the metal shell.

Behind the firing lines, Lt. Kelley yelled above the din. "Remember, headshots or nothing. Aim for the pupil of the eye. Don't shoot until I tell you, but make every shot count. Aim small, Miss small."

Derek forced himself to take deep breaths and tried to calm the rising adrenaline. His mind flashed back to the night at the mall fence. He had made it through that, he would make it through this he told himself.

They watched the things grow closer, step by step. The closest was only fifty feet away when the order finally came: "FIRE AT WILL!"

Twenty-five guns went off at once with a combined roar that made Derek feel dizzy for a second. The closest creatures head exploded at more than a dozen rounds tore thru it. It seemed almost everyone had aimed for the nearest target.

Derek shifted his aim to another and pulled the trigger and was rewarded when it collapsed like a sack of potatoes. He shifted his aim to another and squeezed. It kept coming, he aimed again and fired and the dead thing, a middle-aged woman fell.

He scanned the targets, searching for any that might look like Brandy, but was relieved when none did. He selected another and got it on his second try. He dropped several more before the realization dawned on him that the crowd didn't seem to be shrinking very fast. The thought almost brought on his panic response, but he fought it and selected another target.

Around him, the others continued the relentless slaughter. Derek fired until his rifle clicked empty, pulled another magazine and loaded it. He continued shooting until that was empty, only then sparing a second to count. He had fired sixty rounds and had about half that in targets down. The others seemed to be doing about the same. He could finally see the approaching group's numbers starting to drop.

As with the night in the mall parking lot, it went from terror to habit. Select a target, aim, fire, select a new target and repeat. As dangerous as these things were, simple strategies would win out, and soon it was over.

In the distance, he could still see some of the things wandering about, or beating flutily on the metal doors. Derek counted the ones he could see, less than fifty, but he knew there would be far more than that still inside the breached buildings, contentedly feasting on the people who hadn't come back.

A few dozen yards beyond the fence a mound of bodies had formed as the ones behind had tried to crawl over the ones that had been dropped in front of them, only to then be gunned down, making the pile even higher. The armed group watched the pile intently for any movement. Several times something would appear to twitch and would be obliterated by a hail of fire.

The music abruptly cut off. It's absence allowing the gathered fighters to realize how bad their ears were ringing. After the oppressive noise the actions had made, the quiet seemed strange.

"Police your empty mags and mount up." Called the deep voice of the sergeant. "It's time to get closer and see who is left."

Derek collected his gear and rose to his feet, taking in the fence. What had been a well-maintained fence, was now a tattered ruin with gaping holes where bullets had snapped the wire. He stared at it for a second, awed by the concentration of fire they had put out. He turned and climbed back into the vehicle as it roared to life. To his surprise, it did not back out but instead pushed forward through the ruined fence.

He pretended not to know what the thumps against the front of the vehicle were shortly after. But he knew it was a good way to save on ammo.

Brandy

She eyed the gas gauge as they drove. They had decided against stopping at the station and decided to follow the convoy. The Petty Officer had been quite clear about following, but as the needle dipped into the red again they began to worry. They had no way of telling those ahead of them of their needs.

Brandy's mother had looked at them in confusion when she had tried her best charades to explain, and they had eventually given up. They would have to go on for as long as they could and hope to make it.

Jack leaned over and looked at the gauge. "I would guess about ten miles before she runs out again."

Brandy gave an exasperated sigh. But bit back the remark she was about to make. They were getting close to a town, and that was making her nervous. The numbers of buildings they passed were increasing and they were getting closer together. She had also noticed the roads were getting to be in better condition. All were indicators of increasing population.

A billboard caught her eye and made her smile. It was advertising the county fair, two miles ahead on the left. For the first time in twenty minutes, she knew they would make it.

Sure enough, a minute later, the convoy slowed, then pulled into a parking lot. Ahead of them, armed people began leaping from the trucks and forming a loose circle around them. Brandy pulled the van into the lot and parked.

She quickly stepped from the van and rush to the truck her mother was in as the older woman stepped down. Brandy grabbed her in a fierce hug. They held each other and cried tears of happiness. They separated when Bruiser, jealous that he was not the subject of the affection, squeezed in between them. Brandy distractedly scratched the dog's ears.

"Where is Derek?" brandy asked, looking around for him.

"I don't know." Her mother answered. Brandy could tell her mother was close to tears again. "He left with the soldiers who came here to answer the call for help. They moved a bunch of people from the shelter here, and I guess those... things got in somehow."

"I told him not to run off playing soldier!" Brandy said defensively, worried that Mom would blame her, she was after all the big sister and responsible. "I told him to stay with us!"

"It's okay... In a way, I am proud of him." Mom answered. "I listened on the radio to everything that went on. Nobody on the team got hurt or infected, and it sounds like they saved a lot of people. He was part of that."

They were interrupted by a soldier who walked up and started asking questions about the medical equipment and what needed to be refrigerated now that they were somewhere that was possible.

Brandy stood quietly, waiting. She knew how important it was, so occupied herself with looking out across the empty fields nearby. She could see dark shapes moving around, dragging what could only be bodies into one big pile. She knew one of them was Derek, but at this distance, she couldn't tell which.

As she watched, one of the piles flashed brightly and black smoke gushed from it. Funeral pyres which would have once horrified people, were now becoming the norm. Normal had become a moving target. That thought made her feel nervous. A few weeks again her biggest worry had been keeping her G.P.A. high enough for college, now it was the gnashing teeth of mindless forms coming out of the blue.

"Brandy." Her mother's voice brought her back to reality. "I have to deal with this. Stay here, they are going to be bringing out the survivors soon and I need to rearrange to make room. They want to take as few trucks as possible. We will be leaving in an hour and pushing on to the next safe spot."

Before she could answer, her mother had walked off with the soldier, giving orders.

Brandy walked back to the van, and found Jack having a conversation with the sailor, Mueller. Jack saw her and spoke up. "Brandy, this guy says he can fill us up and we can take the van when we leave." He said happily. Brandy knew it was not the van, but the supply of nicotine inside that he was happy to keep. Jack added, "all we have to do is haul some of their supplies."

"Sounds good." Brandy said unenthusiastically. "I was thinking of riding with Mom now that I have found her."

Jack's face fell into a sad visage. "What am I going to do without my travel buddy?" He asked, trying to hide his disappointment with the joke.

The man in the camouflage asked, "Who is your Mother?"

"Annie Hobbs." Brandy informed him.

Mueller interjected, “Perhaps your mother could ride in your conveyance, she would probably be more comfortable in there than in the back of a deuce and a half. I am sure something can be arranged. She will need at least one member of the security detail with her.”

“And what about my brother? Can’t he do it?” Brandy asked plaintively, she did not relish the idea of hours stuck in the van with a stranger. “Do you know him?”

“I do. He enlisted in the civilian corp and was placed under Lt. Kelley’ command.” The sailor explained in a matter of fact tone. “He will need to remain with his unit for the foreseeable future, but I can assure you he will be well taken care of.”

Brandy crossed her arms defensively. “well you just have an answer for everything, don’t you?”

“I was assigned to logistics for this operation, it’s my job to anticipate the needs and wants of the gathered persons and do my best to fulfill them.” He explained flatly.

She wondered if he was being sarcastic, but decided he was just a very serious person. She considered arguing the point, but he didn’t strike her as someone who could be swayed by emotional appeals.

“I am going to find some grass for the dog.” She added as she grabbed two bottles of water and a bowl.

“Come on Bruiser.” She called and walked away.

“Stay inside the fence for your safety!” called the Petty Officer.

Brandy waved back over her shoulder to show she had heard, but didn’t turn around. She needs some time to decompress. She was mentally exhausted.

She stopped at the edge of the parking lot. It was bordered by a grassy strip of ten-foot-wide and dotted with trees. The sat down beneath an elm in the shade and poured one of the bottles of water into the dog's bowl and sipped from the other as it drank. Eventually, the canine wandered off exploring and claiming the fence as its own property, the way male dogs always do.

Brandy watched the green-clad shapes in the field still about their work of burning the bodies. She picked out one that she was almost sure was Derek and watched him. She had always thought of him as a little kid, but watching him work, she realized he was as big as all the others out there working, and taller than some of them.

"Too many changes..." she said to herself.

"Yeah, it's a lot to get used to." A voice said behind her.

Brandy turned to see Chad standing there, looking down at her.

"I see nothing ate you yet." Brandy said coldly and immediately regretted it. She resolved to not take her anger out people who didn't deserve it. "I am sorry, just been a long day."

Chad smiled weakly at her. "It's perfectly okay, I get to that kind of greeting a lot."

"I said I was sorry!" she said defensively. "what are you up to?"

Chad struggled out of his pack and plopped onto the ground beside her. "Well, since Derek ran off to play army man, nothing. It's boring!"

"Didn't you sign up at the same time?" brandy asked, indicating the rifle he had laid across his legs when he had sat down.

Chad dipped his head as he answered. "Yeah, but they assigned me to sit on my butt not doing anything, so I snuck into a truck going to the hospital." He complained. "It was stupid, I know. But now they won't give me anything to do. I am just supposed to sit in the back of the truck and guard boxes as we drive."

"Well, guarding is important." She said, trying to make him feel better. "You wouldn't want anyone to steal our stuff."

Chad chuckled. "No, I guard the stuff while we are driving. As soon as we stop somewhere, they relieve me."

Brandy thought for a moment, better a slightly obnoxious friend of her brother than a stranger. "I have an idea; how would you like to sit in the comfort of air conditioning and guard something more than boxes."

Chad looked over at her, confused.

Brandy smiled at him, "Come on, let's go find Mom. I think she has the clout to arrange something!"

**Immanuel**

He had ordered everyone down when the shooting had begun. And kept them that way as it faded and was replaced by the engines. The sickening "thwock" sound the things outside made as the vehicles struck them turned even his stomach. It wasn't until he heard the voices of a lady calling from the other side of the door that he had told them to stand up and remove the obstructions.

As the doors had swung open, its hinge had finally failed, and it fell with a clatter to the ground. The brilliant sun streamed into the gloomy room to reveal a group of haggard looking figures holding an assortment of rifles and pistols. The weapons, all of them, were pointed right at him he noticed. Probably because he was the closest to the door.

Immanuel raised his hands in a placating gesture. "Don't shoot! We come in peace." He called and put on his best smile. He heard nothing from behind him, so he knew the others in the room had done the right thing and frozen.

One of the soldiers yelled. "Is anyone here infected or injured?" Her tone let it be known that she was not in a joking mood.

"No, "Immanuel said calmly, "we are all fine."

The soldiers lowered their weapons slightly, and the woman turned to the biggest man Immanuel had ever seen and said a few words he couldn't hear. The man began to bark orders and the soldiers spread out, checking every corner of the building and checking the survivors.

As her troop scurried off, she stepped over to Immanuel and holstered her pistol. "Are you in charge here?" She asked.

"I guess so, no one else wanted the job," Immanuel replied.

Looking around, she added. "You did a good job here. Yours is the only building that didn't fall. I need you to get your people together and get their things ready to go. We are rolling out as soon as we are ready. Keep everyone inside, there are things out there that kids shouldn't see." As she spoke, she took off the helmet and ran her finger through her hair.

Immanuel nodded his understanding but didn't speak. He had employed his sight and was taken aback by the surprise of her red hair and emerald eyes. He found himself reacting to her in a way a man of God should not, and quickly tamped it down.

"I have some of my people out there cleaning up." She continued, unaware of the thoughts he was having. "But it will take a few minutes. When they are done, some trucks will come in, load your people up, and we hit the road, understood?"

Immanuel again could only nod. He became aware that she would soon realize he was no longer speaking and become suspicious, but the large man appeared again, drawing her attention.

"Lieutenant, fifty-three survivors here, Mostly women and children. No untreated injuries or visible bites or scratches" He said in a voice that reminded Immanuel of an actor he had once seen, deep and full of gravel. "There are three armies, two navy, and one airman billeted here, but all were asleep when whatever happened went down."

"Very well." She answered. "Assign them to clean up with the others outside. The rest of you help in here. We want to roll as soon as we can."

The redhead turned her attention back to Immanuel. "What's your name?"

He remembered to lie. "Immanuel."

"Okay, Immanuel. Get your people moving and keep them busy," she advised, "it will help them and us. Let Shrek here know if you need anything."

With that final pronouncement, she turned to leave. She hadn't taken three steps when a yell sounded from outside somewhere. It was followed immediately by a gunshot and scream of pain. Her brisk walk became a run.

The black Sargent was hot on her heels, yelling for the rest of his men to guard the survivors. Immanuel jogged after them despite the soldiers calling for him to remain inside. He had to see what had brought that delicious song of pain.

Outside he saw others running towards the sound and he followed. They lead him to the squat structure at the end of the line of buildings.  He recognized it as the fairgrounds line of bathrooms. At the doors to the women's side, he saw a crumpled form laying on its back, its camo outfit now barely visible in the blood that saturated the cloth. Kneeling over the form was a naked figure of a young lady. Her skin was turning a pale peach in death and was splatter with the blood of an unknown number. He recognized her immediately. His angel.

She looked up at the approaching people with a ruined face, the skin sliced back and hanging like a curtain. Her mouth opened in a wheezing growl. To the right, the men's room door was hurled open and a man appeared, leveled a pistol and fired. Her head jerked violently, and she collapsed onto her meal.

The man took aim and fired another round into the brain of the soldier.  He scanned the area, noticing the approaching military and held his hands up to show he was not a threat.

Immanuel took in the gruesome scene. They had been some of the first to arrive after the scream. He had recognized the man that had stepped out of the bathroom and shot the nude woman. Despite the things he had seen since this started, it distressed him.

. The Lieutenant drew up short of the bodies, with Sarge and a man Derek didn't know right behind them. "What happened here?" She demanded.

"I heard a scream and came running." Derek answered, then added belatedly, "Ma'am."

The man who had exited the bathroom spoke up. "Lieutenant, I was sheltering with several survivors after our building was breached. We heard the shots and vehicles but were waiting for the all clear. I figured it was better to wait to be found than wander out before we knew." He explained. I heard the attack and came out to neutralize the attacker."

She holstered her sidearm before putting her hands on her hips and looking the man up and down. "And exactly why hadn't you made yourself known before now?" she demanded angrily.

"Ma'am," He responded defensively, "When everything went to hell this morning, I was escorting the orphans to the bathroom. I was standing out here waiting for them and saw what was going down and got them all together. I have twenty kids in here with no one else to watch them and no windows to see what was happening."

As he spoke, the door behind him cracked open, and a small face peeked out as if to emphasize the man's point. When it noticed all the people standing there, its eyes turned wide, and it slammed the door.

Lt. Kelley took in the red cross on the man's armband and nodded. "Good work soldier. I need a Medic, you are it" She said and turned abruptly and walked away.

The medic gave a crisp “Yes Ma’am.” And walked over to the only civilian standing there.

“Hey, Immanuel.” He said warmly. “I am glad to see you made it!”

“Same to you,” Immanuel answered, taking the man’s hand and shaking it firmly, “My friend. Let us get those kids out of there.”

**Derek**

Derek watched the scene unfold. The medic and his friend stepped into the bathroom after the children.  Slinging his rifle, he stepped forward to the two corpses laying on the ground. The man now dead had been the next man in the firing line. They had exchanged greetings and once traded M.R.E. pieces, but Derek couldn't remember his name.

"Help me out here." He called to some of the others gathered nearby. "let's move these bodies before the kids come out."

Several came over to help. The dragged the pair around to the back of the bathrooms just as the procession of children began to emerge. Derek noticed a few of them looking down at the blood that remained on the ground, but they kept moving.

As soon as the children had disappeared inside the long building, the soldiers lifted the bodies and started the long walk to the raging pyres already consuming the dead they had put down. Soon one of their own would feed the flames.

Derek watched the others carry off the bodies. He couldn't help the morbid wonderings that ran through his head as they moved away: Would that be his future? To be carried namelessly to a bonfire, or even worse left to wander as one of those... things? The idea troubled him, but he went back to work, trying to drown the musings in toil. It didn't work.

The work was completed by the time the assorted vehicles had formed their line stretching across the open grounds and what remained of refugees were loading in. Derek checked his watch and saw that more than half of the day had passed.

He had overheard the runner who had appeared and given the days plans to the Lieutenant. They were still intended to make the almost two-hundred-mile leg of their trip today, despite the late start. The reasoning being that it would get them out of the "Hot Zone" as it was being called and into a quieter area of the country.

Derek turned to Sarge, who was standing with the others at the rear of the personnel carrier, waiting for the others for the order to load up. "Sarge, why are we still going all the way to Tennessee? Isn't there another place we can go that's closer?"

The big man turned and gave Derek a hostile look that quickly softened. "Cadet, I will give you some leeway because you are C.A.P," he explained, "but I would remind you that ours is to do, not to wonder. Same thing in the Army as in the Air Force, because the lieutenant told us that's where we are going, and because that's where some captain told her to go, and that's because some colonel told him that's where we are going." He placed his hand on Derek's shoulder. "Have faith."

Before Derek could answer, the Lieutenant gave the order to Load up. As one, the mixed group of soldiers, dressed in different camouflage and from many different backgrounds, filed into the back of the heavy steel machine.

Derek made his way and sat down. From outside, he heard a horn begin to sound. He looked outside a noticed a van pulling up, lights flashing. He had just enough time to recognize Brandy behind the wheel and give a quick wave as the ramp sealed them inside. He smiled to himself, he hadn't seen her among the survivors or the dead and had feared the worst.

As the carrier lurched into motion, Derek turned to the man to his left and held out his hand. "Hey, my name is Derek." He said, resolved to learn the names of his comrades. None of them would die unknown like the man at the bathrooms, and he hoped he wouldn't either. He had a family to look after.

**Immanuel**

Immanuel was yanked from his sleep by a lurch of the truck bumping over something and cursed himself for falling asleep. He glanced at the others gathered on the hard wooden benches, but spotted nothing amiss. He couldn't help but notice that several of them showed the inky blackness that ringed their bodies, the mark of evil was on them. He should not have allowed himself to doze off, if even one of them had realized who he was, what he was, they could have ended him.

He could see through the gaps in the canvas cover that the sky was turning a darker blue. It must be getting close to sundown. John the medic had told him the hoped to be at the factory no later than dark, so he had to assume they were almost there.

"Would you like something to eat?" Inquired a voice across from him.

Immanuel looked up to find Claire holding out a flat brown plastic package. He took it from her and studied the printing. It was one of those military meals he had seen around. It proclaimed itself "spaghetti with meatballs".

"Is it any good." He asked, skeptically.

"Well," she answered with a shrug, "its food." She smiled to punctuate the humor and passed him a bottle of water. "they said we are running behind schedule, something about having to move around obstructions. We have about an hour before we get where we are going."

He did his best to stretch in the crowded seat, but the number of people that had been crammed in made it difficult. His back ached and his thighs burned from staying seated on such a hard surface for so long.

"At least there is food and water." He answered, more to have something to say than out of politeness. Immanuel turned his attention to the packet, tearing it open, he was amazed by how many bits and pieces it contained. He marveled at the little plastic bag that claimed it could make the foot warm but decided in the back of a jostling truck was not the time to try it. He said a blessing over the food and began to eat it cold.

Shortly thereafter, he was contemplating the level of research it takes to make everything in the package taste stale when the truck made a turn and came to a stop. He heard a sudden rise of voices outside. He started to stand, but the soldier seated at the back stood suddenly and yelled for everyone to remain seated until the all-clear was given.

Immanuel strained to listen to the sounds outside. He could still hear voices calling instructions and the slap of boots rushing to follow the same. In the distance he could just make out the clatter of chain link being moved, he guessed a gate was getting closed. In the distance, he heard a few scattered gunshots, but nothing like the one would expect if they were being overrun.

The crowded truck was as quiet as a grave as everyone seemed to be holding their breath, waiting to know if they were safe. The guard they had with them held his rifle tightly and stared intently out of the gap between the walls and the flap.

Observing the posture of the man, Immanuel was worried that he was so tense that any sound would startle him. He resolved to be very still and quiet until the man relaxed, lest an accidental discharge of the rifle end him.  The minutes seemed to stretch into an eternity as they waited.

Outside the yelling receded into the distance. The pops of gunfire followed with them. Immanuel counted seventeen bursts before they finally fell silent. On the other side of the canvas, footsteps approached, stopping at the rear of the vehicle. Immanuel tensed for an attack by whomever, or whatever it was. The flap was slung aside, and the passengers gave a collected sigh of relief. A young man dressed in camouflage stood in the opening.

"All Clear." He said. "You guys can come out now." As he spoke, he dropped the tailgate and let it crash down on its hinges with a loud bang. He held out his hand to start helping people make the jump to the ground.

Immanuel stood and waited his turn to exit, happy for the chance to let the blood work its way back into his legs. The ached and the muscles resisted his orders to move. He wouldn't be looking forward to the rest of his trip in this manner. They would all be sore and grumpy tomorrow. He reminded himself to be especially careful in his dealings with them tomorrow.

As he made his way to the end of the truck feeling returned to his leg with the unfortunate side effect of shooting pain returning to his damaged feet. Immanuel found himself wishing for the numbness to return as the pain grew. He had to be lifted to the ground by two of those who were already out and standing on the ground.

They were standing in a large parking lot next to a huge facility. To Immanuel, it looked like a factory, standing about forty feet tall. Its windowless metal construction gave it a purely industrial vibe. At ground level, less than a dozen yards away, large double doors stood open with soldiers standing to each side. The people were being herded through those open doors.

Around them, in every direction he could see from where he stood, was a forest. This location had obviously been picked because of its remoteness. Not even lights could be seen outside of that flowing through the door.

Immanuel reached up into the truck and gather the small bag of belongings he had left, and began to limp his way to the door. The brightness of that portal reminded him of his coming reward, He went to it gratefully

**Derek**

The ramp dropped quickly, and they rushed out into the dark. The last part of the ride had been the normal briefing and distribution of orders, they all knew what to do. Derek followed the others as they scanned the parking lot. They saw no movements, no threats, so they proceeded on to the next item of their list. The approached the doors, and Sarge produced a large prying tool and quickly popped them open.

As soon as the doors were sprung, the men ahead of him rushed inside. Despite his growing fear, Derek rushed in with them, pausing only to flip on the flashlight attached to the bottom of his rifle. He found himself inside a cavernous roof, filled with tall racks containing pallets of boxes.

They moved purposefully across the space, scanning in all direction, looking for threats. On the third aisle, they found them. Several of the creatures were stumbling towards them, arms outstretched. They were quickly put down by a short barrage.

Derek heard several similar volleys in other locations, all ending just as suddenly as they began. The other teams were doing the same thing on the factory side of the building.  They found two other infected as they finalized their sweep, both on a separate aisle, both were immediately put down.

They arrived at the other end of the room and spied an opening in the wall covered by thick hanging strips of black plastic. Sarge stepped forward and extended his rifle. Using the barrel, he slid one of the strips aside and peered thru. Derek peeked under the bigger man's arm into the room beyond. The flashlight revealed a carpeted hallway with several doors off to each side.

Without speaking, they moved forward as one, pushing through the barrier. Together they stalked down the hallway, checking each room as they passed it. The last door was open, and from the smell emanating from it, they could tell that was occupied.

Derek stepped forward and peered into the room. One of the things stood on the other side of the desk that occupied the center of the room, its back to them. It was looking out the window, the only one Derek had seen in the whole building so far as if surveying the trees beyond. He aimed his rifle and fired. The thing collapsed to the ground, dead again. Only then did he wonder why it had not reacted to them.

"Clear" he called, remembering the procedure. Behind him, he heard Sarge rasp the same word into the radio.

"All teams report secure," came the lieutenant's reply over the speaker. "Police the bodies and let's get these people inside."

As if on cue, the lights flared to life overhead, one of the teams had found the generator. Derek was pleased to hear the familiar hum of an air conditioner kicking on. 'This place has potential' he thought to himself.

"Hobbs" Sarge snapped, "get your head out of the clouds and go start getting people inside, Tell them it's all clear."

"On it!" Derek answered and headed out the door at a fast trot.

"Slow down! We have to clean all this up first." Sarge called after him.

***

*Dave Samson stared out the window at the trees beyond and thought about the past. The land he was staring out upon had once been the land of his grandparents. They had moved here from the old country and built their farm here.*

*He could easily remember the hot summer days he had spent there, sitting at their kitchen table. Even though the farm had always struggled, there had always been food on the table and the house was always filled with love and kindness. It had also been filled with the smell of Grandma Carrie's baking.*

*When Dave had inherited the land, he had considered selling it, but had decided instead to use the land in a way that would honor that memory. He had founded the bakery as a small cinder block building in what was now the parking lot and it had taken off from there. They were now the largest distributor of prepackaged snacks in the Midwest.*

*He reminisced as he pressed the necktie against the bite on his hand. He had gotten it from the worker, a guy named Rick, who had walked into the office a few hours ago. Dave's smile of recognition had faded to horror when he saw the blood.*

*Rick had been with them a long time, almost from the beginning and was now more family that worker. The sight of the man staggering into the room drenched in red had caused gasps from those in the meeting, gasps that had been turned into screams.*

*The thing Rick had become had lunged gad Ruby, its teeth on her neck casting a spray of blood across the wall. Dave had rushed to his secretary's aid, but when he had finally dispatched the attacker with the desk chair, she was gone. He had received the bite for his troubles.*

*The cameras connected to his desk computer had shown him what was happening in his building. Dave had watched his adopted family attack and kill each other, helpless to stop it. He felt the change coming on and waited for its relief.*

*Even after his death, his eyes watched what he had built.*

***

**Brandy**

Brandy shifted in her seat, trying to get comfortable. The Cargo vans rear seats did not seem to be made for comfort. She was past beginning to regret agreeing to trade with Chet when the convoy had stopped to refuel. The sun had set already, and the night was descending quickly.

Beside her, her mother snored softly. Chet was doing the same thing in the front seat. Jack was keeping himself busy by continually pushing the next button on the radio, trying to find a broadcast. Other than the occasional pre-recorded message, he hadn't found anything for over an hour.

Right before the sun had settled, he had found music. It had been the song 'it's the end of the world as we know it' by R.E.M., but after it had played five times in a row, they had decided it was somebody's sick idea of a joke and changed the channel. There had been no commercials or deejay, so they had decided someone had turned it on repeat and walked away. Now even that had faded out of range.

Brandy sighed audibly, But Jack didn't seem to notice as he continued hitting buttons. "do you have to keep doing that?" She asked as he hit the button, bringing about another burst of static from the speakers.

Jack glanced back at her. "I am just trying to find something to listen to." He answered defensively. "It's just so damn boring sitting up here listening to everyone sleep."

"Well, I am not sleeping." Brandy responded testily.

Jack glanced back at her over his shoulder and started to snap back, but decided against it. "I am sorry," he said as he switched off the radio, "What's eating you?"

Brandy sighed again, “Nothing. How long until we get wherever we are going?”

“Well, I have no idea,” Jack said simply. “I don’t even know where we are going. I am just following the truck ahead of us and not get run over by the one behind us.”

“Where are we?” Brandy asked, leaning forward to peer out the windshield.

Jack took a drag on his device and exhaled. “Southern Indiana I think. We went through some little towns, but none I had ever heard of. But I haven’t really seen any signs I recognized, just state and county highways.”

“I wonder how much further?” She asked, rhetorically. Beside her, her mother shifted in her seat.

“We are going to some food factory in the middle of nowhere.” The older woman answered. She looked at her watch before continuing. “We should be there any minute.”

“What Kind of food?” asked Chet groggily, waking from his own slumber. “I am starving to death!”

“Snack food,” Annie said distractedly as she looked down at the maps she had shoved into her pocket as they left. Snack cakes, candy bars, pudding pops. That kind of thing. Jack, what was the last road you saw.”

Jack leaned forward, searching for a road sign. “Coming up on highway 421 In five miles.”

“The convoy will turn left there, and then it’s just a couple of miles. We are meeting another group of soldiers and refuges there and moving out in the morning.” She explained. “The colonel wants to get an early start, He thinks if we push we can be at the cove by tomorrow night.”

“The Cove?” Brandy asked her mother.

“Yes, that’s where we are supposed to end up, it’s called Katie’s Cove.” She answered. “It’s in the mountains and supposed to be the safest place they could find.”

It was Chet’s turn to ask a question. “Cove? As in on the shore?”

“No Different type of cove, this is kind of a … sheltered place in the mountain, kind of like a holler, or plateau.” She said hesitantly. Brandy could tell she was trying to figure out how to explain it. “This one is basically a Big flat space way up in the mountains with only one road in. Its surrounded by steep cliffs.”

“Hmmm,” Chet said thoughtfully, “I can see where that is an advantage, no one… or no thing… can walk in easily. Only one road in means it’s easy to watch.”

“I get that part,” Jack added, “But why so far away? If this thing is only out of control in the Midwest, why do we have to go so damn far?”

Instead of answering, she changed the subject. “This place we are going looks nice, they are the ones that make those little cups banana pudding you like so much.”

“MOM.” Brandy said forcefully. “What aren’t you telling us?’

Her mother’s shoulder slumped, and she said nothing for almost a minute, before looking up at the others in the car. Her voice was quiet when she finally spoke. “What I am about to tell you doesn’t leave this vehicle, Understood?”

Everyone agreed quickly, so she continued. “What they have been telling everyone about the situation isn’t exactly accurate.” She paused again, trying to decide what to say. “The truth is that the problem is wider spread than they have been letting on.”

They sat in silence, only the sound of the road beneath the wheels could be heard as they waited for her to continue. Finally, Jack asked, "What IS the truth?"

"There are no safe zones!" she blurted at the question. She buried her face in her hands and her voice turned nasal. Everyone in the car could tell that she was crying. "We haven't heard from anyone from the government or military command for a week. We made all of that up, the evacuation plans, the other units, they were all just random units we found on the radio. None of them have heard from anyone else either."

Brandy, Chet, and Jack listened in shock as the revelation unfolded. They had thought that they were headed to safety, but the truth was that no one had any idea if anywhere was safe. The last three minutes had turned their hope into an uncertain feeling of dread.

Brandy unfastened her seatbelt and scooted closer to her mother, putting her arm around her to give comfort. "And you didn't tell us because you didn't want us to worry." She said as much as to herself as to the woman she held.

The brake lights ahead of them flashed to life and the column of vehicles made the turn towards their destination. Finally, Chet spoke up. "How did they pick where we were going, they had a plan and everything?"

"They were the last three places we knew about. After the Great Lakes Naval Station fell, we knew we had to get out of there." Annie said, trying to calm herself. "We did what we had to do."

"What is where we are going?" Brandy asked.

"A Tennessee National Guard Unit." Was the answer. "We talked to them about a week ago and they told us about the spot. They prepositioned some supplies there, but then most of the members deserted, went looking for family members or something. That's been a big problem everywhere."

Ahead of them, the vehicles were slowing and in the distance, they saw the first one turn into a fenced lot. A large tan building sat in the middle of a large area, its tan metal sides reaching into the darkened sky like a massive mausoleum. As their turn to pull in came, the headlights illuminated a plastic sign built into a brick frame by the road: 'Grandma Carries Cakes and Desserts'.

The van followed the truck ahead of it into the gates and pulled to a stop in its place. Before Jack could even turn off the engine, they heard the first gunshot. Men and women in camouflage were running in every direction. The doors at the side of the building had a clump of fighters standing beside it.

Brandy recognized the large form Of Sgt. Shrek prying at the doors. Beside him stood a tall scrawny figure, Brandy and her Mother recognized him at once, and the blue flash of his name tape on his uniform. They had seen it many times. Their mother audible gasped as Derek shouldered his rifle and rushed inside. It was less than a minute before they heard the gunshots echoing from the door he had just entered.

"Was that Derek?" Chad said in awe. "Bad ass! You guys stay here." He quickly unhooked his seatbelt and stepped from the van. He took a position by the front bumper.

"Should we … do something?" Jack asked.

"We just stay here, for now, someone will let us know when it's clear," Annie said firmly. "I don't see the other vehicles; the other group isn't here yet…"

"Maybe they got held up," Jack suggested. He was staring out the and it was obvious that he was nervous about the activities outside. He was continually running his fingers through his hair and puffing on the vape. Brandy knew him well enough to know both tells.

The action outside was tapering off. Not as many people were running, most now walked briskly. It had been almost a minute since the last gunshot had sounded. From the open doorway, lights suddenly leaped forth brightly. It was much stronger than flashlights, so the power must have come on.

As they watched, a figure exited the doors and made its way to the line of trucks. Seconds later a stream of civilians appeared, walking towards the open doors. Jack opened his door and stepped out. The others in the van did as well. Bruiser jumped to the ground and bolted off into the dark, obviously desperate to take care of his own business.

"Should we call him back?" Brady was asked by her mother.

"He will be fine, it's gated and he will do what he needs to do and then come back." Brandy answered, hoping it was as certain as she made it seem.

They took their time gathering the things they would need for the night. She noticed Jack filling his pockets with a collection of electronic cigarettes and charging cords. She guessed he was going to take advantage of the power inside. She made sure to take the time together with food, the water bowl, and a blanket for the dog.

As they finished gathering the items, Derek appeared. "Hey, Mom." He said, trying to act nonchalant. "Need any help carrying this stuff?"

Brandy reached out and hugged him around the bundle she carried. “Glad to see you survived.”

“Of course, I did!” he said in his best macho voice as he hugged his mother and then lifted the pack she carried out of her arms. He exchanged nods with Jack and Chad as they all started towards the doors.

“They colonel is waiting for you inside Mom,” Derek said as they walked, “He said he wanted to talk to you about plans for tomorrow. When did you become a big cheese around here?”

“I have no idea.” She said, “I didn’t ask for it. I guess since I helped with the organization of the move.”

The first thing Brandy noticed when the entered was the sweet smell that permeated the air. Metal racks formed aisles across the vast space, each seemed thirty feet tall. Each shelf contained thousands of boxes, all bore the logo of ‘Grandma Carrie’s Logo”. Brandy couldn’t hold back a smile when she saw that one whole rack had the words “Carries famous Nanner Puddin’” in bold yellow letters on the boxes.

“I know what I am having for dinner!” brandy said excitedly. She had loved the treats as long as she could remember. She looked over at her mother, who was walking beside her. “Can I?”

“Knock yourself out!” Came her mother permission. “I am going to go see what the boss wants, find us a spot to sleep and save me some pudding.” She said and walked away.

“Derek,” Brandy asked, “What are the sleeping plans?”

“We salvaged some of the cots from the fairgrounds, they are being brought in now. Where do we want to set up, so I can make sure I get some cots there?”

“Somewhere quiet.” Brandy said forcefully. “We all need to have a long conversation.”

“Let’s go claim a space in one of the offices,” He suggested, “Just not the one at the end of the corridor. I can sit with you guys for a while before I have to get back”

Jack, Brandy, Chad, and Derek made their way through the crowd, retracing the course he had taken when he had first entered the building. To their surprise, they found one of the rooms not yet in use. It was a smaller room, occupied only by a copying machine and a shelf of paper, but there would be enough room for all of them.

They all dropped the packs they carried, and the males excused themselves to bring in the cots. Brandy laid out the dog’s food and water and folded the blanket into a pad for him to sleep on. The rest returned as she was finished, each carrying a folded cot.

Brandy closed the door behind them. “Derek, what do you know about everything that’s been going on?”

Her brother looked up at her over the bed he was unfolding. “I guess as much as you do, we are supposed to be meeting a group of people here. I know LT was pretty perturbed that they weren’t here already.” He finished locking the bed in place and then stepped over to help Chad with the one he was struggling with.

“Have you heard why they aren’t here?” Brandy pressed, trying to determine if he knew as much as she did without giving it away. She was engaged in an internal struggle: she had agreed not to tell anyone what her mother had confided, but this was Derek.

“No,” he answered as he struggled to get the cots legs to extend correctly, “The lieutenant and Sarge went to see what they could find out. I guess they will tell us when they find out.”

Brandy Pursed her lips, then asked: “Do you know who we are meeting?”

Derek looked up at her as he finished his project. “Some armored unit out of Kentucky. Why?”

“I am just trying to figure out what’s going on.” She replied.

Chad let out an exasperated sigh, and then just said it. “We know things are a lot worse than they have been telling us. It’s not just here, it sounds like the whole damn country has gone down.”

Everyone in the room turned to stare at chad, Derek’s stare was one of shock, the rest of anger. Jack snapped, “You were not supposed to say anything about that.”

“Geez,” Chad snapped back, “Derek is one of us!”

“Still though,” Brandy said, “There are better ways to say it.”

Derek interrupted, “What is he talking about Brandy?”

She sat heavily on the cot, momentarily alarmed at the squeaks it made, but then panted the space beside her. “Derek, Have a seat. We all need to have a talk.”

**Immanuel**

He was getting his sleeping area set up when he saw the group with the dog enter. They were unremarkable in appearance from all the other groups, except for her. The young woman who walked with them was surrounded by the darkest aura he had ever seen. The blackness that enveloped her seemed to pull the light from the room around her like a black hole. The sight of her caused both a thrill of excitement and a pang of terror.

Her chestnut hair hung in loose curls, and her sapphire eyes stood out against her tan skin and the inky emanation that hung supernaturally around her made them appear to glow with a cold and frozen demonic energy. He felt his skin begin to goosebump as the power hiding within her radiated out.

He stood tensely as her group passed by, unsure if he should strike out at her. "Patience. She will be yours to cleanse.' The voice said in his ear. He relaxed in knowing that the voice was still with him and that it had promised her to him.

He stepped out of the aisle his group had claimed so that he could watch her. They paused and then the older women in the group separated off towards the foreman's office, where the officers and leaders of this group were calling the 'command center'. Afterward, they went thru the doorway to the offices.

Immanuel moved forward purposefully, staying a dozen feet behind them, pausing only at the swinging strips to watch where they went. He saw them disappear into one of the doors inside, so he stepped through.

He had stalked people before and was exalted at the old familiar feeling. The thrill of it had been his greatest reward in the Lord's work, and he felt no sin at the pride he took in it. He knew the Lord would protect him from notice only if he did everything right.

He walked quickly down the hallway, knowing that the best way to avoid notice was to look like you knew what you were doing. He set his eyes on the doorway at the end of the hall and strode towards it. As he passed her door, he glanced inside as the members of her party stepped back out. He nodded to them and kept going. They seemed to pay him no attention.

He reached the door he had picked, and without pausing, stepped inside. He knew if the room was in use, he would have to come up with an excuse, but that was a small matter. Luckily, no living thing was using the room. He swung the door almost closed behind him, leaving a crack no bigger than a quarter inch.

The smell, however, was overpowering. The reek of decay assaulted his senses and he looked around. On one side of the office, a stack of bodies had been hastily built. He noted that the bodies seemed to have been put there quite recently. This must have been where they brought the ones they had found in the building.

Immanuel quickly pulled his sweater up to cover his mouth and nose. It cut the smell considerably, but it was still there. He turned back to the door and peeked out. As he had hoped, he could see into the room where the girl was. Her back was to him as she kneeled to spread out a blanket for the dog.

He considered using this opportunity, rush out and drags her back here. He knew he could do it, one hand over her mouth, one about her waist. It was all about surprise and quickness. And he doubted he would have to worry about being disturbed in the crypt that had once been an office. The desk was even big enough for his needs. He decided, now was his time.

He reached down for the doorknob, but as his fingers closed around it, the door at the other end erupted into the others carrying beds. The came through the hanging strips like figures emerging from the fog. He thanked the powers above for delaying him with indecision.

Immanuel watched as they filed into their room, and as she closed the door behind them. He had no illusions that he could overpower all of them without an alarm being sounded. He had noticed at least three of them were armed.

"Patience" the voice had said, Immanuel reminded himself. Their time would come. He stepped out of the office and walked back down the hall. As he passed their room, he could hear their voices, so he stopped to listen.

He listened for several minutes before he heard one of the boys say something about having to go. Immanuel managed to get out of the curtain door before the boy was even out of the room. He found his way back to the cot he had sat up and laid down.

His mind was spinning with what he had heard. It appeared that the end times were certainly upon them. He had suspected as much, but those people in power had been telling them there was hope. Immanuel knew that the evils of man could create surprising things, and that was what he had decided this was, but now, based on the scale, he knew this was divine punishments for the evils of men.

The young man from her party, the one dressed in the camouflage with the bright blue name tag, walked passed. His face showed a grimace of anger, and he walked quickly to the exit doors leading to the yard, where the soldiers were all setting up their camp. Immanuel wondered if this was the one named Derek or the one named Chad.

He briefly considered following him but thought better of it. Out there was a group of heavily armed people on guard. He thought about going back to the copy room but decided against that. There were still at least four in there. He would have to wait until she was alone.

A voice pulled him from his musings, “Excuse me, sir.” It said shyly, “I noticed you pray a lot, are you a priest?”

Immanuel turned to the voice and noticed it was the woman, Claire. He considered the question, and saw the opportunity. “Yes, my child,” He answered, “Call me Reverend Immanuel. What can I help you with?”

“Well, Father Gene,” she said sadly, “Doesn’t seem to have made it out of the fairgrounds. He led the services at the shelter. Can you… Can you take over for us?”

Immanuel noticed that she was part of a group of people standing expectantly, he counted twelve. He took that as a sign and stood. “It would be my honor. Shall we pray?”

**Derek**

Derek stormed out of the exit doors and into the night. Ahead of him, he saw an open-sided tent had been set up, and his group was gathered under it, eating. The table was littered with plastic wrappers and empty pudding cups. The air was full of laughs.

He stopped in his tracks. He had intended to storm up to the table and confront the red-headed officer and mammoth Sargent, but now he reconsidered. The anger of being lied to burned in his brain, but the realization that telling the others would not change anything. Not to mention that they would wonder how he knew, and that could affect his mother's standing in the group.

Taking a deep breath, he started forward again. He claimed a box of snacks labeled "Nana's Cinnamon Cakes" and sat down on it. It gave a little under him but held up. Only one person in the group had a real chair, the sergeants muscled frame was much too large to be held by a cardboard box of baked goods, the rest either stood or sat on boxes like his. He grabbed a pack marked "Grandpas honey cake" and started eating quietly. The others acknowledged his arrival but continued their conversation.

"So how long are we stuck here?" One of them asked. Derek noted it was one of the professionals.

Of the fourteen people in their unit, about half were soldiers when this all started. Five others were prior military, only Derek and one other were truly civilians. Derek had started out as the Radio Operator, but that had quickly been taken away, he now knew why. The other civilian was named Roger, He had been in some kind of a militia before all this in Illinois.

“One day.” The sergeants answered around a mouthful of something chocolate. “The colonel is trying to get ahold of them right now, if we don’t hear from them by nightfall tomorrow, we move out.”

Another, whom Derek only knew as Chapelle, spoke up. “How many was it coming? What did they have for equipment?”

The lieutenant, who was leaned back on against the wheel of the nearby truck answered as she loaded rounds into magazines. “Three Abrams tanks, four Bradley’s, crews for each vehicle and a maintenance crew with two semis of parts, ammo, and supplies.”

Several low whistles illustrated how impressed the assembled people were. Even a novice like Derek understood what any one of those could do for their survival, much less all of it. A semi full of supplies would take a large burden off all of them. Even as the spoke, one of the crews was trying to hotwire two of the tractor-trailers they had found on the lot. A fifty-three-foot trailer held a lot of food, even if it was just snack cakes and pudding cups.

Derek finished his meal and went to stand beside the woman and started helping refill magazines. He Didn’t feel the need to point out that he had not refilled his own yet from this morning, but he pulled his empties from the pouch that hung at his waist and added them to the pile.

He found the repetitive nature of the task soothing as he listened to the group gossip, tell tales and trade good-natured insults. He listened along, learning what he could. He was just setting down his third full thirty round magazines when the lieutenant spoke to him.

“Hobbs, what’s eating at you tonight?” She asked in a soft voice.

Derek sighed and picked up another aluminum magazine and a hand full of rounds. “I have a lot to take in.” Was all he said.

“It’s kind of a bitch.” She said seriously. “This whole fucked up situation.”

“Yeah,” Derek answered with the only thing he could think to say.

“Look, I know you are getting a raw deal here. Not even old enough to enlist, but put here on the front lines.” She announced. “But you are damn good at it. But I understand if it’s too much for you. What are you, fifteen?”

“Almost seventeen,” Derek said defensively as he added another full mag to the pile.

“That’s young for the kind of shit we have been doing.” She stated in a matter of fact tone. “If you want out, I understand. I know you volunteered, but that was before you knew what you know now.”

Derek started to protest, but she cut him off. “I am not kicking you out, just letting you know I won’t hold you.”

“I Understand.” He answered sincerely. “But I don’t want out. I know what’s going on, and what’s at stake. I want to help. I need to help.”

“Just take care.” She cautioned. “It’s pretty rough, the kind of work we are doing, and not just on the body. We may be at this for a while...”

Derek took in her words and caught what she was trying to tell him, so decided to take a chance. “Lieutenant, when we get where we are going, what are we going to do with no help coming?”

“Survive.” She answered simply. “Make sure you grab some of these for yourself, ten is the minimum.” She commanded, changing the subject. She stood up and stretched before addressing her charges still sitting around the makeshift table, “Get some sleep, we have the night off, but six A.M. gets here awful early.”

“Do we need to post a watch?” one of them asked.

The sergeant answered for her. “Another Platoon has the camp watch honor, they are stationed on the roof with night vision. For us, one person at a time, set up here, two-hour shifts. Decker, Thomas, Porter, Michaels in that order.” He commanded, the added, “Michaels, wake me at 0545 sharp.”

Derek noticed the rest of them making their way towards the closest vehicles. To His amazement, he noted that they were crawling under them. As he watched men crawled into bags placed under the trucks and settling in. Derek shrugged and pulled his bag from his pack and joined them. He understood why when the rain started an hour later. He thought about how lucky he was that he wasn’t on the roof as it poured down.

At some pointed in the night, he woke up to the sound of helicopters. They were incredibly loud, and he knew that meant they were very close. He started to unzip his bag when the man next to him stopped him. It was the soldier named Chapelle.

“Go Back to sleep kid,” He said sleepily, “Those things can’t fly. They are ours.”

Derek listened to the aircraft approaching, knowing that there was no way he could sleep with that noise, but he was quickly falling back into sleep.

**Brandy**

Brandy woke up, not sure where she was, or what time it was. The others around her were still sleeping, so she knew it couldn't be too late. She considered going back to sleep, but a whine from the dog told her that wasn't an option. She pulled on her shoes, thankful for deciding to sleep clothed last night and made her way out into the main room.

Here she found a few more people awake, but the majority snored away in their scattered places around the cavernous area. Bruiser walked ahead of her, leading the way to the exit. Brandy followed, pausing only to grab a handful of the pudding cups from an open box on the way. Her stomach growling had been what woke her up. There was a box of plastic spoons and some cases of bottled water on a table by the door and she helped herself.

The door showed dim light filtering around its panels. It was dawn. She swung the doors open and the canine rushed out. She stepped out and wished she had remembered to grab her coat. The air carried a chill, but the sun was just cresting over the treetops, so she decided it would warm up soon.

A few men were already up and moving around. She could tell by their attire that they were all military. One called out to see if she needed help, but she declined, and he went about his business with a warning to stay close to the building.

Further out in the parking lot, she saw three helicopters. They sat motionlessly, and she wondered when they had arrived. She had not seen them last night when they drove in. Could she have slept through that kind of noise? She decided that obviously she could since they must have come in during the night.

As she stood watching the dog sniff around, exploring for the perfect place to take care of what he had to do, she heard someone walk up behind her. She turned and saw Derek standing there, holding two Styrofoam cups.

“Coffee?” he asked her, holding out a cup.

Brandy accepted it gratefully, feeling its warmth seep into her hands. Her first tip showed that he had even scrounged creamer and sugar, to make it just like she liked it. She put her arm around him and hugged him and they stood together watching the dog.

“When did they helicopters get here?” She finally asked.

“Sometime very early this morning.” He said, then added, “They made one hell of a noise.”

“Who are they?” She inquired.

“Just some more random guys they found on the radio last night. I didn’t talk to them, but gossip moves quickly in this group.” He explained. “They are trying to get as many people as they can. Apparently, these guys loaded up all kinds of fuel before they left wherever they were and took off.”

“Do you know when we are leaving?” Brandy asked.

“I heard last night that the colonel is giving that other group until first thing tomorrow,” he responded, “and then we get out of here.”

Brandy offered him a pudding cup, but he declined. “We ate already.”

“How long have you been up?” she asked incredulously. Derek was famous in the family for sleeping late, sometimes until noon.

He looked down at his watch. “About an hour I guess. We woke up, had a meal, and walked the perimeter already.” He explained.

Bruiser wandered back over to them. Brandy asked, “What is the plan for you today?”

“Well, they are giving us first chance at the showers in that locker room before everyone wakes up and I plan to put on my other uniform. This one is getting crunchy.” He said as he picked something that looked suspiciously like dried blood off his sleeve.

“Wow,” she answered wistfully, ignoring the blood. “A shower would be good right now.”

“You better get inside and sign up quick,” he urged, “they are signing people up for five-minute slots. There is still plenty of water running, but this place doesn’t have a very big water heater by my guess. With a hundred people, it will go quickly and never catch up.”

Brandy slapped her thigh to call the dog, and together they started back towards the building.  She Considered asking Derek for his spot in the shower, but the sight of the blood-stained sleeve stuck with her, so she didn’t ask.

At the doors, he stopped her. “You had better finish that coffee before you go inside,” He urged, “it is a very rare commodity right now.”

She took his advice and hugged him before he went off to the shower. She was conscious of the feeling of the rifle he wore pressing into her arm as the hugged. It felt strange, but it was the new normal, she told herself.

He disappeared inside, and she stood there sipping the liquid. She was determined to consume every drop as she wasn’t sure when the next time she would get any. The coolness of the air and uneasy sleep helped her enjoy it even more. When she had drained the cup, she went inside.

She quickly found a person wearing the red smock of the volunteers and signed up for a shower time. The list was already growing, and it would be more than an hour before her time came.  She made her way back to the copy room to gather her stuff and be ready. She had been warned sternly that arriving late would mean forfeiting her time and being put to the back of the list.

In the copy room, she noticed her bed her mother had slept in was already empty. Jack was sitting up in his cot struggling with his shoes, and Chad was still fast asleep, snoring softly.

“Good morning Jack.” She whispered.

“Hey Brandy.” He answered, also in a whisper. “What’s it look like out there? Is anybody cooking or anything?”

“It’s cold outside.” She said, “The breakfast menu is anything you find out there in a box.” To illustrate her point, she held up the pudding she still held.

“Man,” he moaned, “what I wouldn’t do for some bacon and eggs!”

She chuckled softly. “Yeah, me too. But this is a close second.” She quipped as she pulled the lid off one of the packets and began to eat. “Where did Mom go?”

“That guy in the blue camo,” He said, “the one that tried to shoot us, came in and woke her up this morning. He said the colonel needed to talk to her.”

Brandy opened the second pudding and dug her spoon into it. “I guess I should go find her and see what I can do to help.” She declared. “We are going to be here all day, and I definitely don’t want to just sit here all day, it’s better to keep busy.

“I agree,” Jack said earnestly. “I will help wherever I can. Didn’t you work with the kids before, you could do that again.” He suggested.

“Yes, I worked at the daycare.” She explained. “But these kids have been eating nothing but cinnamon cakes and chocolate cookies since we got here, I will do just about anything else today.

Jack laughed, and it woke up Chad, who immediately asked about breakfast. Brandy tossed him the last Pudding cup as she finished hers. She excused herself and set off to find her mother. She heard Chad pull the lid off the cup as she left the room.

Her Mother was in the office built into a corner of the warehouse. When Brandy stepped through the door, the group of people gathered around the table abruptly stopped talking and stared up at her. Brandy could tell she had interrupted something important.

“Sorry,” she said quickly, “I was looking to speak with my mother, I will come back later…”

As she turned to leave, the colonel called out to her. “Just wait outside for a moment, we were wrapping up anyway.”

Brandy stood right outside the open doorway to wait. The meeting broke up in just over a minute, and people started to stream through the door beside her. Her mother was one of the last ones out. Brandy fell into step with her. “Hey Mom, everything okay?”

“Yes dear,” she said. “we were just getting the morning update. All is well better than we thought. They found a couple of helicopters on the radio last night and they came in last night. They even got a message from that other group that was supposed to meet us here, they will be here soon."

"Awesome," Brandy replied. "Where were they?"

"They had some trouble, Annie said simply, "It held them up."

Brandy thought there was probably more to the story, but decided not to ask. "Have you had breakfast yet?" she asked instead.

"Not yet," was the answer, "I am hungry enough to actually enjoy one of those army meals!"

Brandy smiled, and then took her mother's arm and steered her towards the stack of open snack cake boxes. "Let's feed you and then we can find me something to do around here."

**Immanuel**

He sat on his cot, watching the two women out of the corner of his eye. An internal debate had been running laps in his brain about his next step. The voice was a calm island in the storming sea of his mind. Her abyssal veil seemed to burn his eyes and mock his very existence.

He tamped down his building rage and took deep breaths. The voice had been quite clear in its insistence that she be handled properly. The present circumstances would not allow him to spend the time with her that he knew instinctively knew he would need.

The rumbling in his stomach made him realize that he had been too preoccupied with her, He needed to keep his strength up for the work ahead. He knew she would be his greatest challenge and his greatest victory. He rose from the bed and walked over to the open box of food, and selected several items at random. He returned to his cot to resume his vigil.

From here, he could make out enough of their conversation to get the gist of what they were saying. He was learning a lot. The dark one's name was Brandy, and the other was her mother. The girl was asking about obtaining a job within the group, no doubt to her increase her ability to corrupt the innocents better.

Immanuel had seen the older woman with the military officials several times since they had arrived here, so she must have authority here. He decided to take a chance, and turned to Claire. Her cot was next to his and she sat there reading the bible she had brought with her.

"Claire," He asked in a soft voice, "The woman sitting over there, in the blue shirt, who is she?"

She looked up from her reading and followed his gaze. "I think her name is Annie, she is an advisor to the military. Why?"

"I have seen her with the colonel," He explained, "I was just wondering. There isn't much else to think about right now..."

Claire seemed to accept this and went back to reading. Immanuel spared a moment to ponder what it must be like to not have a direct line of communication with God. He pitied those who had to receive the word from books. He had read the bible many times, but the voice had always been there to direct him when he had questions.

He tuned back into the conversation happening fifteen feet away. More people were up now and having their own conversations, so it was getting more and more difficult to hear. The daughter was explaining something about someone named Derek, who was outside working with the soldiers. Immanuel wondered if this was a relative or lover, but couldn't be sure.

He listened without learning much more until a few minutes later when they both stood and walked away. Immanuel waited until they disappeared around the massive shelves and then stood to follow. He strolled casually around the corner and pretended to study the labels on the boxes, keeping the pair in his peripheral vision.

He followed them until the vanished into the offices. He could still see them through the glass window, but could not hear anything being said as they talked to the colonel seated at the desk. When they took a seat, he determined that he should move on so as not to draw attention to himself.

He meandered back to his cot and sat down. His gaze fell on his pack and the special tools he had gathered. Immanuel decided that he had an opportunity that he hadn't realized. The other side of this building was a factory, and factories normally had maintenance rooms. He decided he would find it, and expand his tool collection. He didn't want to attempt to cleanse Brandy without the right equipment.

## Derek

Derek looked up from the trailer of the semi when he heard the engines approaching. The sun was high in the sky now, and it had burned off the morning's haze. He saw the glint of something coming down the road. From the plume of smoke that puffed from above it, he guessed it was big.

"Sarge!" He said across the bag of flour the man had just handed up to him. "We have Incoming."

The sergeant followed his pointing finger with his eyes. "They are expected, those are the ones we are waiting on."

Derek saw the figures stationed at the gate scrambling to remove the heavy chains that sealed them closed. The blips on the road had grown into the shapes of large trucks. As the came into view, he could see another armored vehicle leading the convoy.

They all watched as the vehicles slowed and turned through the now open gates into the yard. Derek saw the tanks situated on special low-slung trailers. It surprised him, as he had expected to see the dangerous machines driving on their own.

"Hey," he asked aloud, "Why are they tanks on trailers?"

"Two miles to the gallon." Explained Chapelle as he took the bag of flour from Derek's hands and set it on the growing stack. "The trucks haul them close, then the tanks crawl off and do the fighting."

Derek replied simply with an "hmm". That made sense to him, so he took the bag of flour being held out to him and passed it off to be stacked.

He had assumed the plan had been to load cases of snack cakes into the trailers, but had soon realized that the load would be much heavier. They had found mountains of flour, cocoa, and other dry ingredients in a room off the factory, and those were now being scavenged.

Despite the cool morning, the temperature had risen steadily, and all of them now worked without shirts as sweat dripped off them. The morning's shower was already negated by the workload, but Derek didn't complain. Even the lieutenant was toiling with them, her tank top soaked.

She had been quite clear in her instructions to keep their current task quiet so as not to worry the civilians sitting safely inside. Derek wondered if any of those working with him had figured out how bad the situation really was, but decided they must since they hadn't questioned the orders to load tons of flour and canned fruit into the trucks for a short-term problem.

As they loaded the last of the storerooms contents into the truck, Captain bridges appeared and pulled the Lieutenant aside. They had a brief conversation, and when the captain walked off, she turned to her team.

"We Have the watch tonight." She informed them. "We take over at 2200."

Several of those gathered around her groaned at the news, but she cut them off. "Well, it's that or we herd the civilians into trucks at 0600, as for me, I would rather watch from the roof! Get cleaned up and grab some sack time, next sleep you get will be in the A.P.C."

With that, she walked off towards the doors to the building. Derek considered the room remaining in the second truck, and asked the sergeant, "Should we fill up the rest of it with food from the warehouse?"

The deep-voiced replied quickly. “One of the other teams will top it off before they pull out. Lt. Rozier’s crew is supposed to sweep the building for anything we may need and lock up the place in case we need it again.”

Derek nodded his acceptance and hopped down from the truck. He had seen a large sink inside the factory and planned to clean up and wash his clothes. If he hung them up soon, they would be dry by the time they started their watch.

**Brandy**

It was well past midnight when she finally was able to go and collapse it her cot. The others were already out, and she moved quietly so as not to wake them. Around her, their sounds of sleeping were oddly comforting as she kicked off her shoes and settled in.

The last twelve hours had been exceptionally busy for her. Her mother had convinced the colonel to assign brandy to his staff as an assistant, and he had immediately made her his favorite gopher. She had marveled at the number of steps needed in the military machine to get anything done. The man had insisted on reports and forms, despite the lack of anyone to file them with.

She laid her head on the pillow and pulled the scratchy wool blanket up to her chin to combat the chill in the air. She wiggled her body to find a comfortable position and closed her eyes. Instantly she felt a hand on her shoulder, gripping her firmly and shaking.

Brandy sat up suddenly, startled. The sailor, Mueller stood beside her bed. “What!?” she asked in an exasperated whisper.

“My apologies Ma’am.” He whispered back. “It’s time to start getting ready to move out.”

“We aren’t supposed to start until four!” she spat back, a little too loudly. Jack rolled over in his cot, disturbed by the outburst.

The navy man held out his watch for her to see: It showed 4:02. “I am sorry again, but we have to get moving. Colonel Murray is quite insistent that we be on the move at first light, and the sun comes up in just a few hours.” With this, he turned and crossed the room to wake her mother.

Brandy swung her feet over onto the cold tile floor and tried to rub the stinging from her eyes. She had slept almost 4 hours, but she didn't feel like she had been down for more than a few seconds. She pulled on her shoes and rose to her feet.

The next two hours crept by in a blur of slowed time. The civilians were awakened shortly after her and urged to pack up. The cots were carried out and loaded onto the trucks. Eventually, the people have ushered out the doors to the waiting transportation, and she was dismissed to find her ride.

She found the others waiting in the van, all of them looking tired and haggard. As the dark blue sky paled into lighter shades, dozens of engines sputtered into life and began to lurch forward. They passed through the gates and back out onto the road.

**Immanuel**

Immanuel was laying on his back, pretending to sleep when he heard the increase in motion and commotion around him. He opened his eyes and looked around. Soldiers and volunteers were moving through the sleeping forms, gently waking people. With each new person brought back to wakefulness, the sound level rose with complaining and grumbling. Somewhere else among the stacked boxes, a child begins to wail in umbrage of being woken up. Its crying made the task of waking the sleepers much easier.

He set to overseeing the packing up of those in his flock. His twelve had almost doubled during the day, as more and more came to pray with him. He felt the twinges of pride in that, he considered them gifts from God to help him in his holy work. It seemed the end of the world was good for business.

His followers were among the first to be ready, with their packs stowed in the trucks and their cots ready for the men in camo to carry out. Because of this, he was able to get them all into one truck. He considered this another sign of fortune. He would have more time to talk to them, to win them over.

He was praying for them as the truck began to move. Within a minute they were on their way to wherever god intended.

Derek

Derek looked down over the moonlit expanse that surrounded them. The roof felt uncomfortably high, and below him, the shadows seemed to creep across the yard, the only sound was the occasional creak of the metal when someone moved. Creepy was not enough to describe it.

A glance at his watch showed him the activity below would be picking up very soon. He felt a sense of anticipation among his brethren on the roof. He glanced around to where the others were posted around the raised edge. When the unit had been divided around the perimeter, it had worked out to one about every fifty feet or so.

He stifled a yawn and turned his attention back to the expansive grounds. His section overlooked the field opposite where they had driven in and he wished there was something to look at. He passed the time by counting the treetops that stuck up above the sable blackness of the forest and into the barely light darkness sky.

He was well into the hundreds when he heard the foot on the gravel of a figure coming towards him. He turned to see the Sarge's hunched bulky form settling beside him.

"Have you seen anything out there Hobbs?" He asked as he peered out over the side.

"Not a damn thing but trees," answered Derek, "and the occasional figment of my imagination."

"Sentry duty sucks." Sarge agreed. "It's almost over. I came to tell you that at six on the dot, we all pull out to join the convoy."

Derek glanced at his watch again, it was five until six. "Who is relieving us up here?"

"No one." He explained as he stood to move on to the next person. "The ones staying won't be here long enough to need a sentry if it's clear when we take off."

Derek watched the man hurry to the next position and started to pack up the few things he had laid out the previous night. He made one more check of the area his was responsible and found it clear. As he finished, the Sarge called out 'time to go!"

As one, the stood and started to move. As if on cue, the engines of helicopters and vehicles come to life down below. In three minutes, they were loaded up and heading out the gates.

**Brandy**

The last hour had been by far the most uncomfortable. The twisting cut back and forth as the wound up the mountain. It seemed that most of the ride was up roads that were too narrow, and all had drastic drop-offs on one side and sheer cliffs on the other.

Brandy had repeatedly urged Jack to slow down, but her mother had pointed out that it was the truck ahead of them that set the speed. Brandy had eventually given up when she realized the dangers of getting separated.

"Any Idea how much further?" Asked Chad beside her as he clutched the rifle between his legs with one hand and held the handle above the door in a white-knuckled grip in another.

"I have no clue," Annie answered earnestly, glancing down at the map. "I would need a crossroad to figure it out, and well..." She waved her hand towards the window, indicating the three hundred feet drop just a few feet away.

Brandy glanced out the window and down into the floor of the valley and felt slightly nauseous. Growing up in Florida had not prepared her for this kind of landscape.

"What I wouldn't give for a nice level beach with palm trees..." Brandy stated wistfully.

"It's not so bad up in the mountains," Jack added, "I lived in Colorado for quite a while when I was younger. It won't be long until the leaves start to change, and then you will be in for a real treat."

"I love when the trees change," Annie said reassuringly.

They rode on for several minutes before the road changed from a winding slalom to a long straight road. After just a couple of miles, the truck ahead of them began to slow down. Jack let the van slip to the left so that they could see down the canopy road.

The Line of vehicles was just under a mile long, and from their position near the middle, they could see an opening appearing in the trees ahead. They were approaching a clearing in the forest.

The opening in the tree turned out to be the top of a ridge, the other side opening into a treeless bowl set into the mountains. The cove spread out for two miles in front of them and was about a half mile wide. The center was open fields, divided by split rail fences, and they could see buildings set against the edges. The jagged cliffs rose between fifty and a hundred feet and seemed to encircle the entire area. It was their first look at their new home.

The convoy rolled down the roads that ran between buildings and fields until they reached the far end. The Building they pulled up to was a modern structure and stood in contrast against the collection of clapboard and log structures that ringed the area. A wooden sign proclaimed it the "Katie's Cove visitor center and gift shop'.

They came to a stop in the parking lot behind the truck they had followed, and as Jack reached for the door, Annie stopped him. "Stay here," she said commandingly, "They have to search it first."

As she said this, soldiers began to spill out of the back of the truck ahead of them and started to rush off following a pattern only they seemed to understand. The group in the van say similar groups leaving other vehicles around them.

A group rushed past them from somewhere behind them, and one paused long enough to give a quick thumbs up before rushing off to rejoin his group. Brandy waved back, but knew Derek was already gone again.

Chad opened the door and slide from his seat to take his position in front of the vehicle. Brandy was surprised to find herself feeling more secure because of it, it was the first time she thought of Chad as more than a kid or just Derek's friend.

"It's strange," Annie muttered thoughtfully, "When you see them moving like that, it seems like a thousand of them." Everyone realized she was talking about the soldiers.

"How many are there?" Jack asked her.

"forty-three military personnel, most of the infantry." She answered. "There are also fifteen volunteers like Derek."

"I thought we had a lot more than that!" Brandy said, surprised by the low numbers.

"We did," Annie explained. "There were over a hundred that went to the hospital with me and we lost a bunch. About fifty at that mall we used as a staging area, only a dozen of those came back, that's who Derek is with." There was a definite tinge of sadness in her voice as she spoke. "They lost eighty-four while we were at the shelter, scavenging, patrols, and guards mostly. The colonel had three hundred with him in the beginning, he told me last night only half of what we have were assigned to him before this all started."

"That's sad..." brandy said meekly.

Her comment was cut off by a rumbling noise that rattled the van. Brandy's face fell in shock as a tank rolled by, roaring down the circular road at a speed that seemed strange for such a large chunk of metal. As she watched it went around the outside of the fields.

"What the hell?" She asked incredulously.

"It's a Tank," Annie answered.

"I can see that!" Brandy snapped back sarcastically. "Where's it going?"

"Oh," her mother said with a chuckle, "That's our roadblock. It's going to find a place on the road we came in on and park across it, somewhere where the road drops off on one side and has a cliff on the other and sit across the road." She held up her hands and crossed one over the other, demonstrating the idea. 'If anything tries to push past it, it either hits a cliff or falls. Another is going to be on the other road leading in."

"Can't they just walk in through the woods?" Jack asked.

Annie pointed at the cliffs surrounding them. "They would take one hell of a tumble." She answered.

Brandy began to understand why they had come here. The natural set up would protect them better than any building or fence she had ever seen. Despite the end of the world as she knew it, she had to marvel at the number of coincidences and luck had brought them here. She started to think about her father.

"Mom," Brandy began, searching for the words, "Do you think Dad is okay? Do you think he found somewhere like this?"

It took a long time before an answer was given. Brandy was beginning to think her mother had not heard her, but then Annie spoke. "I don't know baby, I hope so, but I don't know."

Brandy says a tear roll down he mothers cheek and felt one welling up in her own eyes. "I think he is alive." She said determinedly. "I bet he ran off with his brother and is having strange adventures in the land of living death."

Despite the tears, Annie laughed. “Yeah, I bet. I imagine the epic stories of folly we are missing about Uncle Mark being chased by bears or your father getting run up trees by hogs.”

The women laughed together. Jack watched them, the look of confusion on his face made them laugh again, the tension they felt being vented in mirth.

“My father,” Brandy explained when she caught her breath, “Is a notorious klutz, and when he follows his brother on their little adventures, it normally ends in someone falling out of a tree, or running from whatever they were after.”

The women fell into giggles again. The dog, finally roused from his sleep looked at the women and whined. Jack shrugged at the dog and sighed, “I don’t get it either.”

Ahead of them, Chad turned back towards them and called out, “All Clear! They are letting everyone out.”

The trio seated in the van looked out the window and saw groups of civilians jumping out of the collection of vehicles. Brandy opened the van door and let Bruiser out. He immediately ran to a nearby clump of bushes and lifted his leg.

“Well,” Brandy said in a matter of fact tone, “I guess this place is officially claimed!”

**Immanuel**

Immanuel stepped down from the truck and took in the scenery surrounding them. The cove spread out to the south of them, green and pleasant. He stretched and stepped gingerly, working the feeling back into his legs.

The stood in a parking lot next to the visitor's center. Several buildings stood around the parking lot, the gift shop was a red brick building that seemed out of place, but the recreation on a sawmill blended perfectly with the others arrayed across the pastures.

Claire stood beside him, helping to steady him. His feet seemed to be especially tender today. He hoped it wasn't an infection setting in, he would have to find John and have him look.

The woman helping him was chattering happily about the beauty of the scene, but he found it difficult to pay attention until he heard her mention 'the pretty little church'.

The phrase made him look up to where she was pointing. The building stood out brightly as its stark white paint threw back the sunlight. It was not large and struck him as quite old. Its wood siding showed the cracks and pitting of weather, and it couldn't be more thirty feet wide and fifty feet long. It was Perfect.

'Go forth and build your flock.' The voice told him. He excitedly turned to Claire and said, "Help me find the colonel!" The pair moved off to find him.

An hour later, Immanuel was finally able to enter his church. The wait for the line of soldiers had move annoyingly slow, and they had told him would have to wait until it was cleared. He had followed behind them the whole way.

Immanuel walked across the ancient oak floors, worn smooth with the tread of generations. The rows of pews were simple constructions of wood, and the alter was just a wooden stand to rest a bible on. It was humble and just enough to serve his needs.

He went through the behind the altar and found the parsonage. It was just a long narrow room with a simple bed and some shelves, but it would serve his needs. The room was furnished in the style of the time the church had been built, but all the furnishings were new. They lacked the patina of age but would serve.

He spent the rest of the afternoon exploring every inch and feature of the building. The carvings were simple but well done. The floor squeaked but felt sturdy. The walls showed their age, but he felt no drafts and say no sunlight leaking through the vaulted roof and no sign of water damage.

His excitement peaked when he found the doors outside leading into the cellar. He descended the stairs carefully, as this section had not been restored. The stacked stone walls stood dirty but straight, and the room was just big enough for him to work. He hurried back to find his tools, here he would purify the evil from angels.

Derek

The minutes after they had burst from the armored vehicle had been anticlimactic. Not a single shot had been fired by anyone, and not a single infected person had been found in the visitor's complex.

They had not found any living people either. The buildings seemed to have been completely abandoned. The searched every space a person could have hidden, but didn't even find so much as a drop of blood.

They stood in a straight line across the width of the cove, each of them about seventy-five feet apart. Not close enough to have a conversation, but close enough that if one of them yelled, others would hear it. The plan was to walk straight across the length of their new retreat, searching buildings and hiding spots as they went. The idea being to make sure the area was safe before moving the civilians into their new homes.

A single blast of a whistle started them walking. Derek constantly checked those on either side to make sure they were keeping the line straight as he had been told.

His line would take him right down the middle of the fields. Aside from a few trees and the knee-high grass, there would be nowhere for him to search. He glanced at the decrepit buildings and thought about the men who would have to search those.

Derek knew they had intentionally loaded the end of the lines with the more experienced troops, and they were closer together than those in the middle with teams to back them up. He hoped that the boredom would be unbroken by the sounds of gunshots.

The end of the line reached the first house, and again the whistle sounded. The line of marchers stopped immediately, waiting watchfully. He could just make out the team that rushed forward and entered the building. In less than a minute, they came back out and the whistle sounded again, signaling the line to move forward again.

This start and stop dragged on for another two hours before the first burst of excitement. To Derek's disappointment, it ended up being on the side he couldn't see very well. As they neared the steep wall that ended the cove, the whistle sounded again, but this time in three short shrill blasts: the signal that the team had found something. He dropped to his knees and raised his rifle, scanning for a target.

His mind raced with the possibilities. Had someone seen something? Was it alive or dead? Had one of those things stumbled out of the woods or one of the buildings? They had not been ordered to stop, so he doubted a team had found something in one of the buildings.

In the distance, he could make out the faint sounds of someone shouting, but it quickly stopped, and time dragged on with no other noise. After what felt like an hour, the whistle blew again, once this time. Obediently, Derek stood and started forward.

They finished their sweep of the cove and were released to wait for their ride back. Derek asked the first person to join him what had happened, but no one seemed to know more than he did.

The mystery was solved when the truck arrived to get them, as they climbed in, Derek noticed a man seated inside between Sarge and the lieutenant. The man was dressed in buckskins and had a long ruddy tangled beard. To Everyone's surprise, he wore a coonskin cap, and the carcass of a deer laid at his feet.

Derek took the seat across from the man and tried to get a good look without starring, but couldn't help himself. The longest rifle he had ever seen was leaned across the man's shoulder, its butt resting on the floor, and still towered over the man's head.

"It's a .48 caliber flintlock." The man said with a smile. "It's sixty-four inches long and weight twelve pounds." The man held out his hand to shake, "Name is Rowdy Rob."

Derek Blushed. He had truly been trying not to stare, and being caught at it embarrassed him. He took the man's hand and shook, noticing the think callouses that covered the hand he held. "Derek." He introduced himself.

"Pleasure to meet you." He said cheerily and turned to the others loading in, "Pleased to meet all of you!"

Several of the soldiers introduced themselves, but some simply nodded, unsure how to take the man they thought out of place. Every part of the situation seemed surreal.

"Couldn't believe my eyes when I saw an actual tank go racing by." He said excitedly. "I was up on the ridge field dressing this critter and looked up to see a gol'darn tank. First one I had ever seen up here, probably the first to ever come up here!"

"What are you doing up here?" Derek asked.

The Lieutenant answered for him. "Mr. Rob was an employee here at the park, a reenactor."

"I was much more than that Missy," He said indignantly, "I am a bona fide mountain man. I hung around here during the summer and answered the question from visitors and such, but I ain't one of them sissy reenactors."

"My apology." She said with just a hint of sarcasm.

Derek changed the subject before the man could respond to the woman, "How long have you lived up here?"

"I have been up here nigh on ten years I reckon," he stated proudly, "Moved up her after that rascal got elected! "

Derek was afraid to ask what rascal he was referring to. "Have you seen any of the infected up here?" he asked.

"Infected?" the man replied incredulously, "These dang things ain't infected, they are dead! But every once in a while, a few will show up. They always come up the road though, so they are easy to avoid."

Derek found that interesting. "Why do they only come up the road?"

“Well,” He answered, “All these gullies and ridges and mountains is like a maze boy. There might be some out there wandering around, but the chances of them getting here are slim. Just as likely to come out in Texas!”

Derek considered this and decided it made sense. He leaned back as the Rowdy Rob began to talk to one of the others surviving in the winters and relaxed. What A long strange day it had been!

**Brandy**

Her position as assistant to the administration kept Brandy very busy over the next several days.  The cove played host to a large number of buildings, some new and some centuries old and in varying states of repair. The newer buildings were move-in ready, but the older cabins needed a lot of work.

She was now acutely aware of the difference between preservation and restoration. The old Janke cabin had been one of the most contentious locations to house people. Its weathered log walls had gaps big enough for the survivors to put their arms through, and the looming weather would be unpleasant if it was not filled with mortar.

They had teams out scavenging for everything they would need, winter clothing, kerosene heaters and the myriad and sundry items that would improve their comfort level and chances of survival.

The crazy wild man that had walked out of the woods the first day had turned out to be quite valuable. His knowledge of the way of doing things the way they had been done when this valley had been settled in the 1830s was had proven invaluable. He was out roaming the settlement somewhere going from home to home showing people how to repair or improve the houses they had been assigned.

They had the food stores the national guard had left behind cached in a cave about halfway down the length of the valley. The cave was packed with food, barrels of fuel, and ammunition. They even located a bladder of aviation fuel towards the back, and a crew was figuring out a way to move the fuel using a complicated system of hoses.

Brandy looked up from her paperwork when the Colonel started speaking. They had set up an office in the visitor's center since it was the only building with solar power to run the radios.

"Brandy," He said, his voice irritated, "The Petersons are raising hell about their cabin. Hank says it's going to be too much work and the soldiers in the church make too much noise, what else do we have for them?"

'Oh great, the Janke cabin again.' Brandy thought to herself, but shuffled through the papers on her desk, searching for the housing sheet. "The only thing left is in the Bower's barn, but it needs a roof."

"Shit," the man said and stood to pace.

Brandy knew the pacing meant his mood was taking a turn downward, and he would soon become quite grumpy. She pitied the next person in uniform to come through the doorway with bad news.

Col. Murray was a kind man, but when the mood took him, he could be quite severe. She was thankful that he always held it back from civilians, but his military personnel would get a firm talking to if they stepped out of line.

Brandy saw an opportunity to move forward on something she had been rolling around in her mind since they had arrived. "Why don't we give them the Hawkins place?"

"Aren't you in the Hawkins place with your mother and those two guys?" he asked, puzzled.

"We are, but it's pretty small for four, and the Petersons are only three people." She said and then pushed the other half of the idea. "We could take the Janke place."

The gray-haired man looked at her with skepticism. “That place needs a lot of work.”

“Yeah, but the roof is in good shape, and the fireplaces work fine,” She said confidently, “and its right next to the Methodist church. That’s where my brother is staying with his unit.”

“I see.” Said the officer. “I have a feeling you plan to wander over there and get them to help you when they aren’t on duty.”

“Exactly!” Brandy answered slyly.

“Okay,” he agreed, “If you can get your mother to agree, its fine with me. Get up with that Rob fellow and make sure you understand how to close those gaps. I still expect you to be here when I need you.”

Brandy felt the smile creep across her face. She had just connived to get a house with her own room, and it would be only a short walk from Derek. She couldn’t wait for her duties to be over here so should could find the others and talk them into it.

**Immanuel**

Immanuel stood in the doors of his church and looked across the meadow towards the other church. The building was a beehive of activity with soldiers and civilians coming in and out of it. He was glad he had claimed the Baptist church early.

Of the two churches in the valley, this was the larger, and in better shape. He and his disciples had spent the last few days cleaning and repairing the ancient building. The dull wood pews were now dust free, and the cobwebs had been cleared from the corners. The soldiers had come across an old family bible during one of the runs to the nearby towns, and it now sat on the altar. He was as ready for tomorrow as he could be.

He felt a level of apprehension about his first services that he was unfamiliar with. Tomorrow morning those who were willing would file in and sit in the pews to hear him speak. He had sat down each night with a notebook and tried to write out his sermon, but the words had not come. He had to have faith that the voice would guide him when the time came.

He limped down the stairs, still having to baby his feet, and circled to the far side of the building. The slanted doors leading down to the cellar called to him, he lifted them and stepped down gingerly down the steps into the darkness.

He used his hands to find the oil lamp he had stashed there and lit it with a lighter from his pocket. The room glowed to life, its rocky walls casting shadows that mimicked the topography of the very mountains it was dug into.

He was pleased to see everything exactly like he had left it. His tools were arranged neatly on a shelf he had built for them. They glow of the lamp made a golden gleam cascade off their shining surfaces. In the center of the room stood one of the dull green army cots stacked atop the crates he had brought from the gift shop made it just the right height.

Satisfied that everything was perfect, he extinguished the light and made his way back upstairs. He still wrestled with his orders to have patience, but he was coming to terms with it. He had come up with a plan.

The fair weather would turn sour soon. The temperatures would drop and people would spend more time at home as opposed to being out wandering. He knew it would be a simple thing to grab her when she was out of some mission for the military and some cold snowy day he would. If he was careful, he could get her here with no one seeing, and then he could take his time with her.

Once she was his, he could strap her down and work. Brandy would be his masterpiece. The evil inside her would have no place to hide when he was finished.

**Derek**

His hands were raw from working the mixture into the gaps. The Mountain man had given the recipe and taught them how to do it before moving on to other projects, and left the group to do the work themselves.

Derek looked down the remaining lengths of the building and sagged. Even with the twelve of them working, this would take all day. The mixture of clay, sand, and ashes dried quickly so they had to constantly stop to make more.

They had tried to find trowels to make the job go quicker but had no luck, so they worked with their hands. To compound the dread, his new friends and himself had patrol tonight. All day in the sun and then the night walking the long loop around the valley meant a very tired day tomorrow.

He spoke through the gap in the wall, to Chad who was working the goop into the inside of the same wall. “Man, this sucks donkey ass!”

The reply was not what he expected when his mother’s voice shot back. “I am in here too,” she scolded, “watch that language mister!”

“Sorry, Mom.” He answered sheepishly. “It does suck though.”

Chad answered back this time. “Yeah, it does.” He said with a sigh. “But thank you for helping. I know you guys didn’t have to.” He added as an afterthought.

“The guys like Brandy and Mom,” Derek explained. “I think they are happy that jerk isn’t going to be staying here. He kept coming over complaining about the noise every time we had we started the carrier or were outside working.”

“Well, now that I will have my own room here,” Chad said back slyly, “I will expect you guys to keep it down. I need my beauty sleep.”

In response Derek flipped a glob of the mortar off his finger through the crack, satisfied to see it splatter on the other boy’s shirt with a wet sound. “You should just be happy you get a room. I am sleeping in a big open room with twenty other people and a curfew...”

“Yeah, it will be nice. Jack snores.” Chad confided. “I like him and all, but this will be much nicer!”

The Janke cabin was thirty feet long and twenty feet wide. It was one of the larger homes from its time, and the only one with more than three rooms. It was laid out with a large center room occupying the middle third of the space, with two sets of two rooms on either side. These would be the bedrooms. The dividing walls were only six feet high with a gap of several feet at the top, but some privacy was better than none.

Derek rolled his eyes at the snoring comment. His living situation at the moment including lots of snoring and with the differing schedules they worked, It was a constant. He decided not to mention that.

“You are going to have to dig the toilet yourself though.” Derek reminded him. “You just cut the end off the barrel and cut a hole in the other, then bury it two-thirds of the way down.”

“Ugh,” Chad said. “Don’t remind me! All the times I have taken indoor plumbing for granted!”

Derek ignored Chad's attempt at humor. “Captain Bridges is going around checking things like that to make sure they are done right.” They had all sat in the mandatory briefing at the last meeting when camp sanitation had been stressed.

Both Derek and Chad well understood the reasons. Circumstances had essentially thrown them back in time when it came to modern conveniences. Everyone had been using the facilities at the visitor's center, but it wasn't hard to see that the simple outhouse style bathrooms would soon fill up and be unusable without the ability to pump them out.

Not for the first time, Derek felt the sting of guilt at not being able to be here full time to help his family in the cabin but knew that his duty with the lieutenant was keeping everyone safe, not just the people Living in this one building.

"Yeah, Yeah, Yeah, I heard you," Chad said. "I will dig it right where you marked, well away from the house and the creek. I was listening, and I sure as fu.. Sorry Annie, sure as freak don't want to catch any of those diseases that medic talked about."

Derek thought back to the speech and shuddered. Cholera didn't sound pleasant, especially with no hospitals, and the thought of tapeworms and other intestinal creepy crawlies made him feel nauseous.

As he moved to the next section of logs, Derek decided he should be extra nice to John, a Medic as a friend could be a wonderful thing to have.

**Brandy**

Brandy admired the work as she finished scrubbing the chink from her hands. The crew had finished the job an hour before the sun had set. She had thanked them all individually and made sure they knew to call her if they ever needed anything.

Her mother had mentioned how nice the inside seemed now. She had marveled out how the job had been done so thoroughly that not even light leaked in anymore.

Brandy tipped the milky wash water out of the metal tub and dried her hands on the shirt. It was too dark to head to the stream to refill it tonight. She would have to take it down in the morning and wash it out to bring water back for the house. The still had a stockpile of bottled water stashed in the cave, but the colonel had decided to make that a reserve since the cold clear mountain water was so available to everyone.

Her outside tasks complete, she made her way inside to set up her brand-new bedroom. She knew it wouldn't take much work, everything she owned had been brought in on her back, but she would make the best of it. She called to Bruiser as she stepped through the doorway.

The room was lit only by the light that spilled in from the single-paned window sat high on the wall, but it was enough to help her move around. She made a mental note to find some candles or a lamp of some kind.

She laid out the dog's pallet and used the last bottle of water hidden in her pack to fill the dog's bowl in case he needed it during the night. Brandy sat up her cot under the window and began to sort her few pieces of clothing onto the single shelf the room contained.

A knock on the door startled her and she felt herself tense instinctively. “Brandy, Its Jack” called Jacks' voice, carrying into the room easily over the wall.

“Come in, Jack.” She said, relieved. The new house had her jumpy.

The door swings awkwardly on its rope hinges and clattered against the logs separating the rooms. Jack stepped in and extended his hand, holding out several small electronic devices. “Can you charge these for me tomorrow?”

She took the electronic cigarettes from him and set them up on the shelf. “Sure, you found the others I left for you?” This was their nightly routine. She worked in the only building with a working plugin, and he wasn’t ashamed to take advantage of that.

“I did,” He said, “thank you. You are a lifesaver!” he turned to go.

“Hey, Jack.” She said, stopping him. “How did today go?”

Jack turned back to face her before answering. “It was okay actually. I met some nice people.”

Jack had started working in the communal kitchen the other morning. It turned out he had a fair bit of experience running kitchens before becoming a golfer, and he had been put to work when the colonel found out.

“I am glad.” She said earnestly. “What’s for breakfast tomorrow?”

He laughed, “Well, our special will be scrambled powdered eggs and something resembling pancakes, but without butter or syrup. Same thing we had yesterday and will have tomorrow.” He said.

"MMMM," brandy said sarcastically as she rubbed her stomach as if she was starving, "Sounds wonderful."

Jack smiled broadly at her joke and bowed dramatically. "We have to work with what we have," he added seriously, "and what we have is tons of powdered eggs and so much flour that we could build walls out of it."

"I know," she said sympathetically, "The colonel swears that very soon he will have the search teams start looking for different kinds of foods. They have to concentrate on other things first." She crossed the room and gave him a quick hug. "Everyone knows you are doing your best!"

"Tell that colonel," he said as he left the room, "If he wants to see my best he can find me some spices."

Brandy smiled as he left and closed the door behind him. She stripped off her pants and changed into an oversized t-shirt before climbing into bed. She felt odd going to bed so early, but it was fast becoming the norm in the community. Candles and lamp fuel were rare, and once it got dark there wasn't much else to do.

"Good night Mom! Sleep well, Jack! Sweet dreams Chad!" she called to the ceiling, knowing that the design of the house would carry it to each of them.

"Night Brandy!" She heard Jack answer, and a "Good night sweetheart!" came from her mother.

Chads answer was in his typically sarcastic style, "Night John Boy, Night Grandpa, Night Ellie Mae!"

"Ellie Mae wasn't a Walton, go to sleep!" Jack yelled back.

**Immanuel**

The day's sermon had left him unfulfilled. Of the almost two hundred people in the compound, less than twenty had made the trek to services. He had felt blessed when they voice had whispered what to say in his ear, and those gathered had come to congratulate him when the service was over for its insights and the joy it had brought them. Immanuel had watched them leave afterward, never knowing how empty it had left him feeling.

He decided he would have to do something towards his goal. Maybe it was time to start his planning in earnest. He would wait for darkness and pay her a visit.

He crossed the field in a crouch, darting between high patches of grass. The darkness of the night made him feel invincible as he made his way towards her house. He thanked the one above for the clouds that had rolled in and blocked out the moonlight.

He could hear the patrol approaching as he reached the single lane of pavement that separated the meadow from the houses. He debated if he could get across before they arrived, but decided not to risk it.

Immanuel melted into the scrub brush around a nearby tree and made himself as small as possible just as he saw the figures materialize out of the darkness and step into the dim light.

He watched the three figures as they moved slowly down the road. He could make out the shapes of their rifles slung casually in their arms and the blocky roundness of the helmets they wore. The details of their faces were hidden from him by the low light, but he watched them intently for any change in posture that would indicate they had sensed him.

To his relief, they moved past without even slowing. His observations of the previous night told him the next one wouldn't pass her for several minutes, so he waited for them to disappear and moved quickly across the road. He took shelter in the line of trees beside the other side of the road and paused to listen again.

When he was satisfied that he was once again undetected, Immanuel crept to the house itself. He rested his hand on the log wall and felt the warmth of the wood against the cold of the night. He knew the warmth was the emanation of the evil that lived inside. Moving quietly along the side of the house he approached the door. It was tied open by a piece of rope to allow the coolness of the night replace the air inside.

Cautiously, Immanuel placed the weight of his foot on the step into the house and thanked God when it stood firm and offered no creak to alert the people inside. He could hear the sound of sleeping coming from inside. He waited for his eyes to adjust to that inky darkness inside as he listened for any change or sounds of waking.

He slowly placed his other foot inside, easing it down onto the boards inside. Then the other foot moved forward and found the floor silently. His third step found him in the middle of the empty room. Here he stopped again, listening.

He concentrated on the sleeper's individual noises. The ranged from a soft breathing to an all-out snore. Immanuel decided that the noises to his left must be coming from the old man and the boy. Those rooms emitted a distinctly male sound, so he concentrated his hearing on the other side.

Despite his best efforts, he could not tell which room his target was in. The girl had to be in one of the two. He stepped to the door closest to him and leaned his ear against the door.

The sleeper inside produced a slow regular breathing, but he couldn't decide if it was the mother or the daughter. He stepped gently to the next door and repeated the process.

An almost identical sound came from this room, but there was something else. A low rumble, almost more felt than heard, filled his ear. he shifted his weight to hear better and his ear moved the door slightly when it touched. The wood made a tiny scraping sound when it slid those few millimeters.

The bark sounded as loud as a cannon against the previous quiet of the house. Immanuel had barely pulled back from the door when it sprung out at him in a violent heave. It pulled the slack out of the hinges and caught, having only moved a few inches and the sound turned into a snarling mixture or growls and barks.

Immanuel abandoned his attempts at stealth and ran from the room. He leaped from the house, ignoring the stair and the stabbing pain in his foot as he made the distance in his sudden panic. Behind him, he heard the house come alive with shouts and calls to each other. He knew it would bring the patrol running.

He trotted across the road and found the bushes in the meadow that had given him shelter before. He sat on them catching his breath. The pain in his foot was increasing and he felt a spreading warmth he knew could only be blood.

The sound of footsteps filled the night as the approaching patrol came down the road at a run. He heard other voices and glanced back to see figures coming out of the church the soldiers slept in.

Knowing he would soon be out of time, he cautiously retraced his steps back home. It had not gone the way he planned, but he had what he needed now. The barking dog had done more than warn them of his presence, it being in the room had told him where the girl was.

Now he could make his plans.

**Derek**

They had heard the frantic barking of the dog and the yells and instantly gone into a run. Everyone had seen the dark figure run across the road, but its hunched figure and unusual gait had made them unsure what it was.

By the time they had arrived at the spot it crossed the road, it had disappeared into the night. Behind them, they heard brandy yell something to someone, and Derek turned and darted towards the sound.

He found his family surrounded by soldiers from the church and talking excitedly. The German Shepherd stood protectively beside them. He ran to them and asked, “What Happened!?”

“Bruiser ran something off,” Brandy explained, “We were all asleep and he just started snarling and snapping and we heard something run off.”

Derek could tell how shaken she was by the tremble in her voice when she spoke. “What was it, did you see it?” he asked.

“No,” His mother said. “By the time I even got out of bed it was gone.”

One of the men Derek had been patrolling with, a man named ward spoke up. “We saw something run across the road. It was big and dark, maybe a bear, lots of them in these mountains.”

The color drained from the faces of Annie and brandy at the words. None of them had thought about the possibility of predators moving amongst them. The idea that four hundred pounds of fur, claws, and teeth coming after them was not sitting well.

"Well, I have been walking around all night in the dark," Derek added to the thought, "and the thought of a bear out there doesn't make me happy."

Several flashlights clicked on around them and scanned the bushes nervously. Several of them expected the see eyeshine staring back at them.

"From here on out," Started the lieutenant, "no one goes anywhere alone. If you go to take a shit, take a buddy. I would suggest you all close every door and tie them shut."

"I don't think that's going to be a problem." Brandy quipped. The return of her joking let Derek know she was calming down.

Sarge added, "AND everyone is armed at all times, even inside." He stepped over to Brandy and pressed a small flashlight into her hands. "When you hear something in the dark, make noise and light. Both will scare off a bear."

Brandy thanked the man and the crowd began to nervously break up and walk back towards whatever they were doing before. Their normal casual walk replaced by a deliberate stalk, eyes moving around searching the shadows.

The trio from the patrol made sure Brandy, Chad, Jack, and Annie got back safely inside and locked the house tightly. They made promises to check the house each time the walked by. The rest of their shift was spent on pins and needles as they moved through the darkness.

There was no further sign of the bear that night.

***

*Captain Bridges Kneeled in front of the opening in the face of the rocky cliff. The beam of his flashlight showed the cave going in only a few feet before it made an abrupt turn to the right. He glanced down at the tracks they had followed here and weighed his options.*

*"What do you see, Sir?" Asked one of the men who stood huddled inside his poncho behind him. The sudden cold snap had taken them all by surprise and complicated the search for the animal they had heard had been brave enough to raid a home in the cover the night before.*

*"Not a damn thing!" the officer declared, irritated at having to spend such an unpleasant day wandering the woods. The orders to comb the area for a bear had been met with general unhappiness. The lack of any kind of bear sign inside the settlement had made the task seem pointless, but orders were orders. "I can hear something, maybe breathing?"*

*"Breathing?" said the other man in their three-man group. "What kind of breathing?"*

*The Captain noted that no 'Sir' had been attached to that one, but decided not to make an issue. The strict military structure was declining into a more casual situation, and under the circumstance he understood.*

*"I am not sure," The Captain tried to think about how to describe the sound he had picked up from the opening, "Almost like a very long, low, snore. Almost like a hum."*

*"So what should we do?" asked the first. "I don't think we should crawl in there after it."*

*"The Colonel told us to come out here and thin the bear population, and this is the first bear tracks we have seen." He*

*explained, "It doesn't matter that we found them miles from camp. I sure don't want to stay here to wait for it to come out."*

*"Can we smoke it out?" Asked the second soldier. "Build a fire here and shoot it when it runs out?"*

*"I have a better idea." Said the Captain suddenly. He reached up to the strap that was fitted across his chest and pulled a grenade loose. "FIRE IN THE HOLE!" he yelled as he tossed the explosive into the mouth of the cave, and watched with satisfaction as it took a good bounce and skittered past the bend and into the darkness.*

*The three moved quickly, seeking shelter against the rock wall beside the opening. As they pressed their bodies hard against the wall, the grenade went off. They felt the rocks move behind them from the blast as a cloud of rocks and dust erupted from the cave.*

*The echo cascade through the trees and back again, but its fading noise was soon replaced by another sound. A buzzing filled their ears, growing louder. The men froze, fearing it was the beginnings of an avalanche.*

*A Black fog shot from the opening and began to spread out, it found the men still frozen in their places and enveloped them. The eyes of the men immediately began to perceive that the fog was made up of thousands of smaller parts, each carried by wings towards them.*

*The unexpected appearance held the men until the stingers began to find their flesh. That was when the screaming began. The three ran in different directions, each smacking their bodies helplessly against the clouds of bees that sought, found and stung them.*

*Search parties sent later would find the spots where each of the men had stopped to shed their bee covered ponchos and equipment, and nearby, the place their bodies had crushed the grass when they died. The bodies were not recovered.*

***

**Brandy**

Shivering, she stared up at the ceiling. The light coming through the window lit the room well enough to see the details of the beams. Her mind studied them, happy for the change after the hours or starring at the blackness that had been there before. Bruiser whined the whine Brandy now knew meant he needed to go outside.

Brandy cast off the covers and got up. She dressed quickly in two pairs of pants and a jacket. The temperature drop had caught her by surprise. It had been a little bit chilly last night, but right before dawn, a cold front must have rolled in. The temperature had dropped to the point where she could see her breath.

She opened the door a crack and peered out, checking the corridor for anything or anyone who might be waiting there, but seeing nothing she opened it the rest of the way and crossed to open the outside doors for the dog. He rushed out into the cold happily.

Brandy followed him out into the dawn-lit yard and surveyed the area. She could see the Methodist church across the meadow. It stood stark white against the browns and reds of the landscape, but she saw no sign of movement there.

The Baptist church was the opposite. Figures dressed in camo moved around the structure attending to assorted tasks. She noted a clump of figures standing around a bonfire as they tried to get warm.

The sound of footsteps inside told her that the others were up and moving, and shortly Jack exited the shelter and came to stand beside her. They watched the dog wander in silence for a minute before he broke the quiet of the morning.

“Did you get any sleep?” He asked, concern in his voice.

“No, you?” she answered.

“I drifted in and out a few times.” He said and punctuated the statement with a yawn. “Id start to slip off to sleep and the house would creak, or something outside would make a noise and bang: wide awake again!”

“It’s going to be a long day,” Brandy bemoaned, “I guess we need to talk to ‘Rowdy Rob’ about how to keep bears away.” She said the man’s name with a special emphasis. She recognized how much help he had given, and liked him. His Insistence on being called ‘Rowdy Rob’ was her only drawback when it came to him.

“Or whatever it was,” Jack said skeptically.

“You don’t think it was a bear?” She asked.

“I’m not sure what it was, maybe it was a bear.” Jack said. “all we know was that something ran across the road that was dark. It could have been anything that kid saw, maybe even a person or a mountain lion.”

Brandy considered his words and realized he was right. She had listened for a bear all night long, but now she wasn’t sure. “Just make sure you keep that pistol they gave you close.”

His hand felt automatically to the waist of his pants and found nothing. “I guess I need to start remembering to pick it up,” He admitted, “I am not a gun person, It's still inside.” He excused himself and went back inside.

Bruiser was walking with his nose to the ground. He had a scent he was interested in and was following it. Brandy watched him closely now. If he was following the trail of the bear or whatever it was, she would call him back before he got too far. The dog was tough, but she didn't want him to risk himself following such a predator.

After a minute, Jack reappeared with the nylon holster on his side and was followed out by Annie and Chad. Chad gave a quick wave and started to make his way to the guard's barracks to wait for his ride to wherever he would be on duty today. Brandy's mother walked straight over to her.

"You ready?" She asked. Brandy saw the tiredness in her eyes and briefly considered trying to talk her into taking the day off to sleep, but knew it was pointless. The older woman would still insist on going.

"I guess," Brandy replied, then added, "I am as ready as you are."

Her mother placed her hand on brandy's back and rubbed affectionately. "Well, call your dog and we will all walk together."

Brandy looked back over where she had last seen the canine and was alarmed to see how far he had gotten in her distracted few moments. She could see him well into the meadow, almost hidden by the grass. "BRUISER!" she called, "COME ON BOY!"

The dog stopped in its stalk and turned to look at her, and then back across the field. He stood indecisively for a moment, and then put his nose back to the ground and took a step away from them.

Brandy felt annoyed as she yelled again, "BRUISER, NOW!" she followed up this last call with a whistle. Across the grass, the dog stopped again, looked up again at the direction of whatever he was following, and the turned and began to lope back towards her.

“It must smell good,” Annie said as the three humans began to walk towards the offices and kitchen set up at the visitor’s center.  Their cabin was at the far end of the valley, so they had a decent walk ahead of them. The fuel was now earmarked for military vehicles and the van sat idle in the yard of their new house.

Bruiser joined them and took his place beside Brandy. She did notice that he kept looking back over the field. She followed his eyes, trying to see what he was. The field was empty from her all the way across to the white church.

“Nothing is there, the field is empty,” she reassured the dog. “Stop being a goober!”

**Immanuel**

Immanuel woke in the morning and pulled his blanket up against the cold. He had gone to bed last night feeling hot after the exhaustion of his flight from the dog and patrols. He must have kicked off the covers.

He tried to roll over and found that his sock seemed glued to the bed. He pulled harder and the fabric pulled free with the sound of Velcro. He peered under the covers and found the sheets stained dark red. The sight reminded him of the pain he had felt when he leaped from the porch the previous night. He must have re-opened his wound. He thanked the one above that the bleeding seemed to have stopped on its own, or he might have bled to death during the night while he slept.

He swung his feet out of the bed and tested the foot with weight. The slightest touch of the blood crusted sock on the floor sent waves of pain shooting up his leg. He ruled out walking to the other church to find John. He would have to await the arrival of one of his disciples to fetch the medic.

Claire had come to check on him when he didn't come to breakfast. She had almost fainted when she saw the blood but had rushed off to bring help. By noon, his friend had arrived.

"I told you to take it easy." John scolded, but then the friendliness returned to his voice. "How did you manage this Gabe?"

"I went down the steps wrong Last night." He admitted, leaving out where the stairs had been. "I didn't think it was that bad..."

"Well," the medic explained, "You busted all your stitches. It looks like you bled like a stuck pig. You got lucky again."

The medic spent some time cleaning the wound and examining it better with all the blood gone before he announced his new plan. "It's been open too long now for stitches to do much good." He explained, "I am going to glue it and load you up with some antibiotics to prevent infection."

"Glue it?" Immanuel asked skeptically.

"Yep," John answered. "It is going to sting like there is no tomorrow, but I think it's the only way to go." As he spoke, he pulled a little metal tube of the adhesive from his pack and used the cap to punch a hole in the metal that covered the end.

Immanuel watched uncomfortably as the man at his feet began to work on him. The sting was as promised, but he tried to not draw back his foot. "Isn't that for broken dishes and stuff like that?"

"It's basically the same stuff they use in emergency rooms," he answered, applying more glue, "But we don't have any of that stuff, so we use this. Works of glass, wood, plastic, and feet."

Immanuel laid his head back, deciding to watch the work was not the best course of action. He didn't look back down until the man was wrapping a bandage around his foot. "Thank you, John." He said sincerely.

"Don't thank me yet," the man said back, "because you aren't going to like this next part. Your other wounds are doing too well, I need you to stay completely off your feet for two weeks."

"I can't," he said, shocked, "I have services on Sundays, and things to do!"

"Consider this doctors' orders," John said sternly, "If these things don't heal, you are a goner." The medic turned to Claire who had stood silently watching. "Can you take care of him? He will need someone to bring him food and keep the wounds clean."

Claire immediately nodded yes. Her house was very close to the church. “I can be here every day.” She said enthusiastically.

John gathered his supplies and packed them away. When he stood to leave, he picked up Immanuel’s shoes and used them to point at the man prone in the bed. “I am taking these with me to make sure you don’t do anything stupid. It will snow today or tomorrow, and I know you won’t go anywhere without these. I mean it, stay off your feet!”

Immanuel watched the man turn and walk out, shoes still held in his hands.

“Let’s get that bed cleaned up,” Claire said and stepped over to help him roll off the blood-stained sheets.

Immanuel didn’t resist her. He watched as his plans slipped away from him. The snow would come, and he would not be ready. He pondered what to do and the voice spoke to him.

‘Patience”

**Derek**

Chapelle walked carefully along the edge of the leave strewn path to avoid stepping in the layers of tracks embedded in the soft soil. He stopped every few steps to study the patterns the passing animals had made. Derek walked in his footsteps and stopped when the soldier. This had been going on for hours.

He could see the overlapping prints made by hooves and feet, but they wouldn't gel in his mind so he could make sense of them. They seemed so jumbled that he couldn't even make out which way anything had been moving.

"Anything yet?" Sarge asked from his position a few feet behind Derek.

Chapelle straightened from his consideration of the spore on the ground. "Some bear, but nothing from today." He said casually. "If you want a bobcat, a beaver or a raccoon, I can hook you up."

"Damn," the giant muttered, "Let's cut back towards camp and see what we can find."

The trio turned back to the west and reformed their staggered line. Derek lost the battle with the yawn he had been holding in and let it out. Behind him, he heard Sarge do the same.

"Stop that soldier." He said half seriously. "When you yawn, you close your eyes. We are trying to find a bear here."

"I thought these mountains were supposed to be full of bears?" Derek wondered aloud.

"Believe it or not, they are," Chapelle said. "Thousands of them. Two or three per square mile is about normal. What surprises me is that one wandered into the cove with all the people and trucks and helicopters coming and going all the time."

"Aren't they pretty mean?" Sarge asked.

"Not at all. In all reality," Chapelle explained, "Your average black bear fears people and their things. But if one came in, why go after a house and not that big kitchen tent or the food cache? It doesn't make sense."

"Well, the big guy heard about it," Sarge asserted, "And said go hunt the bear, so here we are."

"Ours is not to reason why..." Chapelle agreed.

"What does that mean?" Derek asked Chapelle.

Sarge answered before the other man could. "Ours is not to reason why, ours is to do and die. It's from the poem 'The charge of the light brigade.' It's about our place as lowly foot soldiers. We don't get to make the decisions, just do what we are told."

"but what if the decision isn't the right one," Derek asked, "What if it just gets us killed for no reason."

"Faith," Chapelle answered, "Sometimes you just have to have believed in those around you and those above you."

Derek pondered that as they continued to walk. He knew he trusted the sergeant and the lieutenant, and they trusted those who they answered to. It made sense in a way, and that realization gave him a warm feeling.

Shortly thereafter, they came to an abrupt stop when Chapelle raised his fist into the air in the halt signal. The trio raised their rifles and scanned the surrounding woods. Derek couldn't see or hear anything that would have caused them to stop, but the silent signal being given as opposed to the normal ones they had been using all day sent his adrenaline rushing.

Several minutes passed in silence as they watched for something. Chapelle waved his hand slowly and moved it back and forth to get their attention. When they looked, he pointed to his ear, and then made a motion with two fingers like walking feet and pointed back the way they had come. Derek understood: He had heard something walking behind them.

Whatever it had been must have stopped when they did, because there was no noise being made behind them. The two soldiers exchanged several gestures didn't understand, but the situation made him wish he did. When They finished, they stood and moved off at a walk. Derek noted the big black man walking backward, rifle raised and pointed back down the trail.

Before much time had passed, they came to a clearing and the signal to halt was given again. This time Derek's ear picked up the sound behind them, but they stopped suddenly when whatever it was realized its prey had stopped also.

Derek felt the old familiar cold touch of fear creep up his spine. They were being hunted. He ruled out asking what it was, choosing silence over curiosity. Whatever was coming up their trail was smart enough to know what it was doing. It couldn't be the infected, they were machines of low intellect.

Chapelle leaned close to him and spoke softly. "Get ready to haul ass, stay right with me." He ordered.

Derek gripped his rifle and got ready. When the soldier stood and took off, Derek stayed so close he worried he would run into the other man. The crossed the forty yards in just a few seconds.

Chapelle skid to a stop in the bushes on the other side and Derek did run into, but both kept their feet. Sarge came through into the sheltered spot less than a second later.

"Sarge, get to the north side of the clearing, about twenty yards in and find a hiding place." He said urgently, "Derek, go prone here in case it comes straight through, I will be over there."

Derek watches the two hurry off silently before he could ask any questions, and did what he was told. He laid down behind a tree and brought his rifle to point at the clearing.

Minutes passed as he watched the trail the had just traveled. He felt the cold, clammy ground pulling the hit from his body. He couldn't tell if his shivers were from the cold day, the fear, or the adrenaline.

To the far side of the clearing, he heard the snap of a twig on the ground. It sounded like a rifle shot and made his heart skip a beat. The brush on the other edge moved slightly as if touched by something. The rest of the clearing stood as still as a painting.

He shifted the rifle to place the sights on that bush but kept both of his eyes wide open. The bush moved again, and a shape pushed its way into the sunlight. The sudden appearance sent another shot of adrenaline coursing through Derek's body.

The tawny snout came through the bushes and changed to sleek black fur. The fur continued to push through the brush until the animal was revealed in totality. Its shoulders were massive, and its beady black eyes swept from side to side searching for threats.

Derek squeezed the trigger, and the animal staggered back with a bellow and swatted its hide where the bullet struck it like it had been bitten by a fly. Derek fired again, and the bear raised to its hind legs. He was amazed at the size of it, but fired again, aiming for the center of its chest. It collapsed to the ground, but Derek fired three more rounds into it before stopping.

He watched it for any sign of movement, and when it stayed still Derek rolled over onto his back, panting. The rush of fear was escaping him in each exhalation, and he felt the relief forming tears in his eyes. He suppressed the tears and counted to fifty before trusting his still shaking limbs.

He sat up and yelled, "I got him!" to the others.

"I see that," Said Chapelle's voice from the clearing, "You got him a lot..."

Derek turned to see the soldier standing over the carcass of the bear. He must have moved in to investigate while Derek was collecting himself.

Derek stood and brushed himself off before shouldering his rifle and walking out into the clearing. He discovered the creature seemed much smaller when he stood near it. It had seemed gargantuan when it had stood on its hind legs.

Sarge emerged from the bushes and joined them. "So, what do we do now?"

"Bear is mighty fine eating," Chapelle said hungrily. "It's a little gamy, but delicious if cooked right." He drew his knife and offered it handle first to Derek. "Sarge and I Will go find a pole to put this on, you field dress it and we will get it to the camp."

The two walked off and left Derek to his work. He was almost done when they returned. Chapelle knelt by the pile of entrails and found the stomach. He took his knife back and sliced it open, revealing a soggy mass of fur and plant matter.

"Well, the Colonel will be getting a bear," He said, "But this one hasn't been eating our stuff."

## Brandy

The smell of roasting meat in the tent next door had been steadily filling the offices for the last few hours. Brandy found it hard to concentrate on the forms she was supposed to be filling out.

The news of the bear had spread quickly through the camp, and the teams searching for it were all working their way back to camp for the feast. Jack had been especially happy to hear about a new protein source coming in. One of the more engineering mind members of the cook staff had figured out a rotating rack from some old bed frames and the animal was being roasted whole between them. It had been made clear by the mountain man that bear meat was edible, but it had to be cooked all the way to well done to kill the parasites it may contain, so it would still be a few hours.

Bruiser sat on his pallet by her desk, occasionally sniffing the air and whining with hunger. Brandy planned to get him a few bear bones for him to chew on after the dinner was over.

The Colonel came out of his office and asked the man who manned the radio about the teams he had out, and if they were all on their way home. When he was informed that the only one outstanding team that had not checked in was Captain Bridges, Brandy say his pacing routine was not far behind.

"Let's re-route one of the teams still out to his last known location," he ordered, "Maybe he is having problems with his radio."

Brandy decided to distract the man from his worry, "Colonel, I have the sentry reports for you." She said as she held the papers up for him.

He stepped over and took them from her and perused them before setting them back down to sign. He handed them back to her to file. She took them and set them on the growing pile marked 'to be filed'.

The amount of red tape the group created surprised her. Every meal and bullet were itemized and accounted for. Forms of their creation, storage, and use were carefully marked. The scavenging crews even had copier paper and toner on the priority lists. The pile she needed to put away was several inches tall. She sighed and decided to start working on it.

She was just finishing up when the radio call came in about the fate of the Captain and his men. It horrified Brandy that the men's clothing had been found covered in dead and dying bees. She had read once that it could take over a thousand bee stings to be fatal. These men had died chasing her bear. She felt responsible.

She asked to be given permission to leave early, and her tears convinced the colonel to oblige. She left the building and hurried to the trees nearby and found a place to sob. Bruiser sensed her discomfort and tried to lick her face, but when she pushed him away, he contented himself to rest beside her with his head upon her leg, whining softly.

"Why do I always find you leaning on a tree crying," Chad asked as he walked up to her. He extended his hand to her and Brandy took the bandana he offered and wiped her eyes.

"Why are you always following me?" She asked, wiping the trails of the tears from her cheeks.

"You are in my area." He said as he sat down on a tree a few feet away. "I was guarding the playground today."

"What about the Kids?" She asked, concerned.

“I was passing off guard duty when I saw you run out of the colonel’s office.” He explained. “I thought I would come check on you.”

She wiped her eyes again. “Did you hear about the captain?” She asked, as her voice broke again.

“Yeah,” Chad said, understanding now, “I was near a radio when the report came in.”

“It’s all my fault.” She said, ending the sentence with a sob.

Chad laid his rifle down and scooted over beside her. He gathered her up in his arms and held her tight. He felt her stiffen at the touch but relaxed into the comfort he offered. “I know you won’t believe this just yet, but it’s not your fault.” He said softly.

“He went after a bear that came to my house.” She sobbed, “And he died looking for it!” Her voice was muffled by his shoulder, and he felt the tears soaking through.

“Brandy,” Chad asserted, “Those teams went out before you even had a chance to talk to Murray. And he would have sent them out no matter whose house it went into.”

The words worked their way through Brandy’s guilt and found a home. She appreciated hearing them but continued to cry. Chad held her for several minutes before she finally drew away, wiping her tears again. “Thank you, Chad.” She said finally. She still felt guilty, but it was slightly less now.

“I meant it, Brandy.” He said with conviction in each word. “This world sucks, and bad things are going to happen, but we can’t blame ourselves.”

“I must look horrible!” She said shyly.

"Well," He said with a smirk, "Aside from the red swollen eyes, messed up hair and the snot leaking out of your nose, yes. You Look horrible."

"Chad!" she cried and smacked him across the chest and laughed.

He took a dramatic step backward, clutching his chest as a hammy look of pain crossed his visage. "You Have killed me!" he said in falsetto. "I will soon be pining for the fjords! I am coming, Elizabeth, I'm coming!"

Brandy smacked him again, and they laughed together. When they finished, she reached forward and grabbed the front of his shirt, Pulling him in. Her kiss surprised him, and for a second his lips resisted, staying tight and still. Then he gave into it.

They separated and stood considering each other's eyes. Brandy broke the trance, bringing the bandana up to wipe her face and using it to clean herself up. When she felt more presentable, she took his hand and started walking back towards the buildings.

"Let's go see if we can help with dinner." She suggested.

"Can't we go back to sit under the trees?" Chad said weakly. "I Like the trees..."

"Later," Brandy said as she squeezed his hand. "Maybe we can meet in the trees another time."

They walked hand in hand back to the kitchen tent as the snow began to fall.

Immanuel

His feet tingled as he stood watching the medic leave. He had been pronounced healthy enough to walk and Immanuel was happy to be back on his feet after the fortnight of confinement to bed. As promised, His shoes had been returned to him.

The last fourteen days had been a miserable mix of failings. He had insisted on being helped to the chapel to lead Sunday services. Claire had balked but had finally agreed to help him if he sat in a chair to give his sermon.

Immanuel had attributed the low turnout at his first Sunday to the news of him being laid up. When he had been brought out for the second he had found attendance was down yet again. One bold soul had even stood and argued with him during the sermon, finally calling him a "Jim Jones wannabe" before storming out.

The point of contention had been his assertion that the rise of the infected had been God's punishment for man's sins, and the path to redemption lay through purification of the livings blood.

Only three had been in the church when he had ended his last service. Claire, Her bored looking son, and himself. He had laid in bed that night raging words in the sky. Demanding to know why the voice of God had let him down. His answer had not come. The voice stayed silent.

He walked through the doors of the church and stood on the top step, looking out at the snow-covered valley, replaying the conversation he had just finished with John. The medic had been polite and friendly at first, but when Immanuel breached the topic of the evil one in their midst, he had stung Immanuel with his words defending her. In the distance, he could still see the medic walking down the road back towards his next patient. He doubted he would see the man here again.

It all came back to that girl and her demon rider. She had gotten to the others, turned them against him with her lies and persuasion. She would not give up until she convinced them to come after him. It was no longer just the will of God, it was self-defense.

He wondered again if it was her doing, some spell or dark magic that kept the voice from his ears. Could she do such a thing? He walked down the steps and made his way around the building as he pondered. The entire valley was bright with fresh snow, but he could see here taint spreading across it. The white that covered the ground had an oily sheen to it that reminded him of her. The evil she carried was leaching out into the world itself.

He reached the doors to his workroom and brushed the accumulation of snow from it. The doors stuck slightly from the cold and ice, but open easy enough with a good yank.

The room below was just as he left. The cot stood unchanged except for a slight dustiness. His tools occupied their shelf, gleaming in the lantern light. He took his time, cleaning his way around the room.

When the dust was banished, he sat to the task of sharpening each tool again and blessing each again before setting it back in its place. Each tool was handled carefully and lovingly, as one would a child. He took time to speak to each, telling it what its job would be.

The saws knew how they would be expected to perform. He counseled the blades on the importance of keeping their edge away from bones and the tissues that would dull them. Immanuel examined the chisels and hammers, cooing to them about the way they would open ribs and bones.

Satisfied that all was as ready as he could make it, He blew out the lantern. He closed the doors gently so that the noise would not disturb those below so that they could rest until needed.

He went back to the church, he too needed rest.

**Derek**

His feet ached and burned from the snow that had melted into them. He called to the others to stop and wait for a second. They turned impatiently to see what was wrong but soon joined him in removing their shoes and changing into dry socks. In a six-hour shift, the average sentry would go through four or five pairs of socks, and the barracks in the church always had a large number hanging from the mantle drying.

"Good Call Hobbs," Sarge said as he changed his own.

"Feet are your most important tools!" Chapelle said in a drill sergeants voice. Both soldiers laughed, but Derek didn't get it and waived it off as an inside joke.

Derek was just happy to he had been moved up to day patrols. He attributed it to be a reward for bringing one hundred pounds of bear meat into camp and the feast it allowed. Being assigned to work with these two had been a bonus.

The main difference in the day shift was that sometimes they got to go out with the scavenging teams to work as security. Today would be Derek's first such trip and he looked forward to the chance to overcome the cabin fever he had developed towards the valley. As beautiful as it was, it was still the same view every day.

They all finished and tied their laces backup tight and started back on the circuit of the valley. Three teams of three men patrolled the road day and night. The idea is that when things were going right, a team would pass every given spot every half an hour. It made sense to each team, but it was a lot of walking.

Derek glanced down at his watch, it was almost noon. They would stop the next time they passed the visitors center, be relieved and board the transport. Then it would be a chance to rest up until they arrived. They all looked forward to getting off their feet for a little while.

"Do you guys know where we are going today?" He asked, anticipation driving him to ask.

Sarge answered from behind him. "Some big-box superstore down the mountain. One of the pilots spotted it from the air the other day." He answered as they walked. "Apparently it hasn't been looted yet. The roll down doors are closed."

The idea of an untouched store full of food, clothing and all the necessities seemed too good to be true. He wondered how such a place had not been skipped in the fall of society. Derek remembered shopping in such stores before, and they held everything.

"What are we after there?" He asked. Talking was not forbidden on patrol here in the compound, but was still rare. Living and working with the same people meant you quickly ran out of things to discuss.

"Everything," Sarge said. "Anything useful we can fit in the trucks. This is going to be a big one, we are taking the semis, the Bradley's and almost every soldier. The only ones not going are the guards."

Derek realized that would have been him staying here just two weeks ago. The majority of those that worked guard duty were the civilian volunteers, with the enlisted persons acting as the patrols and labor force for the jobs outside the confines of the valley. By becoming attached to the group he had, he had been a hybrid of the two, but the latest move he had moved had essentially moved him up.

“What if something happens here while we are gone?” Derek asked. “Can the civilians handle it?”

Chapelle chuckled. “Aren’t you a civilian?” He said, teasing the younger man.

Derek blushed, realizing his faux pas. But the other man bailed him out. “Derek here isn’t just a civilian,” Sarge proclaimed, “He is and uber-civilian, totally different thing. It’s like a civvie on steroids.”

“Oorah!” said Derek at the compliment.

“That’s the marines.” Sarge scolded, but the smile was evident in his voice. “This is the army.”

From the front of them, Chapelle shouted “Hoo-ah!”

“That’s how it’s done!” Sarge answered approvingly. “Let’s get to the center, it’s almost time.”

They all walked faster, the vigor returning their steps. They were all looking forward to a change of scenery. A trip down the mountain, even at the end of the world, would be refreshing.

**Brandy**

"So, who is he?" Asked Mueller from his seat by the radios. He had been left behind by the convoy to monitor the equipment. It had been a heated discussion with the other two radio operators. All had wanted to go, but it had been settled when the held an impromptu paper rock scissors tournament. He had lost.

Brandy looked down from the clock she had been checking to stare quizzically at the sailor. "Who is who?" She asked, trying her best for sincere puzzlement.

"Well," He began as he stared at her knowingly, "You have been looking at that note every few minutes and looking up at the clock. As soon as you look at the clock, you look back at the note and sigh. So, who is he?"

Brandy felt her cheeks redden and wondered how she could have been so obvious. The note had been on her door when she woke up this morning. It was just a few words from Chad inviting her to join him in their trees when she could get away. He had left it before she had awoken this morning and he was gone by the time she found it.

"Just... somebody." She said.

Mueller smile at her. The smile was full of mischief. "Look, the Colonel is gone for the day on that supply run. There is nothing happening here, why don't you take a long lunch and go see your boy toy."

"What about you?" She asked, unsure. "That will leave you here all alone..."

He pointed to the electronics stacked on the table his feet were propped up on. "If I need anything, I can hit a button and call for help. Just take one of the handhelds with you." He said as he lifted the radio from its charger and tossed it to her. It was one of the simple push to talk walkie talkies you could buy in most stores, but it had proven very useful here in the valley where its limited range didn't matter. "I will call you if I need you."

Brandy didn't take much convincing. She quickly gathered her stuff and clipped the radio to her belt. She lifted her coat off the rack by the door and as she pulled it on, backtracked to give the sailor a peck on the cheek to thank him. She stepped out into the cold.

As the door swung shut behind her, she heard the radio man's voice shout. "Just remember to use protection!"

Brandy saw Chad standing at his usual spot near the swing set. He had often complained about standing in the snow watching over a playground that was far too frozen to use, but he did as he was told.

He saw her and waved cheerfully. Brandy waved back and pointed to the tree line. He nodded enthusiastically and checked around to see if anyone was watching and saw no one. They started for the trees at the same time and met at the same spot he had found her before. Brandy dismissed the dog to wander and explore.

They embraced for a long time, and when they finally separated he said, "Wow your lips are warm!"

"Yours are freezing!" She said, concern in her voice.  She reached into her pack and removed the surprise she had brought. Chad watched in awe as she set up the water boiler and produced two packets of instant coffee. Coffee was already one of the most valuable commodities in the community.

"I should start calling you sugar mama!" he said, licking his chapped lips in anticipation of the warm beverage.

When the device was hissing and popping appropriately, they took their places under the tree. The falling snow was caught by the limbs, leaving a clear dry spot out of the wind for them to sit. They tried to get out here whenever they could, but it was never long or often enough for either of them. They kissed until the coffee was ready, and as they sipped the beverage, she laid against him.

"I think Mueller is on to us." She announced as they drank. "He asked some questions today."

"Hmm," Chad responded, "Maybe we should off him..."

Brandy laughed. "What are you, mafia?"

"Well", he said seriously, "I am from New York. But I have never heard of the mafia, what's that."

He tried to keep his face straight, but her laughter triggered his. As it died down, she continued her thought. "I am serious though. You have been sneaking off guard duty, and I am running made up errands to meet you here. If they found out about us, they would begin to suspect. Not to mention what mom would think, especially with you sleeping right across the hallway..."

"Would she really be mad?" He asked, unsure.

"Mad? No." brandy answered. "But I am pretty sure you would get assigned to a new house rather quickly and with Jack spending most of his nights at that redhead's house..."

Jack had formed a relationship with one of the women who worked the kitchen and they had hit it off. He spent most of his time there with her and visited most nights. The only times Brandy had seen his for the last week had been when he stopped by to exchange dead vapes for recharged ones.

“Yeah,” Chad offered, “But if she keeps making those donuts, she can keep him.” He quipped.

Brandy had to agree to that. He skills had improved the kitchen to a large degree.

They finished their coffee, draining every drop. And he helped her pack up the set up before drawing her in for another deep kiss. Their last kiss before separating again to return to work was always the most passionate, fueled by the longing they both knew would be coming on very soon. He squeezed her hand as she stepped away from him, back towards the office.

“Let’s see if we can get out for a few minutes,” She said as she walked away, “a little after dark… while everyone is in the kitchen for dinner.”

He watched her until she got safely inside before returning to his own post.

**Immanuel**

The roar of the helicopters passing low overhead pulled him abruptly from the dream he was having about his angels. He felt the room vibrate as they went over, and the sound was tremendous. It was loud enough that he was sure they had barely cleared the trees.

He slid his tender feet into his shoes and made his way outside into the snow. As he watched, a line of vehicles made its way towards the exit of the valley. Immanuel noted several tractor-trailers and all the armored cars in the convoy. Normally the military trucks went alone, whatever they were doing was big.

He scanned the circular road around the community and didn't see any of the patrols moving along the blacktop. He sat on the steps to the chapel to wait and see what had changed in the security of the compound.

The other church across the way showed very little activity. Its normally hectic yard showed only one person moving around. Thin wisps of smoke bloomed from its chimney indicating that people were still inside, but not many based on the sparse movements visible through the windows.

After an hour had passed with no appearance by a patrol slogging along the road, Immanuel decided that they weren't bothering with that today. The only movement of the road was the occasional figure moving here or there on their own business. None wore the military garb, and most carried armloads of wood or other supplies instead of rifles.

One person, he recognized as she appeared from the direction of the offices. Claire's figure and clothing made her easy to identify, even from a distance. She carried a basket he recognized as the one she brought his food in, and he was surprised at the sense of hunger it made him feel. He held up his hand and gave her a wave.

She waved back and closed the distance. "I see you are up and moving around!" She said when she was close enough to avoid yelling. "Are you feeling better?"

"Yes," he said warmly, "Very much so. Brother John looked at this morning and gave me back my shoes."

She sat the basket on the step next to him and began to take its contents out. She handed him a bowl of stew and a spoon. "Someone got a deer yesterday, so there is real meat in there." She said happily.

Immanuel obediently took a bite and declared it excellent. She smiled at his praise. He had noticed that she was especially vulnerable to his controls when he gave her praise, so he made a point to do it often. She was his only remaining ally and he still had a use for her.

"Claire," he began after he finished his meal, "I some of the soldiers leaving. Do you know where they went?"

"Some?" She answered quickly. "That was all of them! They took off to get supplies from some big store a couple of towns over."

He considered this, and then asked, "Then who is here protecting us?"

"The civilian volunteers." She answered. Her next statement seemed more to reassure herself than him. "With the infected freezing in the cold weather, they should be more than enough."

"Will they be back by nightfall?" Immanuel asked.

“From what I heard, they will be gone until morning.” She said. “They are supposed to bring back A LOT of stuff in case we get snowed in.”

“I am sure we will be just fine.” He said confidently.

They sat together and watched the snow-dusted world around them as the silence rolled on. Immanuel knew well that she would soon break it with her need to talk. She was quiet for longer than usual before she spoke.

“Immanuel,” She began tentatively, “Did you have someone special before... before all this happened?”

His mind immediately went to the choir of angels that still spoke to him on occasion, and the voice of God, but sensed that it was not yet time to broach that subject, so he asked. “What do you mean?”

“Like a girlfriend,” She said, “or a wife?”

“No,” he answered, “The lord's work has kept me far too busy for that kind of thing.” He left out exactly what the work he had done for the lord was. He could tell she was building up to something, and he wasn’t sure how to handle it.

“I didn’t either.” She said sadly.

The silence stretched again to the point of becoming awkward. “Claire,” he said abruptly, “the world has changed. Gods divine hand has swept across the land, spreading his wrath and judgment. Just as in the flood of Noah, the some of the righteous were taken with the evil, but some of both remain. It is his holy charge that we finish what he began before we move on with our lives.”

“But can’t we do both at the same time?” She asked, expectantly.

"We must keep our thoughts and minds on the task at hand." He preached. "Any distraction could risk our very souls."

He saw a look of hurt and disappointment cross her face, and placed his hand on hers. "There will be time for that kind of thing later." He added and was rewarded as the frown perked up.

Claire put her other hand on his, enveloping his hand in hers. "I understand." She said brightly.

Immanuel took the opportunity to change the subject. "So, tell me of the things going on at work." He said, knowing that it would put her into a gossip-laden monologue and he could use the time to think. Her work at the medical clinic they had established in the old mill kept her right in the middle of news and relationships of the community.

As she carried on, he stared across the field at where his quarries house stood hidden by the trees. 'tonight, is the night' he told himself. No patrols to find him and only a couple of people at the barracks would make it easy.

He caught the name of his nemesis in her gossip and his attention returned fully to the woman's words. He learned all he needed to know.

***

*He removed his coonskin cap and hung it on a broken branch of the tree. The thing was slogging through the knee-deep snow in the valley below. It was the third one he had found today. Rob was happy the cold was slowing them down and that the snow would soon be deep enough to close the passes.*

*A quick glance at the hairs that made up the hats tail told him the wind wouldn't be much of a factor. He pulled off his possum mittens and lifted the gun, careful to keep his bare skin off the metal as he sighted down the long barrel.*

*The click of the trigger and the pop of the powder in the pan always delighted him. The recoil and the bang made him feel like he was living at the time he had been meant for. He skillfully reloaded as he watched the downed target for signs of movement. The figure stayed unmoving in the snow.*

*Rob pulled the mittens and hat back on and started to the next lookout spot. He didn't care for the modern people who had moved into his cove, but then he hadn't liked the people there before.*

*'Newfangled guns and trucks or not, they are people,' he thought to himself, 'and these damned things are not.'*

*Rowdy Rob reaffirmed his mission to himself, he would keep the people in the cove safe, even if he had to walk these ridges and valleys every day for the rest of his life.*

***

**Derek**

The ride in the trailer had been miserable. He and the others had sat in the dark as the road jostled and bumped them around. The thin trailer walls offered no insulation against the frigid winds and the lack of seats made the hard floor almost unbearable.

Derek had no idea how long they had been on the road, but it felt like hours. He had almost cheered the vehicle had finally come to a stop and the beeping had announced that they were backing into the loading bay. The back of the truck thumped into the bumper pads and they all cursed at the sudden stop.

As the engine shut down, the sounds of the helicopters filtered in. he hoped they had already dropped the men on the roof that would clear the store and open the bays for his unit to unload. The lack of a way to open the trailer form inside had been Derek's least favorite part of this plan.

From the darkness, he heard the voice of the lieutenant call out, "Everyone on your feet and get ready. As soon as these doors open, we need to get this thing loaded." She ordered. "Remember the list you were given, get as much of the first items as you can and work down from there."

"Can we pick up other stuff for ourselves?" One of the others in the dark asked.

"Priority to the items on the list." She answered firmly. "But I am not going to be checking pockets."

From the other side of the door, a fist banged three times on metal. Someone inside the trailer answered three bangs of their own and the sounds of rolling doors replaced the noise. Derek saw light flooding into the trailer as the doors opened into the building.

Before the door was even all the way up, he heard those in the front started gagging. Derek had just enough time to wonder why when the smell hit him. A wave of reeking air had flooded into the trailer as the untainted air rushed out into the building.

Inside the store, the months of no electricity had taken its toll. The green sludge that had been produce and the gray slime that had once been the meat and seafood cases had given birth to countless generations of flies that now buzzed about the shelves.

Standing just inside the bay doors, the figure that had opened the doors shouted to them. “Welcome to paradise. Let’s get moving.” Came Sarge’s voice. The waiting people in the trailer moved out into the stock room. Derek filled out with the rest of them but was stopped by the big black man.

“Here,” he said to Derek, “smear this on your upper lip, it helps.”

Derek took the tube he was offered and liberally smeared the toothpaste as he was told. The smell of decay was lessened by the scent of peppermint. “Thanks,” Derek said quickly and handed the tube to the next in line.

He pulled out his list and studied at as his made his way out onto the sales floor. Others would load the boxes in the supply room, he was assigned to clear shelves. As he pushed through the double metal doors, he heard the power saw start up and begin to eat away at the locks on the stores gun safe.

The smell was worse out here and the floor was dusty with the long absence of humans to sweep it. He hurried to the front of the store and stopped dead in his tracks when he heard it. The carts were stored by the front doors, and outside the infected were gathering, drawn to the noise the helicopters made. Their bodies and hands rattled the think metal doors loudly enough that it could be heard everywhere inside, but it was especially loud there.

He forced himself forward and grabbed a cart and hurried towards the right area and started filling buggies with soaps, shampoos, and deodorant. The task went quickly since most of the full looking spots turned out to only contain a few of each product.

He pushed the buggy towards the back of the store and joined several others doing the same. He marveled at how heavy the cart was, and how poorly it performed under the weight.

In the back room, he left it for the ones assigned to packing the things into the plastic totes they had liberated from the store before putting it in a truck. He was amazed at the efficiency of the operation. Two of the semis were almost full and their gapes around the pallets were being filled in with loose boxes.

Derek knew they would soon start the dangerous process of moving the three semis away from the loading bay and moving the three empty ones into position. The fact that they had procured six fifty-three foot and trailers spoke to the scale of the operation. On his second trip, he saw them close one of the doors being closed and heard the heavy truck outside firing up.

Derek checked the next item on the list he had been given and moved off to get another buggy. This would be his third trip to the front of the store, and he felt the dread increasing each time.

He found himself wishing for the bitter cold they had up at the cove. Here in this sheltered spot, the cold did not freeze or slow the dead things like they did at higher altitudes.

He pulled two carts and hurriedly pushed them away from the doors and headed back to the pharmacy section. His list told him to empty the shelves of vitamins tablets and supplements.

His path took him to the pet section. This was where the second buggy came into play. Though it was not on his list, he filled it with as many fifty-pound bags of dog food as it would hold for Bruiser. He had decided the last time he passed it to see if they would load it into the trucks or not, and he didn't like Brandy taking smaller meals to share with the dog. He left the buggy in the pet section to grab on the way back out, stopping only to put a sleeve on tennis balls in his pocket. At least he was sure the dog would get something to play with.

He passed two men sawing thru the metal cage that held the pharmacy supply and was amazed at the distance the sparks flew as the gas-powered cutter bit it.  Two others stood by with carts waiting. He knew they would leave nothing inside behind.

He found Chapelle on the pill aisle, loading a cart with pain pills, cold medicine, and bottles of every description and joined him. When they had filled the buggies, Derek followed him back towards the back, pausing only long enough to push the dog food ahead of him, while transferring the lighter buggy of vitamins behind him. Chapelle grabbed the edge of the buggy and helped him steer it without comment.

**Brandy**

Bruiser chewed noisily on the bone under her desk. Jack had left it when he had come to tell her he wouldn't be home tonight. Brandy wasn't sure why he felt the need to tell her and make excuses, but he did.

She could see the sky growing dark outside through the window and knew that meant they would be ringing the dinner bell soon. This was one of the busiest times in the cove as people finished the day's work and started towards the kitchen to get their last meal of the day.

Brandy walked over to the glass door and looked out at the tent. Sure enough, a crown was gathering. The venison stew they had eaten for lunch had been wonderful, but the promise of tonight's chili had been well received and a source of excitement all day.

The smaller number of meals Jack needed to prepare had meant enough he could make better use of the limited spices, and he arranged this menu as a treat for the people of the valley to take their mind off the absence of the soldiers. It had worked.

A glance at the clock told her it was almost time, so she returned to her desk and sorted through the things she still had to do. With the Colonel gone to supervise the supply run, she knew tomorrow would be a busy day for reports and inventory lists and she wanted to be fully caught up

"You are calling it a day?" Mueller asked from his place across the room.

"I am about to head to dinner," She explained, "then I will come back and finish this up." She looked down at the stack of paperwork she had been too distracted to finish and sighed. "Do you want me to bring you some? It's chili."

"Please." He said gratefully as she pulled on her jacket. "I am going to be here all night with this." He said, indicating the radio that was emitting a steady stream of chatter from the team working at the store.

"Come on buddy!" she called to the dog as she slung her pack over her shoulder. Bruiser looked up her sadly across the deer bone. But obediently stood up and crossed over to her.

"Why don't you leave him here," Mueller suggested. "He is warm and has something to chew on and you won't be gone that long."

Brandy looked down at the dog and considered. Even with his dense coat, he did seem to get cold out there. Finally, she shrugged and said, "you can stay here if you want." Bruiser wagged his tail and walked back over to the bone and settled into the work of chewing the bits of flesh off it.

The cold washed across her as she left the warmth of the office and she stuck her hands into her pockets. Pausing, she looked around at the area around her. The kitchen tent stood a few dozen yards ahead of her, and in the fading light, its openings seemed inviting. The enticing smells escaping those flaps made her have second thoughts of a cold make-out session in the woods.

She could do both, she decided and turned towards the patch of trees her and chad had claimed as their own. The trees cast dark shadows in the dim light, and it was hard to see once she entered them, but she knew the way and wasn't concerned.

She spied chads form sitting at the base of their usual tree. He was huddled up with his gloved hands in his lap and his head dipped down as if protecting his face from the cold.

“You look cold there, stranger,” she said cheerfully, “Want me to warm you up?”

When she got no response, she stepped closer. “Hey Chad, you awake?” She asked and tapped his leg with her foot. The figure at the base of the tree tipped over and fell into the snow.

Brandy dropped to her knees beside him and shook him. “CHAD!” she yelled in a panic. Her hands felt wet where she clutched his shoulders, so she pulled the flashlight from her pocket and clicked it on.

The beam revealed the blood-soaked chest in perfect detail. His face was ashen and his eyes starred unfocused into the sky past ice-flecked lashes. Brandy fell backward onto her butt, driven back from the horror of the lifeless body.

She tried to scream, but the shock had taken the breath from her body. Struggling to her feet, she turned to run for help. That’s was win she say the man standing in the shadows.

The beams swung upon him as he rushed towards her. She had just enough time recognize him as the man from the church as he swung his fist. The blow sent stars spinning in her eyes and then the darkness crept across her vision.

**Immanuel**

The daylight had crawled by after Claire had left. The sun had mocked him in its slow crawl across the sky as he waited for darkness. Only when the shadows settled across the meadows could he begin the trek to get her.

Claire had told him about how she had seen the girl sneaking into the woods with the guard, and how they did it often. Tonight, when she arrived, she would find the sword of God in the trees instead.

If it was not a night for whatever debauchery she committed away from the eyes of the others, he would find her walking home from the office, or get her at the house. He didn't need the now silent voice to tell him that, and maybe her purification would bring the voice back to him.

He spent hours imagining the gratitude she would feel once he had saved her. The things they would do together to forward gods works. When he cut away her evil, he would prove that he could save others, and they would seek him out instead of having to be hunted.

When the time finally came, Immanuel gathered what he needed and set out. He stayed in the shadows as he worked his way through the trees that hugged the edges of the valley wall. The ache in his weakened feet was the price for stealth as he moved.

He arrived in the stand of trees Claire had described and waited. Shortly after the moon rose over the mountains, the boy arrived. Immanuel watched from his hiding place as he called the girl several times and then began to stomp back and forth to stay warm.

The noise of the boy's feet covered his own as he stalked up behind him. Immanuel worked his left arm around the boy's throat and squeezed with the bend of his elbow to prevent a yell for help. He was surprised by the strength of the fight the young man put up.

Immanuel pulled the hunting knife from his belt and plunged it into the struggling figure's chest and wrenched its blade back and forth, feeling the warm blood rush out to cover his hand.

He held the man as its movements began to weaken, and then stop. To be sure, he twisted the arm around the neck until he heard the tell-tale crack and let it slip to the ground.

He looked back in the direction of the offices, listening for footsteps. The only sound that disturbed the night was his own ragged breathing. No one had heard or seen to spread the alarm.

Reaching down, he pulled the cooling figure to the tree and propped it up carefully to look alive. The young man would make excellent bait. As he moved back to his hiding place, he kicked fresh snow over the blood at the sight of the kill. He went back to waiting.

God was with him as the girl appeared in only a few minutes. When she was unconscious, he bound her hands and feet and gagged her. It proved unnecessary as she was still out when he got her home and tied her to the cot in the basement. Immanuel cleaned the blood from her face and dabbed out the wound he had made on her temple with clean water.

He sat in the corner, waiting for her to wake up. He wanted her awake for his search. Perhaps she could tell him where the evil lurked.

'It is my will' the voice said. It's sudden appearance after so long of an absence startled him. He smiled broadly in victory, he had not been abandoned. He was still worthy.

He was still reveling in his relief when he heard the footsteps on the floor above his head. Someone was in the church.

**Derek**

Rushed back out for his last load. He had been warned that the last truck would be pulling out in five minutes and he only had one item left on the list they had given him. He snatched a duffle bag off the rack as he passed the luggage section on his way back to the pharmacy. It would fit what he needed to grab.

He skidded to a stop in front of the condoms and began to sweep the packets and hooks that held them into the duffle. He had blushed when he had seen them on the list, but the lieutenant had launched into a speech about the dangers of childbirth without modern medicine and he had no desire to repeat it.

Once the bag was full, he turned and ran to the back as he closed it up. The bareness of certain shelves in the store struck him as odd and impressive at the same time. So much had been removed in such a short time, but so much remained for another day.

He burst through the metal doors as the last of the supplies were being stacked in the last remaining truck. He was pleased to see the dog food being loaded and tossed the duffel on top of them as the doors were pulled down. He had just made it.

Sarge pounded on the back doors of the truck, and it pulled out in a plumb od thick black smoke. Beyond it, he saw the armored personnel carrier idling as it waited for them. The ride home would be far more comfortable than the ride here.

As the truck moved out of the way, the carrier whipped around and backed closer. When it stopped, the ramp dropped and Sarge yelled, "Go!"

The soldiers standing in the store made the hop to the concrete and rushed over and up it to the belly of the vehicle. Derek sat and looked back towards the store in time to see Sarge and Chapelle slam the rolling door down, sealing the building. He knew they would already be heading for the roof and the helicopter waiting for them.

He settled into the seat and got ready for the ride home.

***

*Claire felt silly, but she knew men liked this kind of thing. She drew the long coat tightly around her, feeling its fabric rub against her bare skin. The cold was barely muted by the lack of layers underneath as she hurried towards the church. She was looking forward to the warmth of the church.*

*She was emboldened by the loneliness she had sensed in the preacher, it matched her own. He always seemed to go out of his to complement her, and make her feel special.*

*The fact that he had not made a pass at her was typical in her opinion. Men like him, good men, never seemed to be able to build up the courage of reading the subtle signs women gave off. She had to be direct and switch from hints to seduction.*

*The lights of the church beaconed her. She peeked through the windows as she passed and saw the chapel was empty. 'good, he must be in the back, that's where I want him anyway.' She thought to herself and instantly felt ashamed for thinking such a thing. She blamed it on the long cold nights in the house with only Ethan and another woman and her child.*

*Claire made her way up the stairs and through the doors into the sanctuary. She paused to take in the warmth of the kerosene heater. It felt wonderful on her cold flushed cheeks. Fear of losing her nerve got her moving again and she crossed to the door to his room.*

*She knocked softly and pushed it open. "It's later..." She whispered as she stepped in.'*

*Claire found the room empty. His bed looked as though it had been slept in, but was cold when she ran her hand across the sheets. She was trying to decide if she should sit on the bed and wait for him to return or if she should just go home when the door to the outside opened.*

*She looked up to See him standing there. His shoulders dusted with freshly fallen snow. He stared at her with a look that made her feel uncomfortable. It was a look of anger.*

*"Immanuel," She said cautiously, "are you okay?"*

*His expression softened as he gained control of himself. "Claire!" he said quickly as he made his way to stand in front of her. "Why are you here?"*

*She screwed up her courage and decided to go for it. "You said later would be time for other things," she said in her best seductive voice as she let her coat fall to the floor, revealing herself to him, "and I figured now was later enough..."*

*His eyes darted down the length of her and work its way back up from the top of her boots, stopping only at her eyes. She would never know that it was not her body he was seeing, but the darkening of the aura she projected to him. "I don't have time for this Claire. Go Home." He said and turned his back to her.*

*She felt tears sting her eyes at the rebuke. "I can be very good to you..." she protested.*

*He started to speak but was cut off by a cry for help coming up from under their feet. Instinctively, Claire looked down at the floorboards. "Who is that?" She asked confused.*

*Immanuel answered by stepping forward and thrusting a knife into her just below he left breast. She watched in alarm as the blade pierced her and sunk to the hilt, only his wrist showed as she looked past her bust.*

*Claire shrieked once and then collapsed heavily to the ground. Her blood escaped her in hot spurts as her vision dimmed. Seconds later she gasped one last time and was gone.*

*He returned with the blanket from his bed and covered her nudity. He kneeled beside her and closed her now sightless eyes by kissing each one.*

*Immanuel lifted her corpse carefully and placed it in the chest at the end of the bed. He wiped up the blood with her long coat and folded it inside with her.*

*"I am sorry, Claire." He said earnestly. "I think I could have loved you."*

*He drove the blade into her skull just under her ear and twisted. The least he could do for her was to make sure her soul was released. Immanuel closed the lid and walked quickly from the room, cleaning the blade with his handkerchief.*

***

## Brandy

She felt weightless as if suspended in a black void as awareness returned to her. Vision returned as if she was coming up out of a deep lake, dark and blurry in the beginning and brightening into detail as she rose to consciousness.

Her eyes slowly focused on the ceiling of the lamp-lit room. The boards again sharpening from blurred strips into the slates of rough wood they were. She tried to sit up, confused when her body didn't obey. She tried to turn her head and was rewarded with crashing waves on nausea.

Her stomach lurched, and she couldn't hold it back. She retched violently as her abdomen convulsed and her stomached emptied over the side of the cot. She commanded her hand to wipe they sickness from her mouth, but it was caught by something.

She tried her other hand with the same result and then tried to kick her feet. She realized that she was restrained and yelled for help. In the room above, she heard a cry of alarm, and then a commotion that stopped suddenly.

Brandy listen for the sounds above to resume as she tried to breathe through the panic. Someone had heard her and would come to help. She looked desperately around the room.

She was in a small stone room about ten feet on a side. It reminded her of the basements she had seen in horror films, but smaller. Its stacked stone walls were broken only by stairs leading up to one side, and a set of shelves on the other held the only light. The oil lamp burned brightly but wasn't enough to truly illuminate a room like this.

The cot she lay on was centered in the room but seemed too tall, it must be on top of something. Brandy struggled against the ropes that bound her to the cot with no results but pain as the cut cruelly into her skin. She felt other ropes across her chest and knees.

She yelled for help again, this time the word transformed itself into a scream of rage and fear.  She heard footsteps above her hurrying across the room and felt the hope of rescue returning. Someone was coming.

Somewhere a door opened and closed, and she could make out the sound of feet crunching through the snow. Another door opened and a blast of cold flowed down the stairs and washed over her. A man came down the stairs and stepped into the light.

Brandy saw his face and it all rushed back to her. Chads bloody body seared into her brain and the face of the man attacking her. That same face now stood leering at her.

"Be quiet!" He snapped angrily. "I had to kill a friend because of your yelling and it has put me in a foul mood when I should be celebrating!"

Brandy's scream was cut off when the man wedged a cloth into her mouth. The cloth felt slimy and tasted like pennies and she felt nausea returning.

"Shhh!" the man said softly, as if comforting a child. "I am here to save you from the evil within, my angel."

**Immanuel**

He stretched the gray metallic tape across her mouth, sealing the blood rag in. he was gratified to hear that her wild shrieking had been reduced to a muffled whimper. Immanuel checked the knots that held her and sat heavily on the chair in the corner.

"If you had just held your tongue another two minutes," he explained, "Poor Claire would not have had to die."

Brandy turned her head to stare at him, her wide eyes showing the fear as she tried to work her tongue past the cloth to work at the adhesive. She cloth was packed tightly, and she couldn't do it.

"I am sorry." He said. "It occurs to me that I have been assuming that you know why you are here, but it occurs to me that you may not." He stood quickly and stepped over to stand beside her.

He lifted the knife into her view. She could see smears of blood on the handle and more on his hand and sleeve. She fought back the urge to vomit, knowing that if she did, the gag would make her choke on it.

"You see, I am special." Immanuel proclaimed as he circled the bed. "God had gifted me with the power to see the evil in people, and I am one of the few he speaks to. I see that evil in you." He paused to run the back edge of the knife up her leg and across her abdomen, tracing a line from her foot up to her throat.

Brandy tried feebly to avoid the knife, but her bindings held her fast. She could only move her hands and feet a few inches, and the ropes across her allowed very little movement.

“I see the terror in your eyes,” he told her, “and I understand. But I assure you I am here to save you, not just your body, but your very soul. I have done this many times before, I have saved the souls of many angels from the wrath of God. Admittedly, I have not had much luck with the bodies, but the souls are the important thing.

He had worked his way back around to her head, and here was the only place she could not see him, but she followed his voice.

“I think in the past, I have been too rushed” he admitted candidly as he walked back into view, “I have to admit impatience is a failing of mine. But with you, I intend to take my time. I will not lie and say it will be pleasant for you, but I assure you that I do this not for my own pleasure. It is for God that I must work, and if that means pain for you, I apologize for the necessity.

Brandy saw his hands pull something from the shelf, but he lowered it to his side before she could see what it was. He continued his slow circling until he reached her feet. He stopped and leaned forward onto the cot. She felt its weight shift as his hands applied pressure to the bed.

“I have come to understand that my efforts have been mere butchery.” He continued. “What I should have been doing is more about precision. I have been looking for something physical. A thing hiding in the body that corrupts. I have come to understand that its isn’t a physical object. The thing I see in you is not tangible or tactile. It is not attached to your body, its attached to your mind.”

As he spoke he pulled off the boots she wore and cast them into a corner, followed by her socks. She saw the scissors when he began to cut the jeans from her legs. He worked the blades gently up her shins as he cut to avoid the ropes at her knees.

"It is not the physical pieces of my angels that I remove that saves them." He explained as the blades worked their way up her thighs and through the waist, making the jeans fall to the side. He switched to the other leg and started again. "It's the pain I had to inflict in the process. That's what purifies them, the pain of the body chases the evil from them. I am sorry to say the level of evil I see in you will require more work than any of the others."

Immanuel finished his cuts and worked the ruined denim out from under her and added it to the pile in the corner. He began to cut away her t-shirt, snipping the bra straps as he went.

"Brandy," He said, pausing to meet her eyes, "the second I see the evil flee you, I promise I will stop. It is only the thing inside I hold malice towards." He pulled the shirt scraps and bra away and tossed them into the corner. He retrieved a sheet from the chair and covered her with it.

"I would appreciate your help and understanding." He said in a sincere tone. "If I take the gag off, can we have a serious conversation?" Immanuel asked.

She nodded quickly, and he took a corner of the tape in his hand. "Now Brandy, I can't have you screaming or calling for help. It is not likely that anyone will hear you, and if they do, I will have to kill them. Do you understand? He asked.

She nodded again, and he ripped the tape off quickly. Brandy spit the wadded rag from her mouth and worked her tongue around, remoistening her mouth before she spoke.

Raising her head, she looked him in the eyes. "Fuck you, Immanuel!" Then she said at spat angrily at him.

**Derek**

The vehicle coming to a stop jolted him from sleep. A quick glance around at the others proved that he was not the only one just waking up. Bleary eyes showed many eyes on the benches.

“We are home.” Called the voice of the driver. “Everyone out so I can put this thing to bed.”

Derek heard the tiredness in the man’s voice and gathered his pack and rifle to his arms. The others were doing the same and they started filing out of the vehicle. The stood in a group at the end of the ramp, waiting for orders to come in.

He noted a clutch of officers standing not far away talking. He knew their commands were starting and would soon begin to trickle down to them. He hoped that they would not have to do much before they could get some sleep.

The stress that had built up in the anticipation during the ride down the mountain, the energy used at the store, and then the decline of adrenaline on the ride home had left him exhausted. Even though they had arrived back at the cove hours ahead of schedule did not seem to have helped.

Derek noted that the three Blackhawks sat idle in the field closest to the visitor’s center. He felt relief knowing that the others had made it home safely. He hoped they had been released to get some sleep, they had earned it.

The officer's pow-wow broke up and they all walked off to brief the clumps of figures shivering in the cold. The Lieutenant approached her group and called for their attention.

“Colonel Murray has asked me to pass on his appreciation for the hard work you all put in tonight.” She began. “He has announced it a complete success, we achieved all of the goals with no casualties or loss of equipment."

Several of those gathered gave a brief cheer. Trips outside of the established shelters were not usually done with no deaths or injuries. To have pulled off a job this big was doubly surprising.

"As for tonight," she added, "Everyone goes home and get some sleep. The trailers will be fine for tonight, we do not have to unload them in the dark. This one met with another cheer, but the officer raised her hands to quiet them down.

"You are expected to be back here at 0800," She yelled over the noise, "to help with the unloading and organizing of the supplies. That's in eight hours. The only exceptions are those with other obligations, specifically patrol or maintenance duties. You are dismissed"

Some groaned at this, Derek couldn't be sure if it was because of the unloading, or the return to normal routine. He knew he would be out walking the circular road at that time, so he would need to find someone to set the dog food aside for him.

They started to break up, heading towards the converted church they now called home. Derek was surprised when he was called aside by the woman. "Hobbs." She said. "I need you for a second."

He stepped over to her. "Yes, Ma'am"? he asked, worried what he had done wrong. He wondered if this was about the dog food.

"The Colonel's assistant," She asked, "that's your sister, right?"

"Brandy?" Derek asked, suddenly more concerned. "Yes, she is, why?"

“She went home and left her dog in the office.” She said. “We just need you to take it home to her.”

“She forgot bruiser?” Derek asked astonished. “That’s not something she would do…”

“Apparently he was eating a bone and she didn’t want to take him out in the cold.” She explained. “We just can’t have it there all night.”

Derek nodded and moved quickly to the office. It didn’t feel right for her to not take the German Shepherd home with her. When He approached the door, he saw the canine standing there waiting. He opened the door and started to call for him to come.

Instead, Bruiser bolted through the gap and began to sniff quickly along the ground, making widening circles as he moved. “Come on Bruiser, you can take a dump on the walk home.” Derek scolded. He wanted to get to the cabin and see what was wrong with Brandy.

The dog ignored him, continuing to smell the snow. Derek was just about to yell at the dog again when it paused and concentrated on one spot intently. The dog glanced up at the nearby woods and growled.

His fingers tightened on the rifle he carried, and he felt a flush of fear. The dog had found something. The Lieutenant, who had been watching from the office door came over and Derek was reassured in his action when he saw that she had drawn her pistol.

“What is it?” She asked softly.

Derek didn’t have a chance to answer as Bruiser started towards the woods in a slow walk, hackles up and his head held low. They followed him into the trees, moving cautiously.

Shortly after the shriek of a whistle blasted through the night, alerting those still gathered around the parking lot. The yells for a medic followed soon after and they descended towards the sound. The medic arrived quickly, but it was already far too late for Chad.

**Brandy**

His slap still stung on her cheek as he wiped her spit from his face, but she set her face in a mask of defiance and held the eye contact. He glared back, his eyes dancing with the flames of rage.

“You should not do that to the one who has just vowed to save you.” he said, regaining his emotions.”

“Go to hell.” Brandy said coldly. “Let me go right now.”

He turned to place the scissors back on the shelf and removed another jawed tool. Brandy recalled the type if not the name. She had seen her father use one many time to trim the bushes in their yard.

“My name is Immanuel.” He said as he circled back to the opposite end of the of the bed. “I had to give them the name Immanuel when they first found me. I had recently had a little trouble with the human law for my work.”

“I don’t carry what your name is.” Brandy said. “Untie me.”

“I am sorry, my angel.” He said with a real sadness. “I can’t do that just yet. Tell me, and please be honest. Do you know when the evil first entered you? Was there an event that you remember?” Immanuel placed the blade of the clipper on the flesh just above her knee and slid it lightly down her skin as he asked.

“What are you talking about?” she snapped at him. “There is no evil you damn psycho!”

The anger flashed in his eyes again. Brandy realized she had touched a nerve with that one and his expression renewed the terror in her. In response. He grabbed her left foot and held it with a crushing grip, his nails digging tightly enough to break the flesh. His other hand brought the clippers into play.

Even over her scream, she could hear the snapping of the bones as it cleaved through her little toe. Every nerve fired as the blade severed the digit where it met the foot. He moved quickly as it fell away and clamped his hand over her mouth, silencing her.

"YOU SHOULD NOT HAVE CALLED ME THAT!" He yelled into her face. He lifted his hand long enough to place the bloody rag back into her mouth. Before she could spit it out to scream again, he had torn a new piece of tape and sealed it in.

Brandy concentrated on breathing deeply through her nose to work out the pain that zinged through her body. Her vision was blurred by the pool of forming tears and she blinked her eyes tightly to clear them.

His face was still over hers, and she realized he had continued talking while her ears had been filled with her own scream. "… so, we will get started. If we can force it out, so be it. If not, I am prepared to go in to find it."

Her eyes were refilling with tears of pain, terror, anger, and helplessness as she watched him move back to the shelf and look at his tools. When he turned back to her she saw the box cutter he held.

"Are you ready." He asked and paused as if waiting for an answer. When she did not give one, he bent over her right leg. Brandy felt the blade bite into her skin and trace a line from her ankle to her knee. The searing pain brought forth the screams again.

Brandy thrashed wildly at the restraints. Her kicking brought another tirade of anger as it mussed the next cut into a jagged slash. "Hold still." He told her and clamped a vise-like hand on her knee as he touched up the spots that had been untidy.

Despite the torment, Brandy felt her heart lift. The binding on her right hand had loosened. The pressure around her wrist still dug into the flesh, but there was more play in it now. The realization that one more good yank could free the arm gave her a swarm of ideas should the possibility present themselves.

She gripped the wooden rail with that hand so that her struggles would not give her away and looked to her torturer. He was circling again, staring at her body. The look he wore was not one of lust, but of indecision. She realized he was picking the location of his next cut.

His circuit stopped at her feet again. She looked down at her foot and saw the trickle of blood that still flowed from her pinkie toe. He too was looking at it, watching the blood flow down the pad of her foot and onto the cut. His expression like that of a child watching cookies bake.

Immanuel brought the blade to the bottom of her foot, slicing along the line made by the blood from heel to toe. He repeated the procedure on the other foot, delighting in the sounds she made at the pain and relishing the parting of the skin as the blade moved.

Despite the lightheadedness, the muffled screams brought to her, and the spasms of pain, she kept her right hand clamped tightly on the rail. Outside, the sound of the convoy returning was barely audible over the noises she made.

**Derek**

The corpse crumpled under the tree looked just enough like Chad to be recognizable, but the sallow skin and odd angle of the neck made it seem unreal. It was easy to suppress the grief with the fear he felt for Brandy.

The secret of their relationship had unbroken more by politeness than lack of knowledge. In such a small community, everyone knew the comings and goings of everyone else. Derek's own mother had been the one to tell him about it, having seen the two first hand from her job in the clinic.

The scene was crowded with people, mostly the soldiers that had just returned from the mission, but a few civilians had heard and come to watch. Their arrival had surprised Derek the most, it had only been a few minutes since the lieutenant had sounded the alarm.

As Derek kneeled over the body of his friend, he listened to the yelling of the Colonel who had just arrived. The man had been put in a bad mood by the event and was now pacing back and forth shouting commands.

His angry shouts indicated his displeasure with everyone trampling the scene and disturbing evidence, but those gathered knew that was his nervous energy. There were no forensic investigators or lab technicians to collect hair samples and analyze blood splatter anymore. Derek knew his real distress was the concern for his assistant.

Bruiser had spent the last few minutes wandering, nose always to the ground. He sometimes made quick trips into the woods, searching, but always worked his way back. The scent of the crowd overpowering whatever he was searching for.

Derek listened as the Colonel gave his orders, and saw those gathered rushing off to the waiting vehicles for the search. They would check every building in the valley for her.

"Hobbs," she said softly to him. Derek looked over at the women kneeling beside him. The Lieutenant had been there with her hand on his shoulder since they had discovered Chad was dead. Her silent comfort helping him. "We need to get moving. The medic will take care of your friend."

He stood, ready to make his way to the waiting truck. "We have to find her!" he said firmly.

"And we will!" The women asserted reassuringly.

The two began the walk to the waiting truck. They had only taken a few steps when the dog burst from the darkness excitedly. Bruiser rushed to Derek and grabbed the sleeve of his coat, pulling him back the way he had come from.

Derek pulled the fabric from its teeth distractedly, eager to start searching. But she stopped him. "I think he has found something." She said quickly.

Bruiser bounded back into the night, and they rushed after it. Hope brought renewed energy to his steps. Twenty yards down the trail the dog took, the beams of their flashlight revealed the first drops of blood.

His officer pulled the radio from her belt. "Go on without us, the dog has found a trail. Pick up Shrek, tell him to start searching the structures to the south." She said in a carefully controlled excitement. "We are traveling the ridgeline moving east."

Bruiser bounded back to them, obviously distressed at the slow pace of the two-legged creature following him. They sped up and followed him as he rushed back off out of the beams of light.

**Immanuel**

He used the fabric he had prepared to bind her wounds. He saw her wince as he tightened them to control the bleeding. Her legs were bleeding from a collection of cuts and punctures he had inflicted, and the loss of blood had begun to worry him as his rage had seeped out in his actions.

"I can't have you bleeding to death on me." he explained to her as he worked, "We have so much work left to do."

He circled her, checking the tightness of the cords around her wrists and ankles. He pulled on the straps that crossed her and seemed satisfied. He pulled the chair over to her and sat in it.

"You will be pleased to know that I have not yet given up." He said. "I am still just as committed to saving you as I was when we started."

Immanuel used the bandage he still held to wipe the sweat from her face and then dabbed at the trails of the tears that ran from the corners of her eyes. This completed he fingered the curls of her hair as if arranging them for a picture.

"We will start again in a minute." He told her. "I apologize for my need to sit, but I am recovering from a rather painful foot injury. All this time on them has given me some seriously sore puppies!" he chuckled at his own joke as if they were having a casual conversation over coffee.

He placed his hand on hers and found it cold and clammy. She tried to pull it away, but the bindings kept her hand from escaping. He squeezed it affectionately, the lean forward and kissed her wrist just below the ropes.

He examined the raw spots the chaffing had created. "This is one of the reasons you should hold still." he scolded as he studied the rope burns. "You have rubbed the skin quite badly."

The building began to rumble as a truck passed by on the road. A second and a third quickly followed. "I guess they have found out you are missing. I have to admit I had expected it to take longer." He confided. "The helicopters got back when you were still asleep. I didn't think they would have a search going until morning."

Immanuel considered her eyes and saw the hopefulness there. "Don't worry my angel." He told her. "No one will disturb us here. No one knows about the cellar here, and it's snowing hard enough to have hidden the doors now."

He saw her eyes go to the ceiling above, and he caught her train of thought. He had remembered the body above also, but was unconcerned. "Claire is well hidden. I will bring her down here once the search is over one way or another. It gets cold enough down here to store her without her presence alerting those above. I can get rid of her later."

Immanuel saw the look of disgust in her eyes. "If I can purify you successfully, you can help me avoid suspicion," he shrugged before finishing the sentence, "and if I can't, you are already down here. Well, let's get back to work!" He finished cheerfully.

Her eyes went wide again, and she began to struggle as he selected another tool. "This one's long curved blade will be perfect!" he muttered to himself and turned back to face her. He used it to open a gash along her upper arm, the curve lining up with the skin of her arm as he pushed it into the skin.

Her muffled shriek at the pain spread a warm feeling of delight through his chest, but the feeling faded when he felt the vibration of another truck. He laid the blade on the cot and straightened to listen.

The truck came to a stop outside. Several voices split the night as the called orders to each other. The sound of feet on the steps to the chapel sounded, and the bang of the door being swung open signal the entry of those above.

Immanuel put his hand across her mouth and laid his chest across her body, pinning her limbs to prevent the rattling of the cot from alerting those outside. His other hand turned the knob on the lamp, lowering the wick and reducing the light to a pale glow.

Under him, the girl struggled against his weight her chest shook with her efforts to alert those above, but he was confident the noises didn't have the power to leave the room. He held her firmly to ensure no change.

He held his breath as the sounds moved above him. The feet rushed through the building then back. Outside he could hear the heavy footfalls of another moving through the snow, and then climbing the wooden steps to join the others searching inside.

The squelch of a radio sounded, and a voice said, "The Baptist church is clear, But the preacher isn't here."

A reply came quickly sounding distant and distorted from the radio. "Copy. He is probably out hooking up with someone... Just like everyone else in this place."

The feet above him moved back out of the church and moments later the engine fired to life and they heard the wheels moving it down the road. Immanuel listened intently for a full minute before relaxing.

"Well," he said brightly as he lifted himself from her, "That worked out well." He turned back to the shelf and selected another tool before crossing to her other side. He jabbed the ice pick into her bicep and smiled at the feeling it made as it penetrated the muscle.

**Brandy**

Brandy Listened to the footsteps overhead. The fresh wound in her shoulder gave her the impetus for the effort to be heard above, but his weight kept her from moving, and the compression of her chest kept even her gag muted screams to whimpers.

She concentrated her attention on the plastic handle she felt against her buttock. She had seen him drop the blade in his distraction of the trucks arrived, and she now struggled to get her fingers on it. His body pinned her arm completely.

Above them, the footsteps receded back to the road and the engine started. He continued to lay atop here for a while, but as he began to raise himself off her, she seized her chance, darting her arm back and grabbing the handle, she slid it under her. As she settled her weight back onto, she felt the blade bite into her skin and the warmth of blood starting to seep from the wound. She stifled the response her body urged.

She watched him move to her other side with a new instrument from the shelf and felt a sense of relief that he appeared to have forgotten the one she now concealed.

She felt buoyed by the feeling of the blade under her, even though it now pierced her skin. The tool was hope, plain and simple. Moments later, when the pick pushed its way into the flesh of her arm, that hope lessened the pain.

Brandy retreated into herself, blocking out the pain as best as she could as he inserted the pick again. She had the knife, but only one free hand. She would have to wait for the right moment.

**Derek**

Ahead of them the dog went quiet and stopped its forward movement. The hurried to its side. Bruiser had stopped and stood looking at the church. His shoulders quivered as Derek reached down to pet the dog. Whether it was from fear, the cold or excitement he couldn't be sure.

"Do you think she is in there?" Derek asked allowed to both the dog and the woman.

"I don't know." The lieutenant answered. "we don't even know what the dog is following." She said skeptically. The long circuitous route they had been lead on had been entirely wooded. Halfway along she had begun to worry that the animal had been following a deer or bobcat.

"He is following her." Derek said confidently. "She must be down there."

She lifted the radio to her mouth and spoke softly. "Lt. Kelley to base. Has anyone checked the Baptist church?"

The reply came back quickly. "Affirmative Ma'am. It was searched less than ten minutes. Do I need to send a team back?"

"Stand by Mueller." She answered. "Stand by, the dog brought us here, we are going to check it out." The acknowledgment came over the radio and she turned the volume back down as she clipped it to her belt.

"Well, come on." She commanded. "Let's get it done."

They stepped out of the trees with the dog keeping step between them. They worked their way around the outside, looking in the windows as they circled. Finding nothing, they climbed the stairs.

Derek put his hand on the knob and looked to the leader. At her nod he pulled it open as she stepped through, pistol held at eye level. He followed her in, rifle raised to his shoulder as he scanned the other side of the room.

The chapel was lit dimly by the oil lamps placed around the room. Even in the weak illumination, it was obvious that there was nowhere anyone could hide. The pews were made of simple boards, and even the alter was small enough that not even a child could hide behind it.

Behind the altar, a door stood ajar, showing a small room beyond. The moved to it and repeated the procedure that they had used to enter the chapel. Derek put his hand on the door and swung it all the way open at her signal. The bedroom was not occupied.

The two lowered their weapons and looked at each other, unsure how to proceed. She reached for the radio to call in their fruitless search. As her hand lifted it to her mouth, they heard Bruiser.

The dog began to bark wildly from somewhere outside.  Over the barking, they heard a roar of pain from below them.

**Immanuel**

The loss of blood was taking its toll. He felt for a pulse and found it weak and thready. Immanuel had feared this and prepared as best as he could. He had been keeping her wounds open only a short time before binding them tightly closed to staunch the flow. Obviously, he had not been quick enough.

"Brandy?" he called softly to her, watching her eyes for a response. They fluttered, and slowly moved to find him and then focusing. "Are you still with me?"

He barely perceived the nod but accepted it. He scanned up and down her body, taking in the bandages that now covered her body. He thought for the first time that maybe he had been too thorough.

Each of the wrappings he had applied showed the red seepage, though he had intentionally been careful about the deepness of the lacerations. The canvas of the cot was saturated. He felt the first feelings of despair at his failure creep into his mind.

"I have failed you," he confessed to her as he fell heavily into the chair. "I tried my best. I swear I did. There were a couple of times when the darkness dimmed, and I thought I had it beat, but it would come back."

Immanuel watched the lazy rise and fall of her chest. He knew it wouldn't be long now. The odds of her surviving an internal search had evaporated. The only thing left to do was pray.

The sheet had covered her from breast to mid-thigh bore its own blood stains now, spurts and drips from the wounds he had given her and cast off from the blade. Each red drip giving testament to his failure. He settled in to watch her, prepared to bear witness to her passing.

Sounds for the outside filtered into his mind. The faintness of them had caused to his mind to dismiss them at first, but he could swear he had heard the fall of feet in the snow. The first squeak of the wooden steps to the chapel confirmed it.

Immanuel turned down the lantern again but knew his angel was too weak to make noise. In an abundance of caution, he placed his hand over her mouth again, comforted by the feeling of her breath on his hand.

The footsteps above him were soft and deliberate. Whoever was up there now was being far more careful. The sound of their feet was almost inaudible in their careful placement. He heard them cross above him, and stop at the door to his room.

A different sound reached him now. A frantic scratching grew louder from the top of the stone stairs to where he now stood. He felt the unfamiliar sensation, fear.

The scratching changed from faint to the sound of claws on the wooden door. Whatever was there had made it passed the snow. And was pawing at the door. The dog became frustrated and began to bark, alerting those above in the chapel.

He felt the girls head move under his hand and started to turn. The low light hid the movement of her arm as it slashed out, cutting a slash across his chest. The shock and pain brought the noise forth before he could stop it.

**Brandy**

The effort of playing possum had been more difficult than she could have imagined when the idea occurred to her. Slowing her breathing had been almost impossible with the adrenaline and pain coursing through her.

She had not known the symptoms to fake, and she was sure that he did. She had learned quickly as the very things she had decided to pretend had begun to happen. That realization had made it more difficult as the fear threatened to take over.

The scratching had come almost too late. She had felt her mind dimming and was worried she wouldn't have the strength to act when the time came. The noise had immediately registered as the dog. She had heard him dig many times, and his bark had been impossible to forget. Brandy had responded to her chance before he blood starved brains had told her it was time.

Palming the knife, she slid her thumb along the blade to make sure she knew was the sharp one and corrected it to the right orientation and readied her swing. Brandy glanced down to double check her grip and the movement had drawn his attention.

As he turned, she aimed for his neck and swung with all her might, feeling the resistance as the blade sliced flesh. Even as her arm followed through, she realized that she had missed. Hooked blade lacerated cloth and meat with ease, but the blood flowed from the level of his collarbones, not the arterial spurts she had hoped for.

Immanuel bellowed like a wounded bear and struck out with both arms, shoving the cot. It toppled over, pushed from its stand with Brandy still securely attached to it. She struck the stone floor heavily and felt her breath stolen by the impact.

Brandy gasped the air back into her lungs as she felt around for the knife that had been jarred from her hand by the fall. She found it and began to cut the cords that still bound her. She heard Immanuel raging on the far side of the room about his wound. The knife was razor sharp and make quick work of the ropes. She was free in seconds. She pulled the tape from her face and pulled the rag from her mouth.

Peaking up over the boxes, she saw him folding the clothes he had cut from her body to his wound, trying to stop the bleeding. He saw her untied and drew the hunting knife from the sheath on his belt with his free hand and smiled.

Crashing sounds filled the room as whoever was upstairs started working on the barred door. The barriers seemed no match for the pounding it was taking, and the cracks that resonated meant help.

Brandy got her feet under her even as the protest as her injuries fought her every movement. She stood and made her run for the steps and the help now stepping through the door. A flash of white burst behind her eyes as the blood loss arrested the sudden movement and she felt the sensation of falling.

Derek

Derek had reached the doors first as he abandoned caution, but she was only a few steps behind on her radio. The slanting portal was embedded in the ground, and still mostly covered in snow even after the dog's efforts.

He brushed the snow frantically searching for the handle and found it. He yanked, but the doors only rattled on the hinges. He pulled again, harder this time, but the only moved slightly.

"It's locked, bash them in!" Lt. Kelley ordered from her place behind him.

Derek raised his leg and brought it down as hard as he could. The door shuttered, and he heard the wood crack. He stomped again, and the cracking was louder. The third time he jumped and brought both feet down. The door splintered, and his body passed through the hole, landing on the steps.

He pulled his feet back and pulled the doors open. A set of steps lead down to a darkened room. He could see the smooth stone floor extending out of view. He flicked on the light attached to the barrel. He glanced back at the women behind him.

Bruiser stood beside her, staring angrily into the cellar. Derek was tempted to send in the dog, but instead, he said "Bruiser! Stay boy, Stay." His voice just loud enough to carry to the dog's ear.

"By the book Hobbs," the officer said calmly. "We go in together."

He nodded and brought the rifle to his shoulder. On her signal, they started down the stairs.

**Immanuel**

'The little bitch cut me!' He thought to himself as he gathered her clothing to press against the wound to slow the blood. "You will pay for that!" he said at the spot she had disappeared to, "You will pay for the blood you have spilled!"

He lifted the wad of cloth and saw the blood still flowing. "You will pay with suffering!" he hurled as he jammed the ruined clothing back against the laceration.

He caught her head popping up over the crates that had recently held the cot and caught her eyes with his. She had managed to free herself quickly. She was not as bad off as she had let on.

He pulled the knife from its sheath at his side, imagining it penetrating her. She would be the third to fall under this blade tonight. The thought gave him a sense of kismet.

The first collision rattled the door. He knew the flimsy wood would not hold out long. With the second, the heard the splintering grow and reacted to his closing opportunity. He moved towards her.

The sound of the door collapsing spurred her to action and she rushed from her hiding spot. He closed the distance as she staggered. He saw her eyes roll back into her head and caught her in his arms.

Immanuel pulled her away from the stairs, using her to cover his body from any attacks those coming down the stairs might be considering. He settled himself into the corner with her back against him and his hand stretched across the cold skin of her breasts.

Across the room, the uninvited guests came fully into view. The lights on their weapons shone brightly into his eyes, but he counted only two. The stopped at the base of the stairs, guns aimed at him.

“LET GO OF THE GIRL!” a female voice commanded.

Immanuel forced himself to laugh and raised the knife to his hostage’s throat. “I don’t think I will do that just yet...”

“DO IT NOW!” ordered the other, this one the voice of a male.

Immanuel felt Brandy starting to come around, and pressed the blade just tight enough against carotid that she wouldn’t do anything stupid. “How about a counter offer?” he said, forcing calmness to his words. “My work is not yet finished. Arrange a ride for me: one unarmed driver with a full tank of gas. I will tell him the destination when we are underway and let the girl go when I am free.”

“You know that isn’t going to happen.” The female said, echoing his calm tone. “Let her go and I won’t kill you here.”

“You won’t,” he said confidently, indicating the walls with a nod of his head. “You know as well as I do that even if you kill me with one shot, the bullet will bounce off these stones and hit god knows what else. Maybe the girl, maybe you.”

He felt Brandy’s leg take her weight from the arm he was using to support her. She was awake again. “Tell them, My angel.” He said to her, but loud enough that all could hear. “Tell them that they need to bring me a car so that you can live.”

When she didn’t speak, Immanuel moved the knife slightly, nicking the skin of her throat. Her gasp told him that he had scored, and the soldiers across from him would be seeing a trickle of red.

“This is your last chance.” The male said. “Let her go or we will open fire! You Have to the count of three. One!”

Immanuel felt a real laugh bubble up at the soldier's bravado. He knew he had them right where he wanted them. He leaned in and kissed brandy on the back of the head.

"Two!" boomed the voice of the soldier. And the urge to laugh again died as she grabbed his wrist and twisted the blade out and away from her. As she side-stepped, she brought her knee up and into his groin. Pain exploded through him as the gunshots rang out and he felt the rounds tear into his chest.

**Brandy**

The world returned to her perception and she heard the voice. One of the soldiers now standing across from them was Derek. She opened her eyes and looked up at him without moving her head.

Her mind worked quickly, and she mouthed the words carefully, so she was sure Derek would see them. "On three." Her lips formed the word soundlessly. As the blade pricked her neck, she extended one finger on the hand that hung limply at her side.

"This is your last chance," Derek yelled to the man that held her. "Let her go or we will open fire! You Have to the count of three."

Her second finger had brought Triggered Derek's call of 'one'. She didn't flash the third finger, but reached up with both hands, grasping the killer's wrist and wrenching it with all her strength away from her neck.

As she had pulled away, the opportunity of the knee had presented, and she had taken it. Feeling the connection and his gasp had been a bonus to her escape from his grip.

The shots had been deafening in the confined space and crashed into her ears like a physical force. She felt them even as he fell, and the ringing persisted much longer.

The exertion brought the swimming back to her head, but she pushed through it to get to her brother as the hand grabbed her ankle. She looked down at the crumpled form on the floor. Immanuel's hand was wrapped loosely around her bandaged lower leg.

Her rescuers were yelling at her to stay back, but she waved them off. “Immanuel,” She said to the man on the floor as she jerked loose from his grip, “I am not your angel.”

She limped to the shelf and lifted the oil lamp that still burned dimly there. Its warm glass was painful on her skin. “I will never be your angel, But I will purify you.”

Brandy threw the glass lamp with all her remaining strength into the wall above him. Curtains of flaming oil fell upon him when it shattered. His screams were loud and continuous as her brother and his boss helped her up the stairs.

Immanuel’s cries continued as they stripped their jackets off to insulate her from the snow. Bruiser came to her side, whimpering softly. She stroked his head as she listened to them. The stopped abruptly as the floor in the burning church collapsed.

Brandy smiled and let herself pass out as Derek and Lt. Kelley attended to her wounds.

## Epilogue

Brandy leaned back in the office chair and stretched her aching muscles. The office was lit only by a single desk lamp and the dim glow of the radio dials.  Beyond the glass doors, the coming spring had melted the snow into patchy blobs scattered randomly across the cove.

She thought about the last few months as she rubbed her emaciated legs. The weeks in the clinic recovering from blood loss had left her weak. The hundreds of stitches and glue that had been used to close her wounds had left her body a maze of fading scars. The infections that had set in days after the night at the church had led to surgeries that had kept her laid up even longer.

The memory of the horror on her mother's face when Derek had carried her into the clinic was still fresh in her mind. The many hours of suturing wound cleaning, and questions about what had happened were dulled by the many drugs they had pumped into her.

In the weeks that passed next, the hours were broken only by visits from her family. They had spent as much time with her as they could, but even an hour a day left twenty-three with nothing to do. Even the occasions when Derek snuck the dog in were not long enough.

The one visit from the colonel is what had preserved her sanity. His Idea to have her trained as a radio operator was his way of saying he would have to replace her as his assistant, but she welcomed the challenge. Studying radio manuals would better than watching the ceiling all day.

One of the radio operators had rotated through each day teaching, and sometimes reteaching her the many procedures involved. Brandy had asked many questions with the purpose of drawing out the conversations, and her instructors had obliged, go far deeper into the theory and practices that made radio waves work.

When the medical staff had reluctantly cleared her to walk, she had begun to work shifts in the office. She had started with a few half shifts, and then the full eight hours with her trainers. She had finally earned the sign off to start working alone. Tonight, was her first solo shift.

She had been calling out on the radio, waiting for an answer, and when none came, adjusting the dials and trying again. Very rarely did she get a person on the other end, and not the one she was looking for.

Absentmindedly, she reached down and scratched the dogs head before starting again. On the third frequency she tried, she heard a faint voice answer. She adjusted the knobs until the voice was as clear as she could get it.

"This is Swamp Tower to unit calling." The voice said. "Please identify yourself?"

Brandy keyed the microphone, "Swamp Tower, this is The Cove calling. Please give your location." She answered. It had been decided to identify simply as The Cove rather than as a military unit to avoid trouble.

A long pause followed before the answer came reluctantly. "We are in north central Florida. I can not give anything more specific than that."

"Understood." Brandy said simply. She knew that many of the groups they had now found were very cautious because of all the raiders that could be listening. She checked the list on the clipboard and saw no reference to a known contact in that area or by that call sign.

“I am calling from a colony in the mountains of Tennessee.” She offered, hoping that her information would build confidence. “I am trying to locate the whereabouts and condition of Sam Hobbs, My father.”

The man's voice started to say something, but the words were cut off and the radio was filled with the sounds of shuffling. A woman’s voice crackled over the line. “Brandy!?”

Brandy felt the tears filling her eyes as she recognized the voice. “Nana, is that you?”

“I am here, Baby.” Her grandmother answered with tears in her voice. “Ken is going to get your father. He is here with us. We are all here and fine.” A pause filled the air before she asked hesitantly, “Is Derek... Okay?”

“Yes Nana,” Brandy answered, “We are all safe and okay. He is out on patrol right now, but he is going to be so excited to talk to you!”

“Patrol?” came the concerned reply.

Brandy didn’t answer but keyed the smaller hand-held radio they used to communicate in the valley. “Derek, Get your butt to the commander’s office on the double!” She said and switched off the radio. She didn’t want to have to explain more. The window to talk to the Swamp might not last long.

“Nana,’ Brandy said into the desktop, “are you still there?”

“I am still here Brandy. I hear your Daddy coming up the stairs, he will be here in a second.” The tinny voice answered.

“I am so glad to find you!” Brandy said, still in tears.

“He is here baby, He can hear you,” Nana said. Her voice giving way to the staticky airwaves.

Brandy waited for a few seconds until she could take it no more. "Daddy, are you there?"

Behind her, the door crashed open and she glanced over to see Derek standing in it. He had a concerned look on his face and his rifle held up ready for whatever trouble might exist. His face softened when the response came over the radio.

"I'm Here." Announced the voice of their father, "It's so good to hear from you."

**Authors note:**

This work was a long time coming. I hope you enjoy it as much as I enjoyed writing it.

As with all my other works, there are so many people to thank that it would be impossible to list them all. To My family, you have supported me through long nights of typing isolated in my office. Without you, none of this is possible.

To my many friends who suffered with bizarre technical questions at odd hours, Thank you for your patience. Those strange messages and obscure thoughts were all part of the labyrinth of an author's mind.

This was a difficult one to write. I had an idea where the story would go, but actually taking it there was the hard part. The toruture scenes were especially difficult. Brandy is not my daughter, but in a way she represents her, and the causing of pain felt the same way.

I do have children, and its hard not to put them into my thoughts as I write this kind of thing. Hopefully they will never experience anything remotely like this.